D1386939

Why so much fear of tears? Because the masks we use are made of salt. A stinging, red salt which makes us beautiful and majestic but devours our skin.
Luisa Valenzuela

TEACH US
TO OUTGROW OUR MADNESS

TEACH US
TO OUTGROW
OUR MADNESS

KENZABURO OE
Translated by John Nathan

SERPENT'S
TAIL

The publishers thank Kathy Acker, Mark Ainley, Martin Chalmers, John Kraniaukas, Bob Lumley, Enrico Palandri, Kate Pullinger, Antonio Sanchez for their advice and assistance.

British Library Cataloguing in Publication Data
Oe, Kenzaburo, *1935–*
   Teach us to outgrow our madness:
   four short novels.
   I. Title
   895.6'35[F]
   ISBN 1-85242-163-0

First published in Great Britain by Marion Boyars Ltd.
Translation coypright © 1977 by John Nathan

This edition first published 1989 by
Serpent's Tail, Unit 4, Blackstock Mews, London N4

Printed on acid-free paper by
Nørhaven A/S, Viborg, Denmark

CONTENTS

These translations are for Mayumi.

THE DAY HE HIMSELF
SHALL WIPE MY TEARS AWAY

I

Deep one night he was trimming his nose that would never walk again into sunlight atop living legs, busily feeling every hair with a Rotex rotary nostril clipper as if to make his nostrils as bare as a monkey's, when suddenly a man, perhaps escaped from the mental ward in the same hospital or perhaps a lunatic who happened to be passing, with a body abnormally small and meagre for a man save only for a face as round as a Dharma's and covered in hair, sat down on the edge of his bed and shouted, foaming,

——What in God's name are you? What? *WHAT?* So startled that he yanked the clipper from his nose with several hairs still caught between the rotor and the blade, and, the pain adding an edge to his anger, he set the Rotex in rotary motion and hurled it at the hairy face, then screamed back, writhing with his chest and shoulders only because the other man's weight on top of the blankets immobilized his legs,

——I'm cancer, **cancer**, LIVER CANCER itself is me! Throwing his robe open irritably he exposed the spidery welts that had appeared on his chest, then thrust in front of him both his bright red palms as well, whereupon the other man remarked, with a cool civility that can hardly have been normal,

——Sorry, I hadn't realized you were bonkers! and abruptly vanished without a sound, like a drop of water sinking into sand.

The only image he retained with eyes rendered uncertain by the tinted underwater goggles he always wore was the arabesque pattern the whirling Rotex had cut along the outer edges of the Dharma's beard. Had the late night intruder already shaved his beard away, he was left without a clue to his identity or whereabouts. Objectively, such was the case, despite the fact that he was ever surer inside himself that he had perceived in the hairy Dharma's features a resemblance to *a certain party*.

[[Must I put down even that kind of silliness? asks the "acting executor of the will," who is taking down his verbal account. As "he" has ceased to perceive those who share only present time with him as people living with him in this world, "he" makes no attempt to ascertain, nor is "he" the least concerned, whether she is his wife, a nurse, or simply an official scribe sent by the government

4

or the United Nations solely to record the "history of the age" "he" is relating. To be sure, should the last possibility be correct, it would be awkward if, reeking of the garlic "he" has consumed in large quantity in an attempt to convert whatever surplus strength "he" possesses now, at thirty-five, as his life is about to end, to sexual energy, "he" attempted to drag her into his bed. But for the moment the entire energy of his body-and-soul is being channeled into talking, continuing to talk. Not even the doctors' regular visits to his bedside, or the medicine the nurses administer to him, though "he" cooperates, are of any positive concern. Why, then, late at night, on July 1, 1970, at 2 A.M., had "he" taken cognizance of the intruder? Because even now it is not clear whether that hairy Dharma had actually appeared or had loomed out of certain hours of the past in his conscious-subconscious which constituted the only real world "he" wanted for his reality. And now, if you please, stop wasting time and get back to transcribing, you know my hours are numbered, I might go into the final coma tomorrow. When that happens you know what to do, it's all in the "will," just call the telephone company–post office in the valley in the forest right away and start the "tape on the occasion of entering the coma." And don't forget to arrange for the plane ticket, if I'm going to beat my mother to the punch once and for all and give her what she deserves, I need that ticket more than anything else, "he" says. Now then, push that pencil, don't eat away the little time remaining this pitiful essence of liver cancer!]]

If, as those in attendance around his bed maintained, the late night appearance of that intruder was a dream, it was his first dream to remain vividly in memory since he had moved to this "final abode" with, like any Bantu tribesman, his liver in ruins despite his tender age, and, he confidently imagined, would be his last.

There were those who reported he often sobbed in his sleep and suggested he was confronting his own critical condition for the first time in his dreams. To be sure, these were the very people who insisted, on the other hand, that he was deluding himself about liver cancer, that all he really had was cirrhosis, and that, while recovery would not be easy, there was still room for hope. On his part, he maintained he remembered nothing of any dreams that would have made him sob. He even claimed he spent his waking hours enveloped in happy thoughts, breathing happiness. Frequently, for the benefit of those who came and went around his bed (who, although they were certain to outlive him, lying in his bed awaiting the moment of his own death as if it had been finally scheduled, were treated by him as if they were already among the dead), not necessarily to flaunt his happiness but simply to enjoy the sounds that reached his ears along his jawbone from his own eccentric vocal chords, and to revel in the furtive, complex sympathetic resonation of his internal organs, pregnant now with cancer cells, he would sing, in English, "Happy Days Are Here Again." Admittedly, since the refrain was strung with high notes, if he mistakenly began too high, his voice climbed to a shrillness that not only threatened those around him but created an uneasiness in himself that seemed to center in his innards. He firmly believed that his liver, soon to complete its transformation into a rocklike mass, functioned in its ample fullness as a speaker embedded in his body, resonating with even the highest notes and filtering the dissonance due primarily to organic factors out of the music of his vital organs. "Let us sing a song of cheer again," he sang, "Happy days are here again," and the refrain went as follows:

__Hap - py   days are   here   a -   gain _____

And now, he thought, just as my *Happy Days* are about to revive at last and I pass the time in excited anticipation there is no one here who shared them with me, and the only person who actually witnessed them, my mother, remains secluded in the valley deep in the forest and continues to send the same high frequency signals principally of hatred to the antenna in my innards, which, now that I think about it, is probably the reason I got cancer, and since that's the case I must be certain to record my *Happy Days* fully during this time I spend alone in a hospital bed, and, to place the record in perspective so that it can outlive my death, to record how, ever since the destruction of those former *Happy Days*, my imagination has been moving back in their direction as helplessly as a model airplane in a tailspin—and this he resolved to do.

However, since he was an invalid at the very brink of death, afflicted with, as he believed, liver cancer, or, at the very least, assuming only what was objectively recognized, an advanced cirrhosis, it was unthinkable that he should put pen to paper himself. At first, when he asserted this and asked for a stenographer, the voices around his bed replied that he was merely deluding himself, that if only he regained the "normal consciousness" that he was in the neurology and not the cancer ward and not so gravely ill that he could not hold a pencil, he would undoubtedly be

7

able to write for hours on end, and even with an instrument as heavy as that giant Pelikan fountain pen which was an ostentatious souvenir from some trip abroad. The fountain pen in question, as well as the discolored brass underwater goggles he wore almost constantly as he lay in bed (the oval glass lenses set into two short cylinders had been covered long ago, before the days of synthetic tape, with dark green cellophane, and were still used that way; clipping his nostrils late that night with the goggles on, he must have looked to the intruder like an alien from outer space, one short, conic, metal cylinder neatly extending from each of his eyes and one nostril), were both mementoes of someone long dead about whom he and his mother disagreed violently yet both referred to as *a certain party*. Not only had *a certain party's* former belongings, now in his possession, been unspeakably insulted by the manner in which they had been described, it had also been insinuated that if he were really about to enter a coma and die, the personal record of his *Happy Days* would be a waste: his anger mounted.

Angrily, he emphasized once again that what he intended to relate was a "history of the age" that would transcend the arbitrary reminiscences of a mere individual. If *a certain party*, who figured in the history, had not been killed in a street battle in a provincial city just before the war ended, he would certainly have been required to testify before the extraordinary session of the Military Tribunal for the Far East that had been obliged to make its way to the valley deep in the forest; the story he was about to tell should, therefore, be of great concern not only to the United Nations but, in particular, to the current administration of his own country, a nation controlled by men who were clearly war criminals who had survived.

8

And now he had an acting executor of the will who took down his account at his bedside, and he had as well the manuscript of a "history of the age" out of chronological order. To be sure, since he wore his cylinder-type underwater goggles like opera glasses with green cellophane covering the lenses regularly, reading over and checking the manuscript, though perhaps not impossible, would have been a fearfully difficult chore.

[[Why do you talk as if you believed you had terminal cancer and were about to go into a coma when all your symptoms contradict that? When I'm putting it all down on paper I have the feeling the characters I've written stand up on the page as fact and push at my fingers as I write, says the "acting executor of the will." The doctor may have ordered you to keep lying to me about my cancer for the time being, but every time that lie jumps out of your mouth it solidifies and floats there alongside your head, and before long you're going to find youself rooted to the spot in the middle of a mosquito-swarm of lies, "he" counters.]]

When he began to feel cancer growing in his body cavity with the vigor of fermenting malt, he also became aware that he was being gradually freed, by nature's own power, from all that fettered him. It was not any accumulation of refusals willed by himself that was accomplishing this; he had only to lay his body down and, even while he slept, the cancer inside him that was an access to freedom continued ponderously to enlarge. What he saw, not only of reality but even in his imagination, was often blurred by fever, but within that vague dimness his cancer appeared to him as a flourishing bed of yellow hyacinths or possibly chrysanthemums bathed in a faint, purple light. At such moments, until fatigue penetrated to the

9

core of his head, he would breathe in and out with particular concentration, summoning to his nostrils the power of all his senses, and attempt to smell those cancer hyacinths or possibly chrysanthemums. The existence inside himself of something growing on its own vitality which, by means of its own internal power alone, was about to conduct him to and beyond new realms he could not fully conceive, and which, moreover, he was able to locate in his body as actual sensations in blood and flesh, seemed an experience more momentous than any since sexual awakening. This *analogy* led to dreams of stirring up sexual embers nearly buried under ash and scarcely warm. Now that death was staring him in the face, he longed to dip up, to reconfront, and to liberate everything taboo that he had repressed during his thirty-five years of life, at which time it seemed likely a whole unexpected world of sex might gush from his rich, yellow bed of blossoming cancer and the purple light surrounding it.

However, becoming bold even to shamelessness required careful stages of preparation. Since he was no born genius at obscenity, transforming his entire body into, as it were, a *vagina* in heat, and then enjoying, heedless of the outrage in the eyes watching him, as if he were a sea anemone set free beneath the water, its tumid wetness and the incessant squirming of its tentacles, was a feat he could not be expected to perform. With the time remaining him limited and new sexual developments merely anticipated, he lay upon his bed like an abstinent mole.

[[Observing that the "acting executor of the will" was unsettled by these remarks, What, are you afraid I'm going to start begging you to masturbate me any minute? Are you afraid if my entire body has become a vagina in heat I may request some grotesque form of masturbation such as jamming a pole into the sea anemone of my body and stirring it around? "he" teased pathetically, half in ridicule but half solicitously.]]

The instant he felt the slightest premonition of pain or itchiness, in his vital organs or on his skin, he screamed at those around his bed to ask the doctor for a "morphine" injection. And he doubted not that the injections he received were always "morphine." In fact, it was only after it had become possible for him to intercept the arrival of pain with "morphine" while pain was still a premonition that he had turned into a man who sang repeatedly a song of *Happy Days*, a happy man. After his injection he would sleep as though in a coma, and it was a sleep he had not tasted since he was a baby, cradled in sweet sensations. Awakening from such a sleep, he gazed at a photograph he had cut from a book by Georges Batailles, of a Chinaman being drawn and quartered while in a narcotic ecstasy. Looking into a mirror, he studied his face to see if it had come to resemble the Chinaman's, which was like a braided rope of agony and pleasure and which, besides, unlike the merely erotic expressions in "spring pictures," was suffused with something purely tragic. His own face, wan, with ink-black whiskers like the spines of a sea urchin sprouting around his lips, the skin particularly drawn because he had been lying on his back and, beneath the skin, scarcely any flesh or fat at all, seemed to have returned to the true face he had somewhere along the line lost the right to possess. Scrutinizing, in a field of vision narrowly limited by the dark green cellophane covering his underwater goggles, a face that had regained even its drawn, comic ugliness when as a child he had submerged after fish in the depths of the river at the bottom of the valley, he was content.

11

Inasmuch as he wanted to experience in its entirety the hopeless situation into which he had finally fallen at the age of thirty-five, there were times when he placed himself quite consciously in a nightmare governed by the fear of death. Early one morning, having made certain there was no one around his bed, he told himself that he was in the grips of the wretched, deluded hope that if he could stave off for just five minutes the slavering jaws of the liver-cancer goblin charging him like a fright-crazed cur, he would also be free of the cancer actually in his body. He began thrashing around, trying to evade the jaws of the goblin dog Cancer that had leaped onto his bed, and when presently he felt the need to urinate and stepped out of bed, he was entirely disoriented. Through the sea-floor dimness he beheld through his underwater goggles he made his way toward the door, which was always left open,' but instead of the open space he expected he discovered, right in front of his eyes, nearly touching the cylinders of his goggles, an unexpectedly solid white wall in gleaming green shadow. The sensation that followed, of total physical enclosure, was death as real and concrete as it could be, its first appearance in his real life. Like a crude mechanical man unable to change direction, he stood in front of the wall in clumsy stupefaction, hands frozen in front of his eyes, unable to touch, as if it were a force field repelling him, the wall. In the reflected brightness, each of his slender, greenish fingertips appeared spatulate and suction-cupped, like frog fingers. Terrified by the game he had begun himself, in a reeling panic, he somehow managed to fall backward onto the bed, but he soaked the sheets with leaked urine.

However, even at times like these, he was able to enjoy imagining dreamily the clamor and bustle when the announcement of death would send all the systems of his body, alive now and metabolizing tirelessly, racing one another to be the first to decompose. At the end of the tape which the acting executor of the will would play when he had entered a coma he wanted to record the following words to his mother, who would be coming alone from the house in the valley: *Please make sure you stay to observe my body decomposing; if possible I would like you to observe even my putrefied and swollen insides burst my stomach and bubble out as gas and muddy liquid.* But it was not easy to deliver such lines without disagreeable masochistic overtones; besides, if the state of his stomach should oblige him to belch just as he began to record and his voice should falter or tremble, he could imagine carrying his chagrin with him right into the world of the dead, so he merely assembled these sentences in his silent head.

When he thought about cremation, particularly cremation hurriedly carried out before the body's cells had fully decomposed, anger stiffened his own still living body. Incorporated in this reaction, he could sense, was rage being demonstrated independently of his own consciousness by the agitated cell systems themselves. He was also filled with disgust and outrage at the thought of his dead body being treated against decomposition and then dissected. Let that which is meant to decompose do so in peace, in its entirety and smallest part; let man impair not the dignity of decomposition! Tenderly pressing with both hands the liver like a stone pillow sewn into his belly, he entrusted the acting executor of the will with the additional, patient task, so as to ensure that nothing interfered with the Copernican rotation in which the cancer lodged in his liver, at the peak of its enterprise, would terminate all life functions and begin at once to decompose, of protecting his injured liver from premature cremation and antiseptic destruction by doctors who retained the experimental spirit of their intern days.

As he thought about that part of himself that would remain in this world after death, he developed an appreciation for the custom of platform burial, in which birds or the wind were allowed to take their course. He also considered what he had seen along the Ganges at the Hindus' sacred Benares, placid corpses decomposing from inside and bloated up like sunfish floating half-submerged down the swift, muddy river, and reflected once again, admiringly, that the wise Hindus were correct, that theirs was a solution befitting the meditative tribe among all the countless tribes of humanity that had meditated longest and most accurately in history, in the climate best suited to meditation.

[[When you traveled to India did you really see corpses floating in the river at Benares? asks the "acting executor of the will." Well now, when I sensed the difficulty in my liver was incurable, I declared my freedom from all bonds connecting me to the real world that was holding me dangling from its fingertips, so there's no telling whether I've actually experienced what I say, correspondence with reality in itself has never meant anything anyway, "he" says. The truth is, I'm heading straight back toward my *Happy Days* in the past, and if bringing some detail in that past sharply to the surface requires it, I'm prepared to alter the present reality however I please. For example, when I'm trying to penetrate deeply into memories of fights I had as a child, I make myself believe that the thirty-five-year-old lying here in bed with a sick liver, and not only his liver but nearly every vital organ smashed and broken, is a professional bantamweight boxer long retired. When I set my internal time machine all the way back to myself fighting the older kids in the valley twenty-five years ago, with the boxing tricks I learned from the cadets who came to my village to tap pine tree roots for oil, my longing to become a soldier and also a boxer revives in me along with the nearly epileptic activity of the brain cells in my feverish young head, and it seems impossible that I could ever have chosen any profession other than boxing right down to this day. If I push myself too hard, a squirt in a torn, dirty, brown undershirt too large for him and short pants easily twice his size that he folded over at the sides and tied with a rope, fighting, with spit and blood whistling between his teeth, against the big kids who came to steal a look at *a certain party's* excrement, his face swollen into a full moon, might just leap from the core of my body and wallop me as I languish here in this sloppy bed, "he" says.]]

Inasmuch as the only limitation he would accept with regard to the present was that he was on his deathbed with a diseased liver, there was nothing to prevent him from postulating any life for himself he chose. And it would have been difficult to think up a set of circumstances better suited to catapulting a consciousness in quest of liberation in the direction of all freedom than lying in a deathbed with a liver like a rock he could scarcely encompass with both arms.

Which was not to say he felt at the same liberty to choose from any number of possibilities those *Happy Days* which were the focus of his past: he was determined that this must not happen. Were he to recall those *Happy Days* as if they were a variety of past sufficiently vague to permit any number of interpretations, he would lose half

15

his reason for continuing to cling to life despite the pain from his liver that constantly troubled his subconscious. Conversely, since he was determined to recreate his *Happy Days* as exactly as possible, he did not hesitate, if the achievement of that exactness required it, to distort the present. Now nothing can have been clearer than this attitude, derived from principle, which he maintained all day and even at night while he was awake, but when he fell asleep he sobbed aloud. To the acting executor of the will it sounded as if he were repeating the word "band," and this she reported to him. Still the nightmares which seemed to carry him back to a specific moment in the past continued, and, as he invariably sobbed the same words, their meaning was eventually ascertained more precisely. To be sure, since he was able to remember nothing of the content of the dream, it was the acting executor of the will who finally discovered what he was sobbing: *Ah, ah, abandoned the man abandoned by the band, ah, ah, abandoned the man the band abandoned!*

II

The words he sobbed in his sleep had been elucidated, but, perhaps because someone else had made the discovery, the sobbing itself was not overcome. There were still times when he sobbed violently, or so another of those in the vicinity of his bed

[[Let's say "nurse" from here on, call it a necessary compromise to lighten the burden "he" places on the scribe. When I know you're talking about the nurse the desire to put down "nurse" tugs at me even though you use some vague phrase instead. This interruption of his account by the "acting executor of the will' was when the trouble began. I should think you might control that selfish need of yours to put down what you believe no matter what I say, especially when I'm going out of my way to use the third person to make your job easier. "He" expressed his dissatisfaction mildly enough, yet the "acting executor of the will" said nothing in reply. This made it more than ever inevitable that "he" go to the considerable trouble in his green-cellophane-covered underwater goggles of reading over that portion of his account already on paper. How could "he" be sure that a single one of the points "he" had asserted with such exactness had not been dissolved in the flux of ambiguity? But what are you so eager to say yourself that makes you want to change the account of somebody else's past? I don't revise one syllable of what is said to me, I'm only asking that you do try to use common nouns, for example, that you say "nurse" when you mean nurse, to make my work easier; if you don't make an effort I'm afraid common nouns will eventually disappear from your speech, and since you almost never reveal even a single proper noun either! said the "acting executor of the will." Whereupon it was agreed that a specific, common noun would be used when referring to]]

the nurse reported. But even after the longest night of sobbing, however brokenly, he was unable to recall what must have been his painful, lonely dream. While he slept, his pulse and blood pressure certainly decreased and his vital organs, including his brain, discontinued a wide variety of their operations. Cancer, however, independently of his conscious-subconscious, continued its cell-by-cell proliferation day and night. If, then, there really was a positive vitality inside him capable of lifting his voice in a scream while he slept, was it not likely to be the vitality of robust, ever-fattening cancer itself? But why should cancer cells sob? One morning at dawn the nurse shook him awake because his sobs were being heard in the next room. Once he was awake he could hear that not only the patient next door but the two hundred dogs kept in the hospital courtyard for use in the laboratory had also been threatened by his sobbing and clearly were howling still; nonetheless, he thought to himself, I am only dreaming; besides, I'm already fully conscious of the significance of those howling dogs because I've written about them, this is no time for howling dogs. At that moment he was in effect beholding himself over the entirety of his thirty-five years of life, from professional bantamweight boxer to author or playwright in reality; at the same time he had shaken off the feeling of having been pulled abruptly backward out of his dream and the physical sensation that lingered after sobbing, and was beginning to tingle with the first indications of his daytime bliss.

Thereupon he began for the hundredth time the game that was his chief source of pleasure now, imagining, with all the fine precision of a timetable, his mother setting out from home on the occasion of his death. The plan was to go into operation just before he entered the final coma, when he had managed to ascertain from the doctors while still fully conscious that death was a certainty within the next few days, when, in other words, the final stage in the accomplishment of his death had been successfully completed.

On that chosen morning, when a cable from the doctor was almost certain to persuade his mother, who never believed a word he said himself, of the objective necessity of setting out finally from the depths of the

18

forest, he would first have the acting executor of the will place a long-distance call to the airport in the provincial city and verify that all flights were on schedule. And he would have her inquire about weather conditions, not only at Haneda airport in Tokyo but also at Itami in Osaka. All in order. He had heard that the pass known in his region as "ninety-nine-curve-pass" was paved now, which meant there was scarcely any likelihood of serious obstacles along the only route out of the valley in the forest to the provincial city on the plain. His mother would leave the valley in a three-wheel truck, emerge from the forest, speed across the plain at the bottom of the pass to the provincial city and be in time for her flight. She would change planes at Osaka on schedule and arrive in Tokyo on schedule, head upright, eyes closed, speaking to no one and, if some overfriendly passenger persisted in speaking to her, pulling from her tight sash the card that had arrived in the mail with her plane ticket. On the card was written: "This old woman does not speak to strangers. In case of emergency, please help her contact the following address."

When it was time at last he would telephone the valley deep in the forest and determine whether the three-wheel truck had left with his mother in it. If she had set out already, the house of his birth, known locally as "the Manor in the valley," would be deserted. In that case the wife of the postmaster (he was also head of the telephone office), who sat all day in front of a switchboard that was still manual, would take his call.

——I can see the three-wheeler coming back across the wood bridge, yessir!, she was certain to report, amused by the strange request phoned all the way from Tokyo, to look and see whether a three-wheel truck was heading for the concrete bridge that crossed to the highway out of the valley. The old lady from the Manor house is setting in it, wearing her urn of ashes of her war dead in a wooden box upon her bosom. She must have went around by the Monkey Shrine to pay her respects before she leaves the village, yessir, and she just now came back across the wood bridge and now they're a-heading out towards the highway, and the old lady from the Manor house is setting straight up alongside the driver, with her eyes closed, and that box upon her bosom, yessir!

——Does it seem as if her eyes are closed because she isn't feeling well? he would ask with just a touch of eagerness, exposing a weakness he could never quite control where his mother was concerned.

——Goodness, no! That old lady doesn't think anybody but herself is human, so she always closes her eyes when it appears she might have to meet somebody in the valley. The subtle, long-felt resentment in the postmaster's wife would dash icy water on the tepid sentimentality rising in him. But there was no danger his happiness would be uprooted. That lady's got no one left but only her one son, and they say he's dying of cancer, so she's leaving for Tokyo with that urn of ashes of her war dead that did her honor twenty-five years ago. And do you know she hasn't shed a tear, and her head is straight up and her eyes shut tight—she's a hard old lady! Of course, she's not one to believe other folks, so she maybe thinks those doctors are wrong and her son doesn't have cancer. And that's what most of us around here think too, yessir!

——It's cancer, all right, *liver cancer,* and it's only a matter of days now! She just learned the truth, that's what made up her mind to leave the valley.

——Have you heard that straight from the doctor? That he's really got himself cancer? Because that's what we've been hearing all along. . . .

20

———That's right, cancer. And I don't have to hear any-thing from the doctor because I'm the son from the Manor house and I'm dying of cancer right now! he would say, then signal the nurse to replace the receiver that had probably become too heavy for him to handle by himself.
———I surely want to beg your pardon, yessir! the voice would whine like a mosquito speeding away, weakly fade, and disappear.

"Wearing" an urn of ashes "upon her bosom" meant that his mother had tied the ends of the white cotton cloth in which the urn was wrapped behind her neck. Toward the end of the war this had suddenly become a style frequently encountered in the valley. But the urn his mother would be taking with her was more than twenty-five years old. Shortly after the disastrous naval defeat at Midway this very urn and white wooden box and cotton cloth, still unusual at a time when the tide of the war had only just begun to turn against Japan, had come home to the village from the Chinese Mainland with a bit of dust representing the "repatriated bones" of his elder brother, the first war casualty in the valley, and had opened decisively the rift between *a certain party* and his mother which was never to close so long as they lived. At the time, *a certain party* had already withdrawn from the multifarious operations of the "committee" directly in league with the military based in Manchuria and was living in seclusion in his native village in the valley. When his eldest son, while attached to the very Japanese division on the Chinese mainland that formerly had been the chief sphere of *a certain party's* activity and influence, had left the front and been shot by the enemy, or possibly a comrade, his mother's hatred for *a certain party* had become manifest. Never again was the word "father" spoken in the house in the valley deep in the forest. Such was the special

21

significance of the urn containing his elder brother's ashes which his mother would now take out for the first time in nearly thirty years and "wear upon her bosom" as she set out for Tokyo in a three-wheel truck, across the dizzying ninety-nine-curve-pass, feeling, in her anxiety at having emerged from the forest, as if a vacuum had formed just behind her and was pulling her back.

When he had enjoyed the supreme game to this point in his conscious mind he decided on a whim to reinforce his pleasure in his subconscious. What if he couldn't remember anything about his dreams when he awoke, assuming it was a fact that he did have dreams, he ought to accumulate at least the physical experience of dreaming while his condition permitted it.

As he was falling asleep again on the single sleeping pill the nurse had given him he tried suggesting toward his subconscious that he would like particularly to dream about ninety-nine-curve-pass. Since childhood he had tried repeatedly to determine whether there were actually ninety-nine curves, but as he climbed the pass the curves and the numbers had always separated in his head. Now, the truth still undetermined, he was about to die. One day at the height of summer twenty-five years ago he had accompanied *a certain party*, unable to move on his own power because of a cancer hemorrhaging badly in his bladder on top of his abnormal corpulence, over the pass in an army truck with ten soldiers who had left the army and come all the way to the valley to entreat *a certain party* to join them, singing in German with the others. And ever since the doctors had begun the final stage of treatment, easing the pain in his innards and blurring his conscious-ness of grief, he had been returning to himself as a kid in that valley drenched in the light of the last summer of the war, and repeatedly had been seeing that little journey over the pass as vividly as if it were a daydream. And who said real dreams could not be dreamed in sleep? If his dreams of himself went beyond himself as a human and were unfathomable to him once he woke up, did that mean cancer itself was in firm control of his body-and-consciousness in his dreams? Even so, he still hoped to recall accurately, in a dream controlled by himself, the climb up that pass which was the only exit from the forest surrounding the valley to the outside world. If this ambition was not entirely unrealistic, it was because he had already become a cancer man!

Yet when he awoke again—can it be he hadn't dreamed?—his body-and-consciousness retained no traces of a dream. 8 A.M.—he tried to determine whether he had been sobbing again, but the nurse would only say curtly, If you don't remember yourself, don't ask me!

[["If you don't remember yourself there's probably no point in my saying anything," wasn't it? Could we make that correction? the "acting executor of the will" interrupts, infuriating him. Correction? For whom and for what reason? If that one correction is made the poison will spread from there and my whole "history of the age" will be ruined. If you're so obsessed with corrections how about imitating those Filipino psychic surgeons and using the spiritual power of that sharp tongue of yours as if it were a knife to *correct* the cancer in my vital organs! Not that I really want to get rid of it, since it's cancer I managed to acquire myself. You said the doctors had begun the final stage of treatment in order to ease your pain and blur your consciousness of grief, but when I wrote that down I didn't accept any responsibility for the truth of it, because you don't HAVE cancer! I don't know

23

what you and the doctors and nurses hope to accomplish by conspiring to lie to me when I'm the patient and I *want* cancer, "he" says.]]

When he asked the doctor on afternoon rounds,

——Why do all of you hide my cancer from me? The doctor flatly denied, as always, that he was hiding anything.

——But that nonsense aside, I see you have an astonishing number of scars and almost all of them look as if you made them yourself, am I right? He did not respond, but after the doctor left he had the acting executor of the will undress him and then carefully examined, using a hand mirror, the old scars that covered his back, buttocks, and thighs. Not that very many small scars could actually be discovered through underwater goggles covered with cellophane. It was rather the various scars in the flesh of his memory that he uncovered. Some dated from the brief period that began with his infancy and ended at the pinnacle of his *Happy Days*. But most were wounds he had received after the destruction of his *Happy Days*, particularly during the first year he had commuted on his bicycle to the postwar high school in the neighboring village. It was commuting on that bicycle that he invaded for the first time in his young life, unprotected and alone, a *territory* outside the valley where he was born and raised. Moreover, the strangers awaiting him outside the valley retained no psychological scars or aftereffects relating to *a certain party*, did not lower their eyes and turn away when they encountered someone *a certain party* had left behind. They were, in other words, total strangers, and it was moreover the most baldly violent group among them who surrounded him on the high school campus.

The echoing effect of the postwar chaos on child

24

society intensified in direct proportion to the children's distance from a major city; and it was in this environment, where all varieties of violence were abundant, that his fearlessness about being wounded and even occasional need to do injury to his body with his own hands gained him for the first time a certain unique freedom. Its acquisition began with an incident just after he had entered high school, when he was summoned, alone, by the leader of the teen-age gang that dominated the school, to the auditorium-gymnasium where the gang waited. The reason for the summons was simply that he was un-mistakably dirtier and poorer beyond comparison than any of his freshman classmates. Although his mother had given him registration fees and tuition, he had not managed to extract from her any additional money for a uniform or club activities. This struck him as unjust. So he sewed the high school badge on the uniform jacket he had been using in middle school and which had belonged to his brother who had been killed in China, and continued to wear it. Since middle school days, afraid the jacket might lead his mother into the clutches of fresh memories of his dead brother, he had kept it hidden, wrapped in newspaper, in a woodshed in back of the Manor house. When it turned cold enough to need a jacket, he would leave the house in his shirtsleeves, go around to the woodshed and hurry into the jacket before going to school. Consequently, he was not able to have the jacket washed or mended, and not only looked unclean but distinctly smelled. He was, furthermore, the only fresh-man without a uniform cap.

By disciplining this youth who was violating school regulations so blatantly at the beginning of the first term, the leader of the gang probably hoped to create the

25

impression among the freshman that he and his friends were not merely ruffians disliked in and out of school but vigilantes upholding justice on campus. Although he forbade the freshmen to enter the auditorium during the disciplining, he required them to gather at all the windows outside. Betraying no sign they felt the slightest affiliation with their lone classmate about to be chastised, idiotic expressions on their faces one and all as they struggled to maintain a balance between cowed curiosity and dull fear, the freshmen gathered around the windows to observe the drama of one-sided violence about to begin inside.

And in the beginning it was one-sided. Seating himself on top of the parallel bars, the prosecutor began by pointing out that his feet inside his torn tennis shoes were bare, in violation of school regulations. Next he charged that beneath his jacket, which was not even a proper high school jacket, he was wearing the most strictly forbidden of all things, a black shirt (he had sewn it himself out of a large black flag, he had no idea what it stood for, which he had pulled from a box full of his brother's personal effects). When the gang leader had admonished him for these and other specific offenses, all of which doubtless had been whispered into his ear by informers among the freshmen, he climbed slowly down from the parallel bars and punched him in the temples, leaving the ground with each blow though he was the taller of the two. Encouraged by the total nonresistance he encountered he then became even more highhanded:

——Your eyes don't show you're truly ashamed even after having been disciplined by an upperclassman, and, sighing theatrically,

——It's really tough to have underclassmen like this; we're the ones who get blamed in the end, right! and fell to punching him again. At this point, the defendant judged it would not do to have his temples beaten further. It was Saturday, and because that afternoon the new students had been assigned the chore of weeding the playing field he had a small sickle wrapped up with his books and notebooks. He stooped and took it out; then he looked the gang leader straight in the eyes and dug the blade with damp earth still clinging to it into the skin between the thumb and first finger of his left hand. Blood gushed, but he did not move an eyebrow. To the leader of the gang glaring at him in confusion the eyes staring back through a mucous film must have seemed incomprehensibly calm. But the effect was that of seeming motionlessness that occurs at the peak of high-speed revolutions: inside he was fighting for consciousness in a frenzy. Submerging then into the quiet revery at the extreme limits of duress he faced *a certain party* and screamed, in a voice so high it could only have registered on a canine ear, *Please drink the blood; it is for you!* and all of a sudden was waiting once again, with those soldiers who had left the army, on the road along the moat that led into the provincial city and the bank, armed with his own bayonet, sweat that was unmistakably from the heat of that midsummer day beading his grimy forehead.

Outwardly, he was confronting the leader of the juvenile gang, lowering the arm that gripped the sickle and extending his wounded, bleeding hand in an ambiguous movement that might have been an attempt to strike back or an overture to shaking hands; internally, he was composed of a lucid part at the clear surface of his consciousness and a murky part that had precipitated down close to the dark bottom yet remained distinct from his subconscious. In the swift wounding of his own flesh

on a bewildering impulse from the hot, pitch-black core of
himself he had felt a deep joy which was not only
unperceived by the hoodlums surrounding him but which
he himself was not even conscious of as joy. At the same
time, however, his head cleared by the blood that had
been let as if the sickle were a medieval surgeon's knife,
he made the fully conscious, practical calculation that it
would not do to let things stand if he hoped to finish off
this opponent from whom he had managed to wrest the
advantage, that, in fact, if he allowed time to pass without
altering his strategy he would find himself in a position
more dangerous than before. To be sure, he had managed
to shock the hoodlums by wounding himself, producing a
queasiness perhaps in each of their stomachs, but none of
them had grasped the lasting significance of that shock.
Consequently, as soon as the momentary physical uneasiness had passed, given their stolidity and forgetfulness,
they could be expected to recover themselves and resume
hostilities. It was therefore essential that he contrive a
means of indicating a way out so simple it would be
understood by the leader of the gang even in his somewhat dazed condition. Once he had the solution in mind
he was merely playacting, an irrecoverable distance now
from that hot, black something that had surged in him a
minute earlier.

He stared at the bloodstained sickle, then thrust it
under his opponent's nose and screamed, as wildly as he
could sound,
——Shall I cut your hand too? I'll fight with this sickle *even
though you don't have one!* And if I start to lose I'll cut my
own throat! With that he deliberately lifted the sickle and
held it against his throat, whereupon his opponent, with a
swift shrewdness more than worthy of someone esteemed

as a leader, even by a gang of hoodlums, solved the riddle he had concealed in his screaming. Turning to his comrades he signaled an end to the formal disciplining.

——He says he's going to fight with that sickle even though I'm empty-handed! And he threatens to cut his own throat if we knock him down. Let's get out of here! There's no use talking to a dirty, wild kid like this. He's a crazy dog, *no rules!* If you hit him too hard you'll catch germs!

With these words, the gang leader had presented him with a passport to his own violence, and now in order to validate it with his signature he ran around the room slashing with his sickle the stuffed mats covering the jumping platforms piled against the wall. The gym teacher, who was almost certainly a man of violence to the marrow of his bones, and who besides had been imme-diately informed of the identity of the criminal, made no accusations at the faculty meeting. One day when he was breaking another regulation by washing his hands at the drinking fountain, this teacher, a smallish man with a head like a shriveled pear and a beet-red face and a perfectly flat, fatless stomach of which he was very proud, bounded up like a long-distance runner and said, coquettishly, in a gentle voice but with exaggerated gestures that might have looked to an observer in the distance as if he were scolding the boy,

——I want you to think of me as a friend, OK? How about if I teach you some killer holds and throws so you won't have to use a knife the next time you fight those punks?

Assuming animals can be called violent, he was spoken of with distaste in and out of school as animally violent; only the leader of the juvenile gang had glimpsed, just behind the roughness he had displayed on the surface, a baffling internal passion by turns turbulent and still. And it appeared that he was instinctively wary of the weird energy he could sense arcing between those poles: in his instructions to his henchmen he put it plainly: watch out for him, he don't care what happens to him; he's like a *kamikaze* pilot that didn't get to die! And so a precariously balanced peace was maintained between himself and the juvenile gang. Had he been judged remarkable for his violence only, the time would have come when the enemy shrewdly sensed they had regained the advantage where violence was concerned, and at that instant his own violence, in direct proportion to its absolute value, would have become a weight around his neck that dragged him gasping to the ground. However, the gang leader had seen in him something his hoodlum friends could never better no matter how they fought to compete, something incomprehensible. And so the gang adopted a compromise policy of considering him a creature beneath themselves, loathsome as the spirit of the plague, and pretended not to see him when he passed.

The day he slashed his hand with a sickle it wasn't long before the pain was hard to bear without crying out. When he wiped the blood away he could see bits of muddy dirt and whitish fat welling out of the wound, and no matter how often he wiped it the blood continued to flow. The bicycle he rode to school, a number 8 which people in the valley called simply "old eight" (he had no idea what the number measured), was the very same bicycle he had been riding since he was a child, on which he had had at least one accident that had very nearly cost him his life, and which even now that he had entered high school was too large for him. When he went to the back of the equipment room where he parked the bike he was so

30

dizzy from loss of blood he couldn't even stand, let alone straddle the high seat. Having gripped the handlebars once, he now stoically released them, so the bicycle would not fall, and then fell himself to the damp, clay floor patched, in just the way that blood vessel tumors would patch his chest when he got to be thirty-five and his liver sickened, with moss of a too brilliant, painful green to his dilated pupils. Struggling somehow to lift himself he grasped some thick weed stumps with his wounded hand, uttered a long, piteous moan, and went limp where he lay. As he watched, with one eye suspended three centimeters above the ground, the blood continue to flow from his hand and seep into the weeds, an extraordinary calm descended upon him and he felt ashamed of the innate violence that had surfaced shortly before with the violence he had consciously created. Shrinking not only with pain but also shame he spoke to *a certain party* again: *Please drink the blood; it is for you!* Surrounding him where he lay on the ground the other first-year students who also came to school on bikes looked on with unconcerned curiosity and disgust plain to see on their faces, as if they were observing a dog die of hunger. No one among them ran to the nurse's office for his sake.

——There's medicine in that weed, that's why he's pushing the hand he cut with the sickle in among the roots like that. Wild animals that have been wounded always do that way. One time there was even a deer that mended a broken bone by wading in a hot springs! The explanation came from the son of the doctor in his village, a freshman like himself who was certain to end up at the head of his class; when he struggled to his feet a minute later and the group fled in confusion the doctor's son was in the lead.

Thus it was that he created a unique lifestyle in the

31

new institution known as the postwar high school. In fact, he had discovered a lifestyle suited to the real world wherever other people were not hampered by psychological scars relating to *a certain party*, everywhere, in other words, but the valley deep in the forest. It was a decisive discovery: not once in all the intervening years until at thirty-five he had been caught by the demon of liver cancer had he found it necessary to shift to any other lifestyle. And this made him think there must be a certain significance in the resemblance between the tumors now appearing on his chest and the pattern of the moss on that damp ground upon which he had fallen and rested while blood ran from his small body. Could it be that he had fallen bleeding onto his own chest covered with tumors now as he was about to die of cancer?

[[I think the doctor had something else in mind, something more direct, the scribe interposes, deferentially to be sure, fatigued by his endless reminiscence. What do you mean, "direct"? I can't say anything definite until I've checked with the doctor, she replies, sidestepping. The way you're acting, "he" says with chagrin, challenging her, I have no confidence you're accurately recording the hundredth part of what I say. I don't abbreviate a single syllable, but the more passionately you speak the harder it is for me to know where your passion is coming from. If I said otherwise I really would be lying, so I want to make that clear to you.]]

III

[[I've just been talking with the doctor, says the "acting executor of the will." Since "he" is meant to be the only speaker in his reality "he" is disconcerted and annoyed that his scribe's mind has been alive and active while his own was at rest. Just what did you discuss? As long as it wasn't discontinuing my "morphine." The doctor inquired about those scars all over your body because he wanted to find out whether you might be suicidal. If it turned out you were, we'd naturally have to arrange for night nurses. Released from one piercing instant of tension "he" begins to laugh, Ha! Ha! Ha! is how it sounds to his own ears, a variety of laughter "he" is aware has never issued from him in all his thirty-five years but which recalls unmistakably a friend of his, a young American Jew from Harvard who had become deeply embedded in his life and who burst into nearly hysterical, self-derisive laughter whenever he was caught in an embarrassing situation he could not explain away. Suicide? Ha! Ha! Ha! This bed I'm sharing with my cancer is as far away as it's possible to be from the need for suicide, "he" says, gradually accustoming himself to this new style of laughter like a stinging in the core of his brain, though clearly the "acting executor of the will" is suspicious. Not that "he" is able to sustain interest in the reactions of those who actually surround his bed. Presently, to regain the breath "he" needs to continue his narration, "he" tries to bring an end to the laughter. But for a time alphabet letters no bigger than ants continue to spill from his lips as faint sounds, *ha!-ha!-ha!*]]

When he pictured himself facing his mother and informing her gravely that suicide's objective was about to be attained though he was not even considering suicide, a life force opposite in direction from the *life force of cancer* that was rapidly destroying him but equally alive with motor energy welled up, particularly from the vicinity of his feverish, itching liver. Mother! I have no need for suicide anymore, now I can sail right past you without having to make that kind of special effort and die legally and morally in every sense! The words were like a musical passage that persisted in moving the performer no matter how often he repeated it. In fact, he had enjoyed this private music of his own words countless times.

——Mother, you didn't knock me flat on my back and rub my humiliation in my face as I lay there, and you weren't able to make me feel instantly with one of those sidelong glances of yours and nothing more that I would never be free no matter where I ran, so that I lost the energy I needed to make the leap to a new world as a new person, Mother, until after you caught me in the act trying to commit suicide when I was almost out of high school. It was like being caught masturbating, and told Look here! a monkey masturbates just the way you do, and having a monkey that was actually jacking off thrust under your nose, a dirty, dwarf monkey with its fur falling out from age and its body misshapen and only that crippled organ wounded in countless battles for male supremacy retaining its vividness as actual flesh and in consciousness, that was the form of humiliation you chose for me, wasn't it, Mother! You did everything in your power to make me feel just how low and shameless a thing it would be for me to commit suicide and leave you behind, and then because you were afraid I might not have received the message clearly enough you continued to beat it into me. You stole my will, didn't you, that they showed you at the police station in the neighboring town. Maybe you'll protest, the way you did before, that, unlike me, you're no thief, but even assuming the police did release that notebook to you as my "guardian," it actually belonged to me, which means you stole it from its rightful owner. Then you let yourself into the mimeograph room in the new middle school in the valley and printed it and sent it to my high school teachers and classmates, didn't you! And in order to emphasize mercilessly how self-indulgent and unpleasant a high school student about to attempt suicide could be, and how many incorrect characters he could write badly in just a few sentimental pages of a will, so that you could double and triple my humiliation, you wrote *sic* all over the stencil before you ran it off. When I found out and went nearly mad with embarrassment and rage and protested, you didn't say a word, just listened in silence and darted glances at me, and the next morning you wrote in the margin of a newspaper with a hard pencil that needed sharpening so I had to hold the newspaper at an angle to the light or bend it backward to read it, *"You have neither the right nor the qualifications to do a thing like that, and you lack the conviction!"* until, by the time you were through, you had me so mortified I was nearly epileptic. Now that I think about it, I had only the vaguest notion beforehand of what might have happened if I failed to hang myself and was severely criticized by you. And then I did fail and you devastated me and after that just thinking about suicide was enough to focus my consciousness on my own softness and immaturity, and suicide became the most unnavigable straits for me. You saw that, didn't you, and you lived your life calmly in the valley all those years supposing you had me bound hand and foot. But now all of a sudden the tables are turned, I don't have to commit suicide or anything else, all I have to do to liberate myself is lounge in bed here! Because my faithful dog Cancer is working around the clock to transform my liver into a pretty fair-sized rock! And you can't combat its vigor, not if you roust up the monkey deity, that Japanese amalgam of Buddhism and Taoism on the hill like an isolated island

35

above the valley that the family has venerated for generations as a private guardian, you're just no match!

[[Does that mean you're not only as far as you can be from the possibility of suicide now but also that you've never really attempted suicide? Ha!-Ha!-Ha! Please don't oversimplify. If a little experiment in suicide that I didn't understand very well myself at the time had succeeded, I would certainly have given my mother the knockout punch she deserves, and almost unconsciously.]]

Since childhood he had ridden a bicycle well, but just once, in his first year at postwar middle school, when he was only barely managing to reach the pedals on a full-size bicycle, he had rammed into the sparkling, flecked-with-mica concrete railing of the large bridge at the valley exit. Because the front wheel wedged itself into a crack in the railing, and because he happened to clasp the bike tightly with his legs at the instant of impact, he only struck his chest and chin against the railing, but if these improbable coincidences had not occurred he would certainly have jumped the bridge head over heels, tumbled down the steep slope through hissing stalks of dog-fig that pushed their leaves and poor, nectarless fruit through cracks in the rocks, and crashed to instant death against the boulders jutting from the quarried river bed below.

Afterward, he stored away in memory a record of the accident which broke it down into details lasting only fractions of a second, like a slow-motion film. At the soft, moist core of the memory was an area of blackness incomprehensible to him at the time but somehow urgent and incalculably sweet, a mood he was able to recreate easily and which led him back to the memory time and time again. And then three years later, when he was a student in high school, he suddenly discovered late one night that he had been attempting suicide on that speeding bicycle, holding himself in a state of vague, near-sub-consciousness as he carefully pumped the pedals, lest consciousness act to restrain him. As the bike accelerated around the steep, downhill curve that became the approach to the bridge his consciousness was screaming Put on the brakes! Turn the handlebars! but his body was numb, heedless of the warnings, and he had perceived the bicycle crash into the railing with detachment. The real significance of the separation of body and consciousness was a surprising discovery, and once he was aware of the simple beauty of the mechanism, his attempt to hang himself three years later seemed awkward and transparently *fake.*

Since he had discovered this all by himself, and just one month after having once again attempted suicide inconclusively, the discovery itself signified his uncoerced endorsement of his mother's earlier insight about him. When he became clearly conscious of his defeat, the catalog of things his mother had been taunting him with ever since his suicide attempt filled him anew with rage which burned the more hotly and unextinguishably now that he understood how unreasonable it was. When he had emptied a tin measuring cup full of ethyl alcohol he had stolen from the high school science materials room, thinking it was methyl alcohol, he left the storehouse where he slept alone now that *a certain party* was gone, stepped into the heavy shadows of the kitchen in the main house and, knife in hand, stood over the even darker mass that was his mother asleep on the wooden floor with the bedclothes pulled over her head. But from his lips, which felt about to sag heavily as a result of the alcohol, even as the boy drunk thought to himself with a *false* sense of control to spare *At least my palate is still alive and my tongue still works,* the following words issued,

——Mother, you and I are the sole survivors here, we must marry secretly and have many children and strangle the abnormal fruit of our incestuous marriage while they are still mewling infants and keep only the hale and healthy and provide for the prosperity of our heirs and thus, Mother, we must make amends for having killed *a certain party.*

Then he began to spin in a truly fantastic whirlpool of bewilderment and fear unlike anything that had ever happened to him right down to the present day, a hole opened in the bottom of his closely cropped head and the blood drained down through his hollow neck and although his conscious world went quite black, his body, invigorated by this superabundance of fresh blood, began to pulse and then to throb and finally to move with a vitality that was as if an arm were growing from his chest, another leg extending from his belly, and was entirely beyond his control. . . .

His mother maintained he had actually been mad since he was three, that although his madness may have been exacerbated by *a certain party's* death, it was important to realize that he had been quite mad since childhood. As he was made to listen again and again to his mother relating, with hatred and contempt, the incident that was "proof" of this, he came to feel that he had stored it away in memory himself, as a very small boy, at the time it had happened. Even now he was able to recall the incident sharply, down to the smallest detail, as something he had experienced personally.

Three years old, he stares at his small hands and stands, not only unable to move but all his fragile muscles taut, riveted with horror. As he stares now at his hands, large and angry-red from cirrhosis yet resembling the child's, he recreates, in the high-noon space in that valley in the forest in the depths of his consciousness at thirty-five, the small child that was himself, musing that if he climbed aboard a time machine and returned to the side of that terrified child in the valley and embraced those small, stiffened shoulders his own hands in present time would also lose their angry redness. Needless to say, since he desperately wants to die an agonizing death from cirrhosis caused by cancer and to deal his mother a blow that will last for all eternity, no time machine of any kind will actually be used.

The small child that is himself has just noticed that his own hands are grotesque, alien, terrifying "things," and, unable to throw them away, stands paralyzed. Immediately he pales, his eyes recede into their sockets and roll upward, exposing the white, while the skin around his eyes beads with sweat like delicate milk. His beautiful mother, in her early thirties, her manner unlike that of the people in the valley because she has grown up in China, holds out her own hands and tries to distract the child,

——Look, mine are the same, the same human hands!

At that instant the grotesque, alien, terrifying "things" press in inescapably, and their number has doubled. The child screams, Aah! and chokes. At the same time, the thirty-five-year old screams in a small voice, Aah! and goes limp with a kind of happiness about nothing in particular.

[[What do you mean by "screams in a small voice"? You seem to have a great deal of common sense where semantics is concerned! I was trying to say "he" pretended to scream, in a small voice! Aah! Aah! Aah! Aah! But what you really wanted to ask was whether I actually went mad at the age of three, am I right? I can tell you this, nobody in that valley would have compared me and my mother and said I was "the crazier," "he" says.]]

Once he stole a look at an old notebook of his mother's and found the following poem:

Should some unlikely suitor make his way to me,
Tell him, pray,
That I am gone to the full-bellied sea,
With a cry of grief for the wind in my sails.

As he knew very little at the time he was unable to determine whether the poem had a classical source or had been composed by his mother herself. (Needless to say it would have been frightening and embarrassing if his mother had discovered him reading her notebook, which is why he had peeked only at the page to which it happened to be open.) But underneath the vision that had brought this poem into being he felt he could detect the presence of something somehow gamey and vulgar and exposed, something which might even be called desire: the stimulation of the poem seemed likely to affect whatever blood in his body he had inherited from his mother in such a way that he broke out in hives.

At the time, hoping to escape to the greatest possible distance from his mother's domination, if only geographically, he was trying to get into a Tokyo university where the entrance fee was a mere few hundred yen and, as soon as matriculation had been completed, it was possible to apply for a tuition waiver and a scholarship. As preparation for the English entrance examination he had been reading paperback who-dunnits. Like the canned as-

40

paragus and canned butter which had also been left behind by the Americans who had come through the forest to the valley in a jeep and stayed briefly in the village in the fall of 1945, these paperbacks were abandoned "issue" of no value whatsoever to anyone in the valley. He had discovered them one day when he had been hired to clean up the storage room at the grange, and had found that he was able to assert himself effectively against their contents with nothing more than the linguistic power he had acquired at high school. In one there was a story about a retired ivory merchant living in London who is murdered by a bee found only in a narrow strip of jungle inland from the Ivory Coast. The first time a person is stung by such a bee he experiences severe pain only, but should he be unfortunate enough to be stung a second time, he must prepare himself for death.

In order to let the blood he had inherited from his mother he had taken every opportunity to rush into battle, and as if that were not enough, had even inflicted wounds upon his own person; but a portion of which he had not been able to purge himself remained, and the sting of his mother's poem now caused this to quicken in him like the venom of the deadly bee. But he was not himself fully conscious that a long incubation period had been instantly spanned. And, it might be said for precisely that reason, he was never able to escape entirely from the hives of this strange poem. Years later he established a sexual relationship with a movie actress who had returned to Japan from Peking a very young woman at the end of the war, and at that time the hives of the poem burst into full blossom.

[[I suppose you think that's a pathetic fib about a sexual relationship with an actress. But in this case my partner has to be an actress, and that's what determines the reality of the past. Which can also mean that it had to be that way in reality too, don't you see, "he" elucidates. The "acting executor of the will" appears unmoved.]].

The trouble began one day near the end of their relationship, when the actress said to him reproachfully in the middle of sexual intercourse,

——Is there something lewd about "a cry of grief for the wind in my sails"? Without that battle-cry you can't even get it up with me anymore, can you! Until the actress had spoken he hadn't even realized he was whispering the poem, which she now asked him to explain so she could also enjoy its "lewdness." But at that instant a lightning bolt crashed across the vault of his slackened brain and, judging that considerable toil remained before the time of her orgasm, he descended toward his penis buried in his girlfriend's genitals and all alone, a vague smile on his lips, ejaculated. Thereafter there was always something oppressive about sexual intercourse with the actress, as if a taboo were being violated, and after intercourse he was not only exhausted but his testicles ached for no good reason, as if they were being squeezed. Since the mere possibility that a man having intercourse with her could experience anything but undiluted sweetness terrified the actress as if she had seen a portent of the end of her career, they had finally separated. A number of years still later she appeared on his television screen in a late night movie playing a woman landlord, and he felt he was seeing a phantom of his mother and looked carefully around the room, his hair standing on end.

By the last year of the war, as he moved from childhood to boyhood, he had already sensed from short, hate-filled exchanges between *a certain party* and his mother that his maternal grandfather had been involved in a plot which had been exposed in 1912 and which, during the war, could not be mentioned. But his mother never volunteered any details, and since she maintained an even more adamant silence after *a certain party's* death, there was no way of bringing the facts to light from inside the family. His mother had grown up on the Chinese mainland and had no relatives in Japan. He did remember that when he was a very small child a young man who said he was a monk from Wakayama prefecture had come to see his mother, but had been told that *a certain party* was in Manchuria and went away. Very likely this had something to do with whatever it was that was being concealed. After the war, when the "human emperor" * paid a visit to the provinces and a large number of students and teachers from his middle school traveled to the provincial city to welcome his Majesty, his homeroom teacher summoned him, though he had not managed to extract the money for the trip nor displayed any very active interest in going along, as if repelled by the negative magnetism the words "human emperor" communicated to the darkest recesses of his consciousness, and gently told him in a hoarse, artificial voice, never looking at him once, that he must not go with the others. He did not speak of this to his mother directly, yet several days later she set out for the teachers' room to protest. And ever after, his homeroom teacher had ignored him entirely. Yet he never asked his mother what precisely it was she went to protest. It was not that he feared the derisive silence that would be her response to his inquiry, it was because he had sensed from the beginning that, with regard to this incident, his mother

---

* In January, 1946, Emperor Hirohito announced to the Japanese people that he was a mortal man and not a god.

KENZABURO ŌE

was justified. Even during the war years there was nothing in his house that had anything to do with the Imperial Family, not even portraits of the Meiji Emperor in magazine supplements. Though he was only a child he knew there were no other such houses in the valley, and in his child's way he thought it strange, especially since *a certain party* was associated with the military and had endlessly asserted the importance of defending the "national polity."

One day early in the war, when the family still held its position of prominence in valley society even though *a certain party* was away in Manchuria, the wife of the village chief who had succeeded *a certain party* paid a visit to introduce her new daughter-in-law, and boasted that the girl's parents owned a *tea-jar* they had received from *a well-known noble.* He was not there to hear this directly, what he remembered was an episode already legendary in the valley which he had been told, not so much because he was the son of the principal figure in the legend as more generally, for his edification as a member of the new generation in the valley; his mother, it was said, using her visitor's west-country accent to her own purposes, countered,

——You must mean persimmon seeds, not *dates!* If they got them from a *monkey* they must have been persimmon seeds, yessir! *

The day he heard this story he asked his mother while they were having dinner why she had said such a thing, but she merely darted sidelong glances at him as if he were some kind of presumptuous stranger who had

---

* Two impossible puns, "dates" on "tea-jar," and "monkey" on "a well-known noble." A medieval Japanese tale has a monkey cheating a crab out of some rice balls by offering the crab persimmon seeds which, the monkey assures him, will soon grow into delicious persimmons.

badly misbehaved by asking, and, sitting there properly with her legs tucked beneath her on the wooden floor of the kitchen in the semidarkness, ignored the question comprehensively.

Among all the eyes he had encountered in his life now about to end, those glancing eyes of his mother's conveyed to him the most sickening denial and mistrust; when those sidelong glances fell upon him, the fragile root of his existence as a human being shriveled like a cornstalk parched beneath the sun, and it was no longer possible innocently to assume his own membership in the human race. When he studied French philosophy at college and encountered the proposition that Man's fundamental state was unhappiness, he had naturally comprehended the condition as that of which he had been obliged to be constantly aware while under his mother's eyes. Even during his *Happy Days?* But that was a time before those glancing eyes had existed. Preparations for their appearance, however, were already complete, and on that summer day in 1945 this particular evil spirit of the eye suddenly appeared where Japanese and American planes were dogfighting low in the sky, swiftly descended to lodge in his mother's eyesockets, and ever after abided there. When he was reading English poetry, again at college, and came across the following lines, he recognized instantly that these were precisely the glancing eyes that had been the object of his rancor for long years, and thus obtained the basis for a sound interpretation of a nightmare which had troubled him incessantly.

> Eyes I dare not meet in dreams,
> In death's dream kingdom.

At the risk of repeating himself he wanted it clear that, unlike the "dreadful eyes" that appear in children's picture books, clean, unblinking eyes or eyes like bottom-less pools of darkness, these, that held a pale yellow light just like a monkey's and stole quick looks in his direction, were the true "dreadful eyes."

Even after he had taken to his sick bed for this final time he often called up, from a pool of memory that could not be muddied, the image of his mother looking at him with those "dreadful eyes" and recreated his struggles with them, struggles which had always ended with his surrender, at various periods of his life, imitating his voice at the time in a strident falsetto.

The villagers respected a certain party and they also relied on him. That's why no one in the village contacted the police or the cadets tapping pine tree roots for oil when he left the valley in that wagon to lead an uprising. If anybody had leaked one word a certain party would have been caught in that wagon like a fat pig, no matter how hard those army deserters had fought to protect him. Because he couldn't get away on foot.

——A wagon! You call that ridiculous box on top of two sawed-off logs a wagon, his mother said unsparingly. And so would someone else I know alongside those deserter hoodlums as they huffed and puffed and tugged that creaky box on logs along, with his *fake* helmet pulled down over his ears and his shirt of woven grass and his old trousers tied with a rope below his knees—lord knows why!—and his straw sandals, so would someone else I know have been caught, like a *little* pig, even if someone else I know had waved around that bayonet he was so proud of!

Then his mother tried to make him recall how, after *a certain party's* group had split over the ideal way to approach the army, he had come home alone to the valley and turned into what was called in valley dialect a "believer," an alienated man who has lost everything as the result of some odd obsession, and had shut himself up in the storehouse, left alone by others so long as he did not bother them, except that some volunteer informer always came up for a look when anything happened, even a small fire on the hillside, and how all there was to eat, since the farm families would not willingly supply *a certain party* with rice and wheat, were those special parts of ox and pig which people of this region did not generally eat, which he bought secretly at an outrageous price.

——The only place in this whole valley that had to swallow gruel without a grain of cereal in it for such a long time was the Manor house, yessir! his mother reminded him, then pointed out his meagre frame, his irregular, ugly teeth, and all the other physical characteristics that were the result of having scraped by on wild grasses and small portions of seed-potato gruel as a young boy, and told him mockingly that these aftereffects of poor diet in childhood would remain with him all his life.

——*But everybody in the village was concerned about a certain party, especially near the end of the war. They all tried to find out what he was thinking by giving me dried yams and things!*

——Because they had you figured for the kind who'd blab his family's shame for a dried yam, yessir! At the end of the war everything was going badly and village life began to come apart. Well, in this valley, when times are bad people always begin to pay attention to madmen and cripples and children who look as if they don't have a chance to survive (the look his mother shot him here landed like a fist in his stomach, pinned as it was beneath the spectre of shameful death which had superimposed itself upon that other, of *a certain party* in the wagon oozing blood from his bladder, which had tormented him with

47

the fall of every night since his *Happy Days* had ended, because it seemed to say that he was certainly such a child himself) and try hard not to miss the omens of change that appear in them. Not because they believe such people are endowed with superhuman spiritual powers, but because they know perfectly well, cruel as it is, that omens of misfortune for the valley will appear earliest in the weakest people in the forest, such as madmen and cripples and children who look about to die, yessir!

Insofar as he desired, young as he was, to maintain his sense of honor objectively, he was unable to argue with the force of a plunge off a cliff that *a certain party* most definitely had not been the object of this variety of concern. The difficulty was that he sensed his mother's blunt assertions endowing each of the incidents of those last summers of the war, incidents which remained in earliest memory uninterpreted, in all their raw multiformity, with specific meaning that fit perfectly and was difficult to deny. But this was not to say he was also able to accept his mother's "correctness" itself. For this "correctness," an unreasonably combative "correctness" that hurt him fundamentally from inside and out at the same time, was every bit as horribly real and even palpable as her glancing eyes.

——*But a certain party wasn't a madman or a cripple or a child about to die!*

——A man who shuts himself up in a storehouse day and night is a madman, yessir! A man who's bleeding from his sick bladder but can't urinate by himself he's so fat he can't move is a cripple, yessir! And a man who'd set out on a long trip in a wooden box with some deserters when he had no possible chance of returning alive is even worse luck than a dying child, yessir! And for the crafty farmers of the valley to have taken an interest in him because he was that kind of pathetic character, that was a disgrace, don't you understand that! Or is it foolish to talk about disgrace to someone who's been picking up the garbage other folks threw away and eating it since he was a child, Ah!

As he recalled the sound of his mother's voice that day his emotions instantly rose, even as he lay abed with cancer, all the way to the desperately high water mark of the actual moment in the memory, when he had seized a hoe without a handle that was lying nearby and tried to attack his mother. The sudden climb produced a disorder related to hysteria in his eyes behind the underwater goggles, and he began to see everything as tiny particles like poppyseeds. Despite the resistence of the goggles themselves, which were cutting red circles into his skin, he shut his eyes tightly and silently rolled the words upon his parched tongue: yes, I was the young boy who picked up seed-potatoes discarded along the edges of certain fields I can still recall, and who cut the good parts out and used them in gruel, *but you ate them too, Mother!* Perhaps it was foolish to speak of disgrace to someone like himself, his mother had moaned as if stricken with grief, but the truth was he had already developed his own unique sense of honor, and it was that which finally had prevented him from speaking the words the day of their dispute. Thereafter, for more than twenty years, time and time again, trembling with chagrin, he had tasted the flavor and overtones of those words he had been unable to utter that day.

[[Why do you keep calling him *a certain party?* Can't I change to "father"? When you say *"a certain party"* he sounds like an imaginary figure in a myth or in history,

49

says the "acting executor of the will." My mother may have insisted on calling him *a certain party* beginning on a certain very special day precisely because she wanted to debase him to the level of an imaginary figure. When I left the valley once and for all and moved to a place where there were no traces of *a certain party*, I gradually began to wonder myself, possibly because I'd been influenced by my mother's repudiation of him, if I hadn't created *a certain party* entirely in my imagination. But even if he was a product of the imagination he still managed to be infinitely troublesome. At times I've thought to myself maybe I have been mad since I was three just as my mother says, and someday if I recover my sanity the phantom tormenting me I call *a certain party* will disappear. But I feel differently now; if I'm a madman, fine, I'm resolved to stay that way and continue sharing life with my favorite phantom, *a certain party*. Ha! Ha! Ha! But you know something? As time passed after the surrender and various military journals began surfacing, official and unofficial, particularly in reactionary quarters, and being published, I came across *a certain party's* name frequently in accounts of anti-Tojo operations within the Kanto army. I even saw a photostat of one of his poems, which couldn't have had less to do with the military by the way, written in his own hand with brush and ink. There's never been anything special about my family, but we have produced a number of calligraphers; *a certain party* must have been proud of his calligraphy. Anyway, if I truly exist here and now, and I do, *a certain party* certainly existed, too. To make someone sound like an imaginary figure can be a way of debasing him, but it can also be a way of exalting him into a kind of idol. So please don't change to "father," keep on writing *a certain party.* I wish you'd even write thick characters and blacken them with your pencil until they look like gothic type.]]

IV

The examples of *a certain party's* hand he had discovered in photostat copies of various so-called secret military journals were easy to read, even though they had been reduced in printing, because they were written in phonetic script in the style of the great calligrapher Hekigodo. There was a period when the area inside and around the forest surrounding his valley was alive with amateur calligraphers in the school of Hekigodo or Fusetsu. To say that he came from a long line of calligraphers would have been a silly boast: *a certain party's* style had not evolved down through successive generations of the family but was simply an example of an amateur style to be found all over the region. The clearly dated entries had been written at the end of that year when the war, which had sustained around itself a vast feeling of mutuality based upon the phantom of nation that covered the entire sky he could see from his valley, and which indeed had made him long, notwithstanding his secret fears and misgivings, to die a mutual death, had unmistakably been placed in a noose by the defeat of the Imperial navy at Midway and the still more pitiful devastation at Guadal Canal. The date immediately evoked for him concrete images of a moment in the past which existed for both himself and *a certain party.* For it was on New Year's Day of the following year, 1943, that *a certain party* had unexpectedly appeared in the valley again, gone straight into seclusion in the storehouse and stayed there, fattening from insufficient exercise and a monomaniacal appetite, losing finally even the strength to stand by himself as his bladder cancer progressed, not to appear again before the people of the village until a few days before the defeat, when he had left the valley in a wagon together with the ten deserters who had come for him and his young son.

Neither the boy he was at the time nor, he supposed, his mother, had any idea of the circumstances which suddenly had brought *a certain party* back from Manchuria on New Year's day. He was of course equally ignorant of *a certain party's* reasons for walking straight into isolation, as if his long journey home ended with a final step into the darkness of the storehouse. In fact, he now realized, for as long as *a certain party's* self-confinement in the storehouse had lasted, his young brain had been entirely occupied by the actual presence of that giant body; by the time he had begun directing his brain to active thoughts about *a certain party* himself, *a certain party* no longer existed, an emptiness with the volume of one obese adult had opened in this world, and he had discovered with his entire small, thin body that this emptiness was packed with nothing more than August heat and light. Once this void began searching for a meaning, it proved to be a vacuum powerful enough to pull in all of his thirty-five years of life that protruded from his *Happy Days*.

However, since his mother was ignorant of the meaning of *a certain party's* extraordinary behavior toward the end of the war, or at least insisted she was ignorant and then lapsed into silence, a performance she maintained for as long as he was in the valley, there was no possibility of uncovering any new facts while he remained in the depths of the forest. Accordingly, it was not until he had moved away to a big city that he had the pleasure of encountering for the first time, albeit in suspicious books such as *An Unofficial History of Manchuria,* not only examples of *a certain party's* hand but a variety of brand-new information.

Late in 1942, burdened with the hopes and expectations of those "loyal subjects of Empire" who were the invaders in Manchuria, *a certain party* had boarded a special plane and secretly had returned to Japan as a member of an underground group determined to bring about a meeting between Prime Minister Tojo and General Ishiwara, who had already left the army and was living in seclusion in the country. The core of the group were those former Kempei [secret police] officers who had massacred proletarian activists at the time of the 1923 earthquake. A meeting was in fact held, but it began and ended as a kind of zen dialogue which yielded not the smallest hint about anything practical to be done; the former Kempei officers and their subordinates flew back to Manchuria at once and adopted the new strategy of spreading false rumors that Prime Minister Tojo and General Ishiwara were working together.

Of the entire group, only a *certain party* had taken leave of his "comrades" and remained in Japan, never to visit Manchuria again. How had he separated from them? When the meeting was over *a certain party,* representing the "Manchurian Committee to revere Basho the Master," had traveled to Iga-Ueno, Basho's birthplace. There he had drafted with ink and brush the inscription for the memorial the Committee was planning to erect. His composition, which had survived in a photostat but had never been inscribed on any stone, was as follows:

What kind of frog or possibly toad
Did the Master follow down country back road
Through hilly daley and ferny frondy
To that ancient, waiting pondy?
Or was it no frog at all but a wop
Who dived in with that eternal plop?

Reading this doggerel he remembered the day the son of one of the tenant farmers who worked for his family, a man who had made a good business of doing piecework for a munitions factory in his small machine shop, came to request a sample of *a certain party's* calligraphy to frame. It was during that brief interval just after *a certain party* had confined himself in the storehouse, when he still commanded the dregs at least of general respect rather than what his mother called "concern for the weakest man around," a time just before the abrupt commencement of his *Happy Days* when communication between his mother and *a certain party* had not yet run dry. When the villager had been led by his mother as far as the high threshold at the entrance to the storehouse he called out solemnly,
——Squire, I'd be obliged if you'd write me out "Prosper but be not proud." However, when his mother presently emerged from the storehouse trying so hard not to laugh that all the skin of her narrow, egg-shaped face was stretched across her cheekbones almost to transparency, she held a piece of Chinese drawing paper on which was written in large characters in the style of Hekigodo, "Hibernate but be not proud." * Admittedly, this memory, like others, was certain to be a compound of something he had actually witnessed as a young boy and valley legend ingested at a later time.

---

* An outrageous pun, *tomin shite* (hibernate) on *tomite* (prosper).

[[Your whole family loves puns, don't they, says the "acting executor of the will." Don't think I didn't know where you're aiming those roundabout missiles of yours, "he" replies. They say that certain manic-depressives are fascinated by puns and anagrams. You're suggesting I'm that type of madman, and that all my chatter until now has been nothing more than a madman's raving, that everything recorded here about my past is therefore untrue, that even my insistence here in the present that my liver is a stronghold for cancer is merely a madman's delusion—that's the elaborate logic you'd like to apply, isn't it! I meant something much less elaborate, says the "acting executor of the will." But "he" laughs—Ha! Ha! Ha!—and keeps her at a distance. The reason there are so many puns in my account is that nearly all my childhood memories are influenced by oral legend from my valley. In a valley surrounded by a forest, every little scrap of inside information gets turned into a new legend as people pass it back and forth among themselves and fiddle with it. And silly puns are the only rhetorical ornaments they have to dress a legend up with as they pass it on. If someone like my mother actually makes a clever pun, that in itself is enough to make whatever it is she may have said the most fashionable legend in the valley for a time. The importance the valley still places on puns got me into all kinds of trouble when I was studying foreign languages at college, I kept getting tangled up in silly associations that never bothered students from the city, and they'd occupy my head and lead me off on daydreams. For example, all I had to do was see the word *mori* in Latin class and I was off and flying back to the "forest" [in Japanese, *"mori"*]. For all I know, whatever rhetorical skill I may have even now originates in simple puns. Still, I'd appreciate it if you'd put me down on paper just as I speak, without changing my rhetoric into something more creative than it is. Maybe I have liver cancer and maybe I'm just a madman obsessed with anagrams, either way I'm pathetic enough to deserve sympathy, don't you think? Ha! Ha! Ha! That isn't what I was trying to say, either. Even at the height of the war there was at least one moment of harmony in your family, and it occurred to me that it might have been built around your parents' special gift for puns. I imagine in the beginning it was probably your father who loved puns, and as your mother went out of her way to accommodate his tastes she must have developed her own skill at that special kind of mental gymnastics. And in that way, two of the very few educated people in the valley shut off from the world by a forest, and bitterly critical of everything around them, your parents did try to maintain a unique style of life in their isolation—that's what I wanted to say. It just doesn't seem possible to me that they always felt the intense hatred for one another that colors your whole story, as if they were sworn enemies from the beginning. Could it be that you leave out the positive aspects when you talk because you don't want to recognize any link between your parents that had nothing to do with you? Beginning a rare slide down an incline toward foul humor, "he" braces himself against his hands resting atop his hardened liver and digs in his heels. Even if you're right, that wouldn't affect my *Happy Days!* As if to demonstrate the truth of this, "he" softly sings a bit of his specialty, *Let us sing a song of cheer again, Happy Days are here again!*]]

He did not intend to deny that there was a period when his mother and *a certain party* had a perfectly normal relationship as man and wife. But except for his memory of having approached madness when he was close to

56

three, he had almost no memories of life at home during that period. Nor was this simply because he was too young. It was as if, in the gloom, even in daytime, of those rooms beyond the earth-floor entrance of the house of his birth, known as the Manor house, the child he was had not yet truly existed. Direct memories that felt real and had substance began at the moment of a certain "birth" which suddenly had illuminated that gloom of nonexistence and had transformed it into a solid consisting of tangled memories in lurid color. Memories which preceded the moment of this "birth" were therefore all legends in the valley which he had recreated as memory in his own body-and-soul. Once, he had tried stirring up the depths of memory rooted in his very flesh itself, hoping to revive some direct proof of his existence prior to those several festival days during which the "birth" was accomplished. It was a long and difficult experiment in which he employed mnemonics and other techniques, and at the end of his labors the pallid memory that finally appeared in the darkness as though in the beam of a distant flashlight was of himself as a part of the entirety of the valley, organic and inorganic objects included, that did not possess consciousness, a part of what the French philosopher called the *être-en-soi*. A small child, submerged in a pool in the river that ran along the bottom of the valley, he was peering, with eyes so shadowed they merged with the dark water, at the freshwater fish known as *ida* in his region, that lived in the cracks between the rocks and the sandy river bottom. The school of minnows had aligned their bodies, their pursed, gill-breathing mouths all pointing toward the faint current flowing behind the rocks. Their eyes, lit with a pale, yellow light the color of saffron, seemed uneasy about the boy observing them, suspended

57

there as long as his breath held out, his uncovered eyes opened wide in the water, and again seemed completely indifferent. In fingers long since bleached and puffy from the water the little boy grasps a spear gun, but the harpoon tip is not attached and the rubber bands on the firing mechanism have rotted away. And so he only stares at the minnows, unblinkingly, a pale yellow light gradually appearing in his own shadowed eyes, and, as if he is already beyond the need to breathe, makes corrections ever so slight in the alignment of his body so as to remain facing the current that flows into his nostrils and communicates the smells of all the numberless, vital substances of the valley. The child in this very earliest memory of himself, he had recognized, was actually not even so much a child as a fetus before the "birth," and with this realization he had lost interest in uncovering memories that preceded the "birth."

His memory of the "birth" itself, at least of its sharply defined beginning, must have been a dramatic reconstruction he had later incised upon his memory. In actuality, he was far too young to have perceived immediately the significance of the arrival of the telegram delivery man; nonetheless, when he poured fresh blood into his memory of the "birth," the opening scene that instantly rose to his mind was a bird's eye view, as if seen through a telephoto lens, of the delivery man puffing up the rise at a slow, persistent trot from the boat-bottom flat of the valley toward the Manor house. Assuming the angle was possible in reality he must have been looking down at the man from the village office where formerly *a certain party* had served as the youngest village chief in the prefecture, atop the only other rise in the valley, or peering into the distance from the top of the hill which his mother

58

regularly climbed in order to maintain the monkey shrine. However, since even the inside of the storehouse in which *a certain party* sat facing the other way in his mechanical barber's chair was distinctly visible despite the gloom, it was clear that the bird's eye view in his memory was imaginary. Because he has read the telegram, the delivery man lurches up the hill without giving his short legs a minute's rest though he is gasping for breath, but clearly he would love the opportunity to race back down the steep stone path into the soft, planted fields and from there to flee, with the fabulous speed of the kangaroo that once visited the valley with a circus troupe, into the depths of the forest, as if it were a certainty that he would be ambushed and killed by the people of the Manor house. No longer a baby and not quite a boy, about to experience the true "birth," he looks down from the rise and, as if he were tracking the man with a directional microphone, distinctly hears him utter the lament reserved by people in the valley for moments of direst emergency. *Lordy! We've gone and fetched it now!* It says right here the eldest son at the Manor house has deserted in China. *Lordy! We've gone and fetched it now!*

[[That's it! That's the other thing you shout when you cry in your sleep! says the "acting executor of the will." It's such a disheartening thing to hear at night, it makes me feel like running out into the moonlight in the hospital courtyard and screaming myself. But you know, that delivery man's distress can't have infected me, because unlike everybody else at the Manor house, I was as lively and full of spirit as a river shrimp just netted after that telegram arrived. The first thing that happened was that I was sent running to send cables to Manchuria, by *a certain party* and my mother separately. It was the first time I had been recognized in my own house as a person who could have some actual effect, it was my "birth" in that sense, too. What struck me as peculiar in my child's way was that my mother and *a certain party* were each trying to help my deserter brother in their own way, by separate routes. It was one thing for *a certain party* to have contacts in Manchuria, I was amazed that my mother seemed to know people too, and inside the Kanto army! Of course I know now that she was raised in Peking as the foster daughter of a man who took her in despite the fact that she had some connection with an act of rebellion against the emperor, and that *a certain party*, who had been smitten by her on his very first journey across the sea, had brought her back to the valley and married her formally as soon as he had left his wife from his days as a young village chief. Then, when he had seen to it that she was securely tethered in the depths of the forest for the rest of her life, he set out for China again and remained there, active at something in Manchuria for years. My mother's telegram must have been directed at contacts related to her foster father. Before long, she and *a certain party* began shouting at each other in the storehouse, for the first time. My memory of that quarrel is a reconstruction later, when I finally managed to form a clear impression of what they were talking about by relying on rumors in the valley, but the way I "remember" it now, my mother said,

——*If he doesn't get over to the other side quickly, he'll be killed* and burst into tears. A *certain party* became furious, and shouted back,

——*What are you saying! This only happened because I permitted him to be raised by the likes of you, with a traitor's blood in your veins! I'm doing everything in my power to have him shot quickly and treated as if he'd died in action so at least his ashes will come home to us.*

——*You're trying to have that child killed before he reaches the other side? You want your own child shot in the back on orders from hoodlums like —— and —— and that's what you requested in your cable? That child is running as hard as he can, all alone, trying to reach the other side, and you want him shot in the back!* my mother shouted, still crying bitterly, and it went on that way. Much later, when I began reading military journals, I discovered that the names my mother had mentioned were the last bigshots in the Kanto army. To tell the truth, I was too young to grasp the real meaning of "the other side." A child who'd been raised during the war may have known what "enemy" meant, but he simply didn't have the imagination to resolve an image of real people and a real society on "the other side" of the front. All I could picture to myself was a cliff rising straight up on the horizon of a vast plain. One alone young soldier runs as hard as he can toward that cliff. If he can reach it, not only will all values be reversed and everything instantly allowed, the soldier will be extravagantly praised and find salvation—that was the scenario I wrote in my mind. Anyhow, *a certain party* had only two children, myself and my older brother, and my brother happened to be the child of his first wife, the woman he had divorced. In other words, my mother seemed to be working herself into a frenzy over her stepson! But this heated family battle lasted only a week. A notice arrived, and silence fell over the Manor house and hung there. Then, early one morning, my mother set out in mourning, and just before nightfall she returned with the ashes of the valley's first war casualty in a white wooden box tied around her neck with a piece of white cotton cloth, "he" says.]]

The boy who was no longer a child after the experience of this week went along with almost everyone else in the village to meet his mother at the bridge that led

61

out of the valley to the highway, but his mother ignored him just as she ignored the others waiting there in a scraggly line, and for a time stood in silence on the bridge where he had almost died, her head upright, and darted glances at the valley with the eyes of a hawk surveying its adversaries with the purest contempt. Probably she halted there to recover her sense of firm ground after the long, rough ride she had hitched from the provincial city in a truck driven by Korean forest workers. Presently she narrowed her eyes, creases rippling across her thin, flat, egg-shaped face so terrifically white and dry it appeared to be a scrap of paper and, looking right through the faces in the ring of people she approached and cut across, each step a swift kick so that her hissing sandals just skimmed the surface of the ground, she headed for the Manor house. When she had passed under the great roofed gate at the entrance with the boy, who was now the only one following her, she halted at the base of the giant black pine where the paths to the main house and the store-house divided. Then, as if only now she had become aware of his existence, although he had made no effort to muffle his footsteps as he followed her all this way, she wheeled around in the dusk as though startled and stared down at him with her flashing eyes. And in unfamiliar accents entirely unlike those of the valley she snapped,
——Don't think *a certain party* (it was the first time his mother used the phrase) hiding in the storehouse has any right to these ashes; they haven't come back to him!

Without another word his mother hurried toward the main house once again, and as he dug in his heels against the pull of her small back that seemed to have dwindled swiftly, resisting with a force of his own sufficient to shred the thousands of leaves on the black pine, he shouted

62

something altogether unexpected, in a manner that communicated his outrage at having been ignored by his mother all this time,

———*I don't have no traitor's blood in my veins! You can take the ashes of that coward and throw them in the feed trough, yessir! Now I'm going into the stor.house too, and forget all about them ashes! Because I don't have no traitor's blood in my veins!*

His mother, though she disdained to answer these shouted words, did look around for just an instant and toss her head at him, but he turned his back on the white, dry paper of her face that appeared to flutter and dance through the gelatin filter of his tears and the dusk, and pulling his *fake* helmet down over his ears just as she described it when she ridiculed him, the figure of a valley brat in his shirt woven from hemp and his old trousers tied around his legs like knickerbockers, he headed alone for the storehouse. The bayonet strapped to his hip with a hemp cord, his grandfather's in the Russo-Japanese war which early that morning, just after his mother had set out in her black kimono, he had hunted up in the barn and cleaned of rust himself, reassured him as he walked along.

[[In my child's way I sensed that people from the outside might try to destroy the *Happy Days* in the storehouse that were about to begin for me and *a certain party* and no one else, and if they did appear I intended to fight fearlessly with that old bayonet which had been used for cutting fodder and was like a pitch-black iron bar, "he" says. You seem to have had a marvelous time in that storehouse, was your father glad to have you there from the beginning? Certainly not, I didn't even try to talk to him. There was a naked bulb hanging from the lintel at the entrance, wrapped in a black cloth as a precaution against air raids, and when I turned it on and stepped inside, where it was pitch dark, *a certain party* was wearing the underwater goggles with cellophane covering the lenses that I have now (he had originally prepared them to observe a solar eclipse in Manchuria) and staring into the back of the storehouse, I suppose he had already resolved to prevent anyone from reading his expression ever. All around the mechanical barber's chair he was sitting in there were piles of big books in a foreign language. They were probably books about agriculture. According to the military journals I read later, he had plans to bring his "comrades" back to the land in the valley and to have the skirts of the forest cleared for cultivation. But by the time I joined him in the storehouse he must have lost his will to read those books, otherwise he wouldn't have kept the goggles on day and night. With these goggles on I don't imagine he could distinguish a single object in that storehouse. He did sense an annoying light when I switched on the bulb at the entrance, though, and he immediately scolded me with an angry Shhh! as if he were shooing a chicken away. In my haste to turn the light out, and in the darkness, and because I was still worked up after my proclamation to my mother, I caught the frayed heel of my straw sandal on the sill at the entrance and tumbled onto the dirt floor about two steps lower and rolled across it head over heels and finally cracked my rear against the raised wooden floor of the room where *a certain party* had installed his chair. But this time *a certain party* didn't even hiss, it was as if he had fallen asleep the minute I had turned off the light, he held his large, looming head perfectly upright in the darkness and didn't move a muscle. I opened my mouth wide and exhaled a ton of breath to keep from crying out, the bayonet on my hip had dug into my stomach and it hurt so much I could hardly stand it, and I wept truly forlorn tears and wet my scraped cheeks and the dry dirt of the floor. For quite a while I stayed just as I was, unable to get up. But from that night on I had a place to sleep in the storehouse. To make *a certain party* think I'd chosen to roll across the dirt floor as a way of locating the best place to sleep, and not simply fallen, I made a bed of straw and boards and old blankets directly on the floor where I had come to rest, and that's where I slept. After that I only went back to the main house to get the meals I brought to *a certain party*. My mother was isolated, and not just at home, either. From the day those ashes returned, as if the only temporary bond between the outsider she was and the valley had been maintained through her stepson gone off to war on the Chinese mainland, she began to ignore every man, woman, and child in the valley even when they were right under her nose, and effectively vanished from society. Which left me, a kid, to run around the valley, with my grandfather's bayonet on my hip, collecting our rations and keeping my small eyes peeled for extras and making sure that my family, and particularly *a certain party*, who was gradually becoming obsessive about his food, had enough to eat. Now that I think about it, there has never been a time since when I've taken so much responsibility for my own family's daily welfare. On my own initiative I went down to the village office and received the plaque that said "A son lost in battle" and nailed it up with old nails, not to the main house but to the fire door of the storehouse. With the bayonet rattling at my side, I stood on my tiptoes and swung a large, heavy hammer, and when the kids from the valley who had followed me from the village gathered around in curiosity I waved them away with my hammer as if it were a scepter, "he" says.]]

V

[[Claiming sudden physical exhaustion, "he" spends the entire day either sleeping or looking at animal picture books. At the same time "he" tries to demonstrate to the "acting executor of the will" that "he" has not lost interest in narrating his "history of the age." Look at this wild boar in Ceylon charging down a valley of dry brush with half a dozen baby boars, even though the parent in front is a female in this case, these little ones with their heads lowered as if they were lost in thought but their legs churning as they try to keep up remind me perfectly of myself in the days when I was at *a certain party's* side. Do you suppose the Ceylonese wild boar has long hair growing around its eyes? This bunch is running at such terrific speed the picture is out of focus, maybe that makes it look all the more like hair—anyway, fierce as these characters are they have deeply shadowed, mournful eyes that don't really fit them, and look how hard they stare at the ground just in front of their flying hooves, doesn't it give them a solemn, fussy look? A human being never looks this intelligent when he's running. I don't feel I spent my *Happy Days* like a human being running, I was more like one of these little boars with a giant head and spindly legs and a huge mouth clamped cruelly shut in a melancholy face. I even imagine there must have been bright melon stripes down my back in those days. I'd like to put a belt around this baby boar's middle and hang a bayonet on it from the Russo-Japanese war, I bet he'd manage the heavy, clanking thing somehow and keep

66

right on running, even if he had to shorten his stride a little. Ha! Ha! Ha! Under cover of the animal pictures, "he" speaks obliquely about his *Happy Days* and seems about to resume his account, but continues to say nothing about actual life in the storehouse. There is a constant feeling of bloating as his liver fattens, and although precious little flesh or fat remain around his stomach it is as if, "he" complains, a bomb of gradually increasing size were biting into the soft layer beneath his skin, making concentration impossible. It would be so refreshing if this hard bomb that used to be my liver would just fall out of its present location by mistake! The way things stand, the bloated feeling of this rock maturing inside me even governs my subconscious while I sleep, not even my own sleep belongs to me! The "acting executor of the will" is becoming actively interested in the history. I wonder if the difficulty you've begun to experience in telling your story might have nothing to do with your illness. I wonder if there's something hidden in your life in the storehouse that you don't want to talk about, even though you speak of *Happy Days*. Could it be, she speculates, prodding at the same time, that those unpleasant memories are creating the bloated feeling that's making even your subconscious uncomfortable? Ha! Ha! Ha! I consider that period in my life the first *Happy Days* in my thirty-five years, alongside these final *Happy Days* as I lie here dying unhurriedly but swiftly of cancer, "he" says. Will you ask the doctor to give me an injection to concentrate the life-force left in me and make it burn up quickly? Don't you agree the patient should have the freedom to choose diluted life over a long period or concentrated life briefly? Anyway, tomorrow I may feel rested and my fever may be down, let's start again then, "he" says, beginning to sleep.]]

He helped *a certain party* build a radio receiver the size of a horse. In Shanghai in the 1930's, *a certain party* had shipped home two of the finest European receivers available there at the time. Now he installed in front of his mechanical barber's chair a broad, rectangular platform which had been used originally in the breeding of silkworms and still reeked of their body fluid, and on top of this he took apart the two sets and reassembled them as one receiver. When he was finished, he attached headphones to his large head and sat listening to the radio all day. The construction of the receiver took three months to complete. Once it had been assembled *a certain party* scarcely ever removed his underwater goggles for observing solar eclipses and the headphones which made his large head bulk even larger. Trapped in the paranoid certainty that to someone peeking into the storehouse *a certain party* would look like a spy transmitting secret messages, he walked careful rounds around the building with the bayonet at his side.

[[So you couldn't hear the radio yourself? the "acting executor of the will" inquires after waiting in silence for a considerable interval while his shoulders heave and "he" labors to regain the energy which even this short fragment of narration has cost him. I had no desire to listen to the radio, my main tasks during those *Happy Days*, as *a certain party* sat there listening to the radio and pondering, were to gaze at the back of his giant head and to guard him from the volunteer informers in the valley who would have loved to discover a spy or two for the glory it would bring them. Besides, I wasn't really interested in radio equipment. Then how can you have been any help assembling the receiver? All I did was pick up screws that had rolled off the work table onto the floor so *a certain party* didn't have to keep getting up from his mechanical barber's chair. Not that it was easy finding little screws in the dimness of that storehouse, it wasn't a job a dog could do, "he" says.]]

To provide food for *a certain party* and his mother, and for himself, he struggled. Standing on the left side of the large number 8 bike whose pedals he couldn't quite reach even when the seat was lowered all the way, he would step with his right leg beneath the bar that supported the seat until his right foot rested on the right pedal, then push off, tilting the bike sharply away from himself to compensate for his weight, and "side-pedal" long, perilous hours until he reached the neighboring town down river, where he would buy in bulk, at the only butcher shop in the vicinity, according to *a certain party's* instructions, the oxtails and pigs' feet which no one in his region would eat except the Koreans who worked in the forest felling trees. Oxtails sold out at once and were often impossible to get; the pigs' feet, unshaven, made a bristling, bulky package which he tied to the back of the bicycle and transported home. This shopping for meat was actually the first task *a certain party* had assigned him. For days after he had prepared his bed on the earth floor of the storehouse he had been ignored. Then one morning he awoke with a faint sensation of anxiety to find *a certain party* towering over him on the raised wooden floor in front of his mechanical barber's chair, gazing down into the face. Only partially awake, he gazed back and smiled, and was immediately dismayed at his own forwardness and, because the smile had been ignored, ashamed. As he lay there in what was now indignant silence, *a certain party* addressed him for the first time. *Can you ride a bicycle?*

Down a midsummer road white as snow beneath the

powder of crushed rock, the same long road he had dreamed of reapeatedly before and after, he "side-ped-aled" to the butcher shop in the neighboring town and that wasn't all: stopping on the way home at the shack of the forest workers who had been brought forcibly from Korea and were kept in isolation, barred from living in any other community no matter how wretched, he had to receive from the Koreans a few strands of garlic. Because he had the feeling both the oxtails and the pigs' feet would have been food for the Koreans if *a certain party* had not managed to cut in ahead of them, he was afraid they might notice the packages loaded on his bicycle right in front of their shack, and when he finally managed to cross the bridge back into the valley, he was careful the strands of white garlic tied with a cord to his bare stomach beneath his shirt were not discovered by the other children. When the word spread among these valley brats that the compost pool at the Manor house had a queer smell and they came reconnoitering, he took his position in front of the drain cover of the outhouse attached to the storehouse for *a certain party's* exclusive use, and brandishing his Russo-Japanese bayonet as if it were a carving knife, he kept the persistent enemy away and finally sent them running altogether out of the territory the people of the valley referred to as Manor-house-rise.

The day he delivered his first oxtail on bicycle number 8 *a certain party* made one of his rare appearances outside the storehouse, to do the cooking himself. The cooking shed stood alongside an uncovered well with the giant black pine behind it, between the storehouse and the main house, which was a good thing both for his mother, who had no desire to behold anything so ominously exposed as an oxtail, and for *a certain party* himself who, in

70

becoming a temporary cook, could not help losing a measure of his dignity. His face stubbly with beard, wearing an African explorer's helmet and a khaki "citizen's jacket" buttoned up to the collar, his underwater goggles on, useful as protection against the midday summer sun and the spattering from the giant heated pan of the crude lard his mother made, *a certain party* emerged from the storehouse with a step reminiscent of the wooden soldier dolls, popular in those days, that tottered forward in a kind of simulated walk when you placed them on an incline. Slowly he approached the cooking shed; dangling from his right fist, in which he clutched it by the butchered end, bright red meat and yellow fat and white bone showing, was an entire oxtail with black hide still matted with blood and filth; in his left hand he gripped a short sword in a scabbard of white wood. The boy, whose headlong journey clinging to a bicycle had drenched his shirt and short pants and model helmet in sweat and who had washed them in the river and stuffed them into a red-willow stump to dry, was waiting in the garden in just the outfit valley children always wore when they swam in the river, a cotton loincloth and nothing more, his bayonet in hand. As *a certain party* passed, his large moon face looking pale and puffy in the sunlight, he spoke an order in a soft, hoarse voice,

———*Pick me some smelly wild grass, pick all that grass you won't even feed the goats because you say the smell is too strong.*

Naked as he was, he bounded off at once like an animal on the run. But when he stepped into the thicket of hot, damp underbrush at the edge of the forest and began actually picking "smelly grass," he was stricken by the sudden feeling that this was an unlawful act no respectable person in the valley had ever committed before, maybe

71

even an open betrayal, a desecration of all the plant life thriving in the forest. Then his exultant pride at having managed to obtain the oxtail meat *a certain party* required seemed to spoil, to deteriorate in the direction of a very nearly indelible shame. Nonetheless, though he had never so much as touched wild scented grasses, he managed to gather, guided by the instincts of "one who eats," a *bouquet garni* as opulent and fragrant as any to be had in the valley, including even withered tomato plants covered with yellow fruit the size of ping-pong balls which he pulled up roots and all, and ran back to *a certain party*.

[[Before long I became experienced at making oxtail stew myself, and do you know when I think back to the "smelly grasses" I gathered that day I get the feeling my *bouquet garni* included everything indispensable to oxtail stew but impossible to obtain in that valley, not only celery and parsley but even dried laurel. I even get the feeling *a certain party* must have had a bottle of wine hidden away, to use in stewing the oxtail he'd sauteed in lard, or that he'd prepared soup stock in advance and could actually move effortlessly to stage two of the preparation, cooking the whole stew. I realize I'd be inviting my mother's ridicule if I left things in writing so obviously counter to the truth, so I won't include it in my account but it does feel real to me, "he" says.]]

What appeared to him in his memory, as if in an overexposed photograph, was a huge frying pan in heavy shadow on top of a stove that glowed ruby red in the fading light, and the face, also in deep shadow, and shiny white helmet of *a certain party*, his large head lowered mournfully as he peered down into the frying pan through his underwater goggles, which must have been fogged by the rising steam. Several steps behind *a certain party*, his

72

head and body bared to the sun, he listened to the meaty, sizzling joints of oxtail jump and bump in the pan, and smelled, with revulsion, the indescribably cruel, animal odor of the meat. Sweat rolled continuously down his back and felt as if the pointed ridges on a dinosaur's back were being chiseled into his own. For a long time he stood this way, stock still beneath the summer sun, and presently, as always happened in the valley, the sun's position passed a certain point above the forest, dusk came and was gone in a flash and heavy darkness abruptly fell, the fire in the cooking stove glowed even redder, and the scrawny dogs that had gone wild and lived in a pack at the edge of the forest began to howl.

Finally *a certain party* turned around to him, his shadowed face pitch-black except where the rims of his underwater goggles bluntly gleamed, and asked in a perfectly sober voice, as if his raptness over the cooking stove had been the work of some entrancing demon that now had dropped away, *Can you support my weight?* Shivering in the chill wind from the valley below he stepped forward tensely, still aware in his nakedness, though his sweat had dried long ago, of what felt like the scars of those ridges on the dinosaur's back. *A certain party* placed his hand on the top of his head as though he were grasping the end of a pole, and began walking, step by step, toward the entrance to the storehouse. Even now he could recall, with extreme vividness and reality, thinking his neck must break beneath the weight if he continued walking this way, and, ridiculous as it was, wanting to shout Long live the emperor! so that *a certain party* would acknowledge that it was his young son who was the true heir to his blood.

[[The "acting executor of the will" begins to fidget

73

and "he" asks reproachfully, Do you think I'm making this up? I'm a man dying of liver cancer, why should I have to tell made-up stories? Furthermore, I'm coming to the part about how the valley doctor discovered that *a certain party* had bladder cancer. When I'm getting ready to talk about cancer it seems to me you could show a little respect, not to me but to my cancer!]]

Slowly they advanced toward the entrance to the storehouse, but *a certain party's* feet, ponderously lifting and lowering like the leg of a circus elephant stepping up onto a barrel, simply could not step across the broad, high threshold of the many-layered fire door. And when the boy dropped to his knees on the ground that retained the midday warmth and threw his arms around the calf of the thick pole of a leg *a certain party* was still laboring patiently to lift and tried to lend him strength, *a certain party* fell over on his back as unceremoniously as an infant but with a thud that shook the ground. Then his large, pitch-black penis sprang from the long-since buttonless fly of his "people's" overalls, and he energetically urinated. The boy remained on his knees, chilled with a sense of failure, and the smelly urine wet his naked side and right buttock. Hesitantly he had wiped his fingers, and then, because they were sticky, had rubbed them on his chest and was just perceiving uneasily that something thicker and more mucous than urine remained, when *a certain party*, lying on his back on the ground and attempting with one hand somehow to put away his penis shrunken now after urinating and hard to distinguish on top of his wet trousers, spoke an order in a voice more than ever sober and composed: *Fetch that quack doctor and tell him my bladder is bad.* Jumping to his feet he raced down the stone path just as he was, not stopping to rest until he reached the doctor's house, and when he saw in the light that spilled through the glass door from inside that his naked body was drenched in blood he burst into tears.

[[And from that summer in 1944 until that special day the following summer when the soldiers who had left their barracks came for him, *a certain party* didn't venture a single step out of the storehouse. That night, when the old doctor from the valley who had been examining his bladder since before the war arrived at the storehouse, he informed *a certain party* immediately, with a mournful helplessness in his voice, Squire, you've finally gone and fetched yourself bladder cancer, yessir! "he" says. When the blood in *a certain party's* urine got all over my hand, which was when the commotion that went on most of that night began, I had a premonition that it must be some kind of important omen, and then twenty-five years later when I found out cancer had caught me, too, I took a careful look at my hands, which had turned bright red, and I understood the significance of that omen in blood. My life has a splendid continuity, don't you agree, especially in the details? What happened to the food? The food? The question catches him by surprise and flusters him. To cover his embarrassment, and because "he" is still unsettled, his head a blank, unable to form words clearly, "he" begins to laugh. Ha! Ha! Ha! Your job requires that a person be realistic above all, I realize. Still, if you're not aware of any difference in importance between bladder cancer and stew because you think everything I tell you is made up and take it all relatively, no matter how bloody, that's a bit of a problem! But you know I love oxtail stew, I've helped you fix it many times. And as long as that saucepan full of oxtail is still on the fire, it's on my mind. Ha! Ha! Ha! People who still have a long life ahead of them are so cheerful and easygoing, their feet are so firmly on the ground! "he" says. My mother was that way too, that night, someone with a long life ahead of her, who didn't come to the storehouse to visit the invalid even though the doctor had announced that he had bladder cancer, but was thoughtful enough to see to the oxtail stewing in the cooking shed. Even though she had no desire to see anything as horrifying as oxtail, she was probably moved by the respect paid to food in general in those days. The next morning, when I went out at *a certain party's* bidding to look in the cooking shed, the stew was ready. Since I had no idea how to serve it out of the smaller pot my mother had put it in, I carried it pot and all to *a certain party* where he lay in the storehouse in the room with the wooden floor. Then I wanted to take care of my own stomach and had no choice but going to the kitchen in the main house. Since my mother had continued to prepare noon and evening meals for the recluses in the storehouse, my share of the previous night's meal, of which I had eaten nothing, should have been waiting for me that morning. I went in through the kitchen and found my mother in the adjoining room, repairing and polishing the ornaments to be used in the autumn festival at the monkey shrine. Ever since my brother's ashes had come home, my mother had cast a cold eye on the valley and everything in it, even the scenery, she scarcely even lifted her eyes to see where she was going, but she had begun to look after the monkey shrine with real devotion, and to this day she still does! When I asked for my breakfast, my mother answered me stiffly, as if she'd rehearsed the lines, lifting her eyes only to dart glances at me as she spoke,

——*The vegetables I set aside to make enough gruel for the whole family to eat were all thrown into that pot of filthy oxtail,*

76

consequently there is nothing left for us. So I grabbed two chunks of something that passed for bread, finely ground corn steamed with just a touch of wheat flour, and took them out into the garden, thinking I would eat them with the vegetables that should have sunk to the bottom of the broth remaining in the large pot. But when I stuck my hand into the pot I found that everything in that muddy broth had cooked away, leaving only bunches of fiber, and for just an instant the horror seeping through my fingers stirring around at the bottom of that pot came close to making me sympathize with my mother's outrage. As a matter of fact, even after I had finished washing down that corn bread like board planks with some water I drew from the well, I didn't go back to the storehouse for a while. Partly it was *a certain party* tearing into the oxtail stew the morning after his bladder cancer had been discovered, lifting those joints of oxtail whose baleful odor had overwhelmed the *bouquet garni* I had gathered at the edge of the forest, holding them by the ends between his thick, round thumb and first finger, ripping the meat away from the bone and devouring them one after another without offering to share the smallest morsel with me; partly I was afraid that, eaten in a valley surrounded by a forest, and early in the morning besides, the smell of a thing like that would draw down upon us all those ghostly creatures that had dwelled for years in the forest's depths. After that, on the rare occasions when we got hold of an oxtail, and even when all we had was pigs' feet, I had to do the cooking myself, because *a certain party's* physical condition no longer permitted him to leave the storehouse to cook or do anything else. To be sure, I followed his instructions, and the procedure was simple enough: all I did was throw the meat into a large pot of boiling water in chunks, just as it came from the butcher, wait a while, add barley or some other grain, whatever vegetable scraps I could sneak away from my mother, who was no longer ever careless about leaving her onions and carrots unattended, some salt, and a few beans of a substance that never under any circumstances made its way into my mother's kitchen, garlic. Possibly *a certain party's* instructions for that simplified cooking were a reduction of his experiences on the Chinese mainland designed to permit him to relive them in the valley; certainly there was no one anywhere in the valley whose diet was closer to that of the Korean forest workers. The Koreans held up well under labor conditions that would have to be called harsh, and *a certain party*, too, despite his advancing bladder cancer, grew, thanks to that unique meat-pot with garlic, in the manner of a landslide, fatter and fatter until there was no covering him, "he" says.]]

VI

[[Once August begins, "he" is in a state of constant agitation. Apparently not even sleep releases him, for although "he" no longer sobs aloud as before, it seems that "he" repeatedly cries out as though in great anger. However, "he" insists to a dubious "acting executor of the will" that "he" continues to have no memory whatsoever of his dreams. These past few days you've frequently expressed concern over whether your mother will be able to survive the heat of this summer, I wonder if your dreams might have something to do with that? It could be, now when I'm finally in a position to really let my mother have it for the first time in my life, I don't know what I'd do if she died a step ahead of me, "he" replies with

78

objective calm. But a minute later "he" is agitated once again. The fact is, my mother could decide to violate our contract and commit suicide cleverly enough to make it look like natural death of old age and I wouldn't even be able to go into the field to investigate. She's easily capable of starving herself and starting whatever organs inside her were sufficiently weakened rolling down a gentle slope they could never get back up, she has more than enough malice for that! "he" says resentfully. You and your mother promised one another you wouldn't commit suicide? When I was in high school my mother made certain I would never be able to try suicide by hurting and humiliating me so deeply my basic attitudes toward society around me were bent all out of shape. How can the force she had to exert against me to achieve that not bounce back at her? And doesn't that amount to having entered into a contract? But in order to denounce her effectively for her contract violation I'd have to catch her in the act of attempting suicide just the way she caught me! As the day in August approaches when twenty-five years ago the ten officers and soldiers who had deserted from the army led him and *a certain party* out of the valley in a wagon, his agitation is high from before dawn until late at night and the "acting executor of the will" must go to the nurses' station frequently to request treatment to calm him down. Insisting that he must re-experience that midsummer day under weather and atmospheric conditions as similar as possible, "he" has the air-conditioning in his private room turned off. You know I can never experience that summer day again just as it was, how can you try to cheat me out of that final summer? "he" says. But in the un-airconditioned hospital room his exhaustion accelerates, "he" spends the entire day sighing, then tires and falls asleep without having narrated a word, dreams, and cries out in anger. The morning after such a night, "he" complains of a kind of difficulty "he" has never before admitted. When I try as hard as I can to remember clearly the officers and soldiers who loaded *a certain party* into a wagon in spite of the bleeding cancer in his bladder and hauled him out of the valley as if they were pulling a root up out of the ground they sometimes appear in my memory, especially the officers, dressed just like Occupation GI's! I've always had a double image of soldiers, part Japanese infantry just before the war and part GI during the Occupation. And while the two images are separate they have a way of merging subtly, I could never describe the uniforms of those young officers and soldiers who came to the valley with any concrete accuracy. Yet that part is crucial! Without it I can't make you accept what I say as anything but make-believe! The radiant culmination of my *Happy Days* originates there, everything I ever did from that time on was affected by the force emanating from there, even my death so close at hand glistens in the light from there and nowhere else! Thus "he" laments, and, helpless to control his mounting agitation, trembles. Yet when the "acting executor of the will" tries to help, hunting up, for example, photograph collections of wartime styles and manners so that "he" can verify his memory objectively, "he" is, if anything, resentful. I intend to narrate a "history of our age" which I myself have experienced definitively, the experience of which continues to live inside me; if I start dressing up my own uncertain memory with photographic records made by someone I don't even know, you tell me how I'm going to produce a "history of our age" with any real power over me and my mother! "he" shouts in irritation, his eyes red as plums. The truth is, it's not easy, all these years later, to reproduce in words just how it felt late that afternoon at the height of summer, when those officers and soldiers appeared in the valley and crossed the bridge from the highway and drew up in a solid line, and I heard them declare, as I stood among the adults who had evacuated to the valley and were too lazy to work and the other valley kids, that they had come for none other than *a certain party*, and then ask to be taken to him, and happiness seemed to charge me with static electricity so that every particle of my flesh and blood stood on end, even though I was thunderstruck by that sudden and unexpected development. And going back through the way those soldiers moved, their stiff quickstep even when they only had a few paces to go or their no-nonsense voices when they shouted orders to themselves, to the valley boy inside myself that was me in August, 1945, and reviving him gradually with fresh blood until he has regained his former health entirely is no easy job, either. For one thing, my mother attacked precisely that ecstatically happy boy inside me with such persistence she finally drove him to the edge of extinction. For a long time it was as if destroying him was the sole objective of her remaining years, she went about it with a fury worse than the cancer gnawing at my liver! But you must have resisted? So if you recall all the things inside yourself you tried to protect from your mother as a child and talk about them one by one wouldn't that give you all the leads you need? Say, I notice recently you've been doing more for my "history of the age" than just transcribing it! For very nearly the first time since taking to his sick bed "he" expresses something like genuine gratitude. In his excitement and irritation "he" is also revealing an unexpected openness. Because

I'm afraid if you lost interest in this project now you'd sink so deeply into the liver cancer in your imagination you'd never surface again, says the "acting executor of the will." Ha! Ha! Ha! Once again on guard, and cunning, "he" tries kicking sand with his hind leg to cover the openness "he" has just revealed. I didn't realize you could be so exquisitely sentimental! Now "he" has regained his grip on what he needs to speak about himself with cool objectivity, and in the process, no doubt aided by his desire to oppose the "acting executor of the will," a measure of vitality as well. For the moment, however, "he" will reply on this vitality to help him fall asleep. When "he" awakens from this shallow sleep and his strength and spirits are at such low ebb "he" cannot fall asleep again, in the middle of the night, if his scribe on her cot next to his bed will also wake up and keep him company, "he" will resume his account.]]

As he led the officers and soldiers up the stone path toward the Manor house at the top of the rise, followed by nearly all the children in the valley, whose friendliness toward him had been instantly restored by the appearance of the strangers, he perceived, with a flicker of uneasiness that intruded for just an instant on the excitement rioting in his head, that his mother was hurriedly closing the double rain doors ordinarily used only a few times a year when a typhoon was approaching, not only on the ground floor but on the second floor where no one lived and even in the attic, as if it were an attacking army he was leading up from the valley, and, hoping to preserve his high spirits, he lowered his eyes to the path as he climbed. At the roofed gate at the entrance to the Manor house, one of the officers yelled at the children to go back. There was nothing unusual in the valley about voices being raised, but if someone did shout, in any situation except a family

82

quarrel, he shrank with shame at his raised voice, which had reached the ears of the things lurking in the forest depths, and ultimately compromised himself though he may have been entirely in the right. The other party, however, no matter how large a concession may have been made to him, far from forgetting that he had been shouted at, retained the memory rancorously. In the communal society of the valley, the label "the one who raises his voice" amounted to an official coup de grace administered to someone who had been judged irretrievably antisocial. The sound of voices being raised quite shamelessly by *outsiders* at a crowd of valley children thus filled him with resentment and disgust and a certain sense of injustice, and then at the entrance to the storehouse where he was living with *a certain party* it was his turn to be told in a loud voice, Stay Out Even so, he somehow managed to contain, temporarily, his anger, and humiliation at this outrageous impropriety and, when he had opened the kitchen door to the main house by lifting the latch inside with an old nail, he went in to "challenge" his mother where she huddled motionlessly in the darkness of the adjoining room.

——Mother! Mother! Just like I thought, just like I thought, Mother, the army has come for *a certain party* just like I thought His voice as he spoke into the darkness was shrill with excitement, but his mother ignored his mood, answering only,

——Just *as* I thought, the least you can do is speak properly, you must have a *little* shame left!

Yet he managed to contain forbearingly even the antagonism this venomous response provoked, and continued his appeal for a dialogue based on exultation they could share:

——Mother! Mother! I have a piece of paper hidden in a

secret place with a list of all the people who said *a certain party* was a spy or who spread rumors that he wrote letters to the newspapers saying we would lose the war, and Mother! I've been thinking about that list ever since the soldiers came for *a certain party* just like I thought!

——*A certain party* doesn't have the ability to be a spy. And he doesn't have the gumption to come right out and say we're going to lose the war, either! Oh, he wrote in to the papers all right, something about making Saipan and Tinian and Guam permanent strongholds against the enemy and moving the Imperial palace out there, even if it meant leaving all of Japan defenseless against the American attack, nonsense like that, Lord knows why or who he thought he was a-talking to, and then he hid himself in the storehouse because he was afraid the secret police would come to arrest him, but all that happened was a few country cops came out to tell him to stop it, yessir!

——Mother! Mother! The army came for *a certain party*, Mother, just like I thought! Just like I thought! When he had sung out these final words into the darkness that retained the heat of day where his mother sat motionless and probably sweating he dashed outside again into the early evening light and snuck around to the back of the storehouse, nimbly evading the soldiers despite the glare of the still-reddish sun which tightened his chest and stopped him in his tracks for just a minute, like a blind rat, then scrambled up onto the outhouse roof, got down on his hands and knees, and tried to catch a few words of the conference the officers were having with *a certain party*. Before long his leg was grabbed and he was pulled down off the roof by a soldier who had been walking around the storehouse, possibly to guard it, possibly because he was bored; unable to find another hiding place where he could continue to hold out alone against the world he raced back

84

yet again, undeterred, to the dark kitchen entrance of the main house, and reported, in a voice so strained and shrill he might have seemed to be weeping, *Mother! Mother! the situation has become critical so they're going to revolt and a certain party is going to lead them, just like I thought, just like I thought, we're in a crisis situation and they've chosen a certain party as their leader! We'd better have a good look at the list of people who said a certain party was a spy or someone who wanted us to lose the war, and we'd better total up their names, Mother, we're going to have our hands full, because Mother, Mother, it's just like I thought it would be!*

This ardent speech he delivered deliriously, but his mother might have been asleep, so complete was the indifference and silence in which she enclosed herself in the darkness where she sat on the wooden floor with her legs beneath her. Ignored, he rose and closed the door at the entrance to the kitchen from the inside, then sat down on the raised sill of the room with the wooden floor, his back to his mother, his bare feet dangling above the dirt floor a step lower, and, staring vacantly into space in front of him, his eyes rolled up and partly hidden beneath his lids, his hammer-head pulled down between his shoulders and angled obliquely upward, in just the pose his childhood pictures always caught him, he tried to daydream with a bit of concrete detail about his own role in this crisis situation as a youthful soldier armed with a bayonet, and began to wait. Dusk had suddenly descended and children's voices and animal cries fallen silent in the valley below when one of the officers threw open the wooden door at the kitchen entrance and half leaned inside, his broad shoulders and head framed from behind in a faint, golden light adjacent to pitch darkness, his body black as night, and called out,

——Mrs. ——, the Squire is asking for you!

Mrs. ——! It was a last name he had never heard. And he was about to announce that the name was a mistake, having finally been presented an opportunity to satisfy his longing to be of some real service to the soldiers, when unexpectedly his mother responded from the darkness with a perfectly commonplace reply, then stood up and seemed to be adjusting her kimono.

[[Even now I remember perfectly clearly the way my mother emerged from that dark room, and the sound the stiff cloth of her *obi* made when she tightened it, and the soft fall of her footsteps. But when I try to focus on the uniforms those soldiers had on when they appeared, I see only a vague picture. Sometimes I think they must have been wearing army uniforms of that khaki cloth that seemed so very thick, and sometimes I'm sure they had on dark brown shirts open at the neck that were so stained with sweat they frightened us, with their stripes pinned on their collars. His brow knit, "he" speaks with effort, in a way that evokes the empty space in his imagination behind the underwater goggles where decision is being deferred. Since the last thing "he" expects with regard to this problem is an active response from the "acting executor of the will," her attack comes as a complete surprise,

——It's only natural you have no clear memory of how those soldiers were dressed. The day they came to the valley not one of them was in military uniform, full dress or combat or any other kind, not even the officers. Instantly "he" is aware of grave danger. A specific anxiety "he" has not tasted in a long time, the special tension of the feeling that an entangling malice was threatening to pulverize the very bedrock of his identity, an anxiety which, moreover, like the memory of an odor, could be revived inside him at any time by any one of numberless experiences of his childhood, now rises inside him to flood level along with something else that envelops and presently will transform it into a sense of utter helplessness. Wait a minute! "he" protests, his voice straining pitifully. If a group of soldiers had been traveling openly without their uniforms during the war, they would have been stopped by the police in the provincial city before they ever reached the valley. It also happens there was an army garrison in that provincial city, which means, for your information, that secret police must have been all over the place. And those soldiers didn't make any attempt to hide the fact that they were soldiers! The war was over on that day. The war had just ended! You talk about leaving behind a "history of the age" like a last testament, with nothing in it but the truth, you slave away at it until your physical strength and your spirit are nearly worn away, and then in the most crucial part you imbed a lie that's immediately apparent to the person you want to read it most—I can't understand that *either*, says the "acting executor of the will." I honestly can't understand it *either*. Those soldiers drove up to the bridge leading into the valley in their army truck on the evening of August fifteenth. They couldn't cross, because the bridge supports had been partly washed away in a flood at the height of the war and hadn't been repaired. They took you and your father back to the provincial city with them the following day, August sixteenth. By the evening of August fifteenth, the war was over. That's a fact as plain as day, so you can't very well blame that particular mistake on your memory. It seems your descriptions of the wooden cart they took your father in and the clothes you were wearing when you left and all kinds of details like that are accurate, it seems you consciously distorted only the date. But why you would go to so much trouble to keep repeating a lie like that I can't understand *either!* Lying in bed on his back alone and helpless, "he" longs to open a hole in the sheets, wriggling his neck and hips like the lowliest bugs that live in the soft, shallow earth, and burrow into the mattress. How long has it been since my mother arrived here at the hospital from the valley? Long enough for her to have read the entire account so far? "he" moans softly.]]

VII

[[The soldiers came on August fifteenth, yessir! That's a fact. And they left, with *a certain party* and this child, the morning of August sixteenth, yessir! The person crouching nearly to the floor in the far left corner of his sickroom speaks with calm detachment, in idiocentric accents which create the impression overall of chill objectivity despite the emphatic suffixes of his valley dialect. Not without surprise, "he" listens to the voice directly for the first time in just ten years and discovers not a trace in it of the veiled hostility and hinted ridicule that had saddled him for so long with the aftereffects of a persecution complex; the impression created is of a simple old country woman talking. There is a mild, respectable ordinariness about the voice, a feeling of benign old age, and "he" must wonder if the image of the aggressive mother that has cast its loathsome shadow over the better half of his thirty-five years is merely a delusion of his own. Nonetheless, "he" replies directly to no words that issue from his mother's lips. In front of his mother "he" is embarrassed for the first time about wearing the underwater goggles covered with cellophane, but so long as "he" gazes up at the ceiling

88

through the cylinder lenses she cannot possibly enter his field of vision. Perhaps, to that extent at least, "he" can refuse subjectively to accept her unexpected appearance. Not that his mother addresses him directly; she is speaking solely to provide the person taking down his "history of the age" with evidence, extremely negative evidence. His own main objective in interrupting her, similarly, is to educe and examine details of the "history" in order to corroborate them. It was early in the morning and they were singing all together, not an army song either but some song in a foreign language, maybe they were trying to say they weren't soldiers anymore, and they loaded that tub of lard with bladder cancer into a wooden wagon and even took this child along, for a hostage maybe, it was mean and low! And they set out from the valley and even dragged this child along, with his *fake* helmet down over his ears and a rusty old broken bayonet tied at his side, lord knows what he was thinking! It was the morning of August sixteenth, and they were singing a Bach aria they'd learned off a record, yessir! Taking radios and phonographs apart and putting them back together was about the one thing *a certain party* could do a pretty decent job on—he was at least average when it came to working with his hands—and he had a radio and a phonograph in the storehouse. The night of August fifteenth everybody knew there wouldn't be any more air raids, so the mood that was general all over the valley was lights uncovered and blazing away and folks gathered around their radios, but we were the only ones with a phonograph that wasn't broken and even a few records, yessir! And that whole night long the soldiers who had come for *a certain party* listened to records while they drank the *saké* they'd brought with them in the truck. *A certain party* had been collecting Bach records since before the war, but he'd sold them or traded them for food and he couldn't have had more than two or three left, but the record those soldiers listened to over and over until the next morning and even learned the simple chorus of it by heart before they left happened to be Bach, yessir! I say soldiers, but the young officers were just college boys and still making a big fuss over the Victor red label!]]

Since his elder brother's ashes had returned, his mother had scarcely ever walked the stone path down to the valley. Besides, the radios that survived the war in that valley in the depths of the forest were in general capable of producing only a noise no bigger than the whining of a mosquito. How, then, from Manor-house-rise, can his mother have heard those radios in front of which people had gathered in a mood that was "general all over the valley"?

[[Late the night of the fifteenth I went around to four or five houses in the valley, that had bicycle carts, and each place I stopped I says Tomorrow morning those *former* soldiers who just lost the war will be coming to commandeer your cart! hide it in the forest! in China it used to happen all the time! There was supposed to be an important broadcast on the fifteenth so most families sat outside on the porch listening to their radios most of the night. Naturally there were no interesting programs, there sure as fire wasn't any broadcast with enough truth to it to teach anybody in that forest what he ought to do from then on. But folks wouldn't leave their radios, because every once in a while a little bit of voice would work its way through the static. When I made my rounds everybody did as I suggested and hid their carts, which is why early the next morning the soldiers had to saw logs into

90

wooden wheels and attach them to a wood fertilizer box and line it with pillows and load him into that. If it had been any time before August fifteenth, the folks in the valley would have had their lights masked and they would have been listening to the radio quietly away at the back of the house, and the general mood in the valley would have been entirely different, yessir!]]

Then yield for the moment, assume those soldiers who refused to accept defeat rose up with *a certain party* as their leader on August sixteenth. Young as he was, his sense of date cannot have been very certain, after all. But that in no way changed the essence of the incident. Young officers unwilling to acknowledge the war's end and the men who followed them formed a group that refused to accept defeat and came in quest of *a certain party's* leadership—surely there was nothing unnatural about that! And considering that vast amounts of data and evidence were destroyed during the Occupation, it is not at all unlikely that on August sixteenth a triumphant American pilot buzzing a surrendered city should have strafed an odd wooden cart carrying a man dressed up in a "people's jacket" and even holding a military sword. In short, the basic problem was not affected by the fact that the incident occurred on August sixteenth and not before the fifteenth. As a matter of fact, officers and soldiers were more likely to have entrusted the leadership of an uprising to a civilian after the war, dissatisfied with the surrender, than to have left their unit to join a civilian while on active duty in wartime.

Anyway, one morning in August before the sky was even pale, the boy and the soldiers loaded *a certain party* into the wooden wagon they had improvised and set out across the pitch-black valley at a turtle's pace, one step at a time. At the mouth of the valley they hoisted *a certain party* into a truck, wooden wagon and all, and started up ninety-nine-curve-pass, now a band of insurgents. And while the truck sped along, the soldiers sang in chorus, in no particular order, over and over again, the bits and pieces they had learned of a song in a foreign language. The only one who could not join in at first, the boy wiped, again and again, with old diapers he had carried in by the armful and even stuffed into cracks in the wagon, the sticky urine and hemorrhaging blood that kept soaking *a certain party's* abdomen and crotch. But he could not wipe around his obese, planted buttocks without help from the soldiers, and before long, the pillows on the floor between *a certain party's* buttocks and his thighs were submerged in a pond of faintly evil-smelling blood. He was terrified that all the blood in *a certain party's* body would drain away, but it was impossible to communicate his fear to the men, for, although they continued to support the swaying, creaking wooden box on the truck bed on all four sides, they had temporarily turned their attention away from *a certain party* with soldierly courageousness and were singing at the top of their voices. The pain must have been severe, but *a certain party* endured in silence, his eyes closed, his obese body crashing back and forth against the walls of the box like a rubber ball inside a cube. Afraid he was dead already, the boy pressed his face against *a certain party's* thick neck, his nose filling with the odd sweetness that underlay the sickening odor of sweat and blood, and shouted What's the song mean, huh? Whereupon *a certain party*, who not only had never answered his questions during their time together in the storehouse but had seemed unlikely to allow him even to ask a question, with beads of sweat sliding down the unwrinkled porcelain of

92

his wan face, his eyes still closed, his huge body smashing against the wooden boards as before, unexpectedly explained with fatherly care. To be sure, what he retained directly in memory was only a small portion of what was said. *TRÄNEN means "tear," and TOD that means "to die," it's German. His Majesty the Emperor wipes my tears away with his own hand, Death, you come ahead, you brother of Sleep you come ahead, his Majesty will wipe my tears away with his own hand, that's what they're singing. I wait eagerly for his Majesty the Emperor to wipe my tears away with his own hand, they're singing!*

[[The "acting executor of the will" confers with a doctor who knows music, determines the title of the Bach cantata and borrows the record. I have the feeling this cantata is part of the reason I didn't study German in college, "he" says, listening to the record and groping, guided by the verses printed on the jacket, for the lines that have been echoing in his internal ear for twenty-five years. I wonder if I wasn't afraid subconsciously that, if I learned to understand German, the singing that day that remains in my head might not begin to convey a meaning just the reverse of *a certain party's* explanation!]]

Though he had just taken his first step into that intricate passage that connects childhood and youth, he understood everything *a certain party* said atop the truck that day. In his small head inside a *fake* helmet, aflame not only with the heat but also the matter that had been enfolded in it, he understood. *A certain party's* words ignited his child's passion at its very source, and his ten-year-old body-and-soul, truly alive atop that speeding truck, shook, radiant and electrified, as though it had been struck by lightning. As the army truck emerged from the valley in the dense forest and started up ninety-nine-curve-pass, they were released from the deep green darkness of the evergreen trees that had walled off their view, and could look out across an expanse of young deciduous woods that were dry beneath the summer sun but retained a pale green luster. And now he gazed at the scenery with the new eyes of a bird, a sharp-eyed bird, a hawk or a peregrine falcon. Tree-leaves, as far as he could see, were trembling ceaselessly. What he had never noticed while he lived in the valley surrounded by a forest, that tree-leaves trembled continuously even when the wind was still, he now perceived distinctly as he finally left the forest depths and at ten was about to end his life. *The leaves on the trees are always moving! I'll remember that until I die, until I die fighting in the army a certain party is leading into revolt!* As he was thinking this, a fighter plane appeared from the direction of the provincial city, coming in low over the pass, and the soldiers began shouting,

——Look how reckless he is, he doesn't care what happens any more!

——We'd better get the planes we need fast, before those bastards crash them!

——We need at least ten, then we can all fly over the palace and skyrocket ourselves!

——Our objective is *junshi* *—death as allegiance—it's *junshi* for us all!

It's junshi for us all—the hot thorns in the words pierced his small heart, lodged there and continued to burn. And the heat originating inside him empowered his strong eyes and he was able to see, from one corner to the other of the slopes that dropped steeply toward the pass which the fighter plane had just circled and left behind,

* The suicide in the emperor's name that was the goal of the Kamikaze pilots.

the hundreds of millions of leaves tilting upward in the strong wind that had risen and to see, vastly and distinctly, the undersides of those hundreds of millions of tilted leaves shining with a silvery gray light. *This must be a signal! A certain party will lead our army in an uprising and we will all die. And these soldiers are singing that they want to die as quickly as possible, and are waiting for his Majesty to wipe their tears away with his own hand.* His heart pumped vigorously and the pressure in his blood vessels surged until his eardrums sang and all he could hear on the other side of that curtain of piercing sound was the silence of all things. Like a ferret he lifted his head and rotated it, gazing at the soldiers with love and pity through eyes about to dissolve in tears. In contrast to all the other soldiers who had come to the valley during the war, including the cadets who had tapped pine tree roots for oil, who had treated "small citizens" with excessive kindness, the soldiers on the truck had been cold and rough with him from the beginning, had even behaved as if he were unclean. Also they had been drinking steadily in the storehouse since the previous night, and singing drunkenly, and were in general a far cry from the image of the soldier he had cherished until now. But such impurities as these he forgave and accepted with utmost tenderness, and saw in them the very model of "true" soldiers. For these were soldiers not merely unafraid of death but awaiting death eagerly, and he was able now to confirm unwaveringly a choice that had been made with them already somewhere along the way, that he was about to die as a member of their band, and thus effortlessly to transcend the source of his shame for several years, both the hesitation he could confess to no one in his regular answer to the daily classroom question Will you die happily for the Emperor? *Yes, I'll die happily,*

95

and his fear late at night when he pictured actual death in war. Before long he was even imitating the officers and soldiers and singing along in his shrill voice.

Komm, O Tod, du Schlafes Bruder,
Komm und führe mich nur fort;

[[Lying there in bed singing away like that I don't know if this child is serious or what, but there's no way *Heiland* can mean "emperor"! And as for having their tears wiped away, those soldiers had worked themselves up to where they were ready to bomb the personage that was supposed to do the wiping, yessir! When that officer came to the main house he called for me by the last name of my real father, which made me suspicious enough to go over to the storehouse, and when I got there *a certain party* couldn't even look me in the face, because he was about to make an outrageous demand on top of having brought me there with his little trick. But the soldiers spun his barber's chair around unsparingly, yessir! so he lowered his eyes right quick, and then drunkenly, his face beneath his stubble of beard beet-red from the *saké* they'd poured into him, he had the nerve to say to me,
——*We'll accomplish what your father tried and failed to do. We're going to steal ten fighter planes from the army airfield, and disguise them to look like American planes and bomb the Imperial palace. There's no other way left to make the Japanese people rise up again and protect the true essence of our nation!* After all the bigshot talk about some crazy dream I wondered what was coming next, and the first thing I knew I was being asked to hand over my stocks for battle funds. Well, he was so mean and low I felt I couldn't listen to *a certain party* a minute more, so I set my seal to the forms just as he asked me to, yessir! I didn't know it at the time, because we still

couldn't get telegrams or anything, but the day the Soviet Union had entered the war my foster father had shot himself in Harbin. It was my foster father who had given me the stocks! He'd chosen them because he figured they were stocks the government would help the stock exchange honor even if we lost the war. He must have had control over the bank in our region, he arranged for the bank to take care of everything. Well, *a certain party* had me put my seal on the papers that released those stocks, and he had me write a letter of agreement on top of that, and then he took the papers and those soldiers took him and carted him off in a ridiculous wooden box with sawed-off logs for wheels. He was hurting bad, and I suppose he must have taken the narcotic drugs he'd bought in China and maybe stuffed them in his nose, because he was reeling like a top, yessir! It was a cruel business, but I didn't go out of my way to interfere. But in my heart I kept a-thinking to myself, Now you'll see! Any minute now you'll see! Ah, what a cruel business, how cruelly the bigshot is going to be used! The child, who of course had no inkling of any of this, he was clutching old diapers for to wipe away blood from *a certain party's* bladder, his bayonet clanking at his side, so grim and determined he was pale, lord knows what he was thinking! Well, if you're wondering whether the soldiers who took *a certain party* with them really drove that truck onto an army airfield and stole fighter planes and flew to Tokyo, they did no such thing! There was a shootout at the bank entrance, and *a certain party* and all the soldiers were killed, yessir! None of the officers was killed but they never turned up again, and I don't know what happened to the stocks, maybe they couldn't be sold in the confusion after the surrender and maybe they were sold and someone made off with the money, no stocks or money turned up again so I reckon those officers took the money and ran. And I bet that's what they planned to do all along, yessir! I think *a certain party* had sensed it, too, and what he planned to do was go through the motions of that *fake* uprising and then climb back into his wooden box and come home nursing his bladder and announce *The officers betrayed me, the boy knows the whole story!* and then hide away at the back of that storehouse again! But someone thought *a certain party* and his bunch had gone into the bank to rob it, or maybe they were planning to rob it themselves and thought someone was there ahead of them, anyhow, instead of notifying the police in that chaos after the surrender they drove up in their own army truck and shot down *a certain party* and his bunch as they came out of the bank. In his right hand *a certain party* held his army sword, and he was waving his left hand frantically as if he was shouting Stop! Stop! but they say he was shot down before he could actually shout a word, yessir!]]

It was truly a pitched battle in the streets, and overhead, fighter planes, possibly Japanese and possibly American, probably both, swooped so low their roar shook the streets. The only one who experienced the entire battle and understood its significance fully was himself. And now, examining once again, in light of the true significance of that battle, the fact that the uprising actually occurred on August sixteenth, he saw for the first time the importance of that date and no other and understood more clearly than before the structure of the festival culmination of his *Happy Days*. August fifteenth, 1945, the Emperor swiftly descended to earth to announce the surrender in the voice of a mortal man. August sixteenth, his Majesty was circling upward in a swift

98

ascent again. Though it was inevitable that he die in a bombing once, now truly he would revive as the national essence itself, and more certainly than before, more divinely, as a ubiquitous chrysanthemum, would cover Japan and all her people. As a golden chrysanthemum illuminated from behind by a vast purple light and glittering like an aurora, his Majesty would manifest himself. Who is to say that the many gods who have figured in the history of our land did not on that day require of the Emperor who had descended to speak in a mortal voice, in order that the dignity of our national essence be elevated once again, the ritual purification of death by bombing at the hands of martyrs in a plane?

In fact, the palace was not bombed. Instead, *a certain party*, leading a small, select unit, not on horseback to be sure but in a wooden box mounted on sawed logs like pulleys, confronted the enemy head on, military sword held high, and was shot down. And what if the battle did take place in front of a bank from which some funds had been peacefully withdrawn and not at an airfield where fighter planes to be disguised were being seized, how much can that have depreciated it? Was there a street battle fought anywhere else in all Japan on August sixteenth, 1945, even if it was at the entrance to a bank, that could have resulted in *a certain party's* death? Although they would have been justified in resorting to any means whatsoever to raise the money they needed to achieve their objective, *a certain party* and his army went in to get it lawfully. Whether they succeeded is unknown, for as they emerged from the bank with the wooden wagon bearing *a certain party* in the lead, another army that had driven up in a different army truck opened fire, even the fighter plane flying low overhead joined the attack, and *a certain party's*

99

army was annihilated. Why did the other army attack? Wasn't it really a unit controlled by spies of the Allies, afraid their maneuvering to end the war might backfire in the final stage? *A certain party* was planning to disguise Japanese fighters as American planes, why shouldn't someone else have tried the opposite experiment? Very likely *a certain party* was strafed, and killed, by a plane disguised to look like a Japanese fighter but flown by an American. It was probably the very plane that had appeared as they were crossing ninety-nine-curve-pass, which had continued following them and finally had attacked.

And *a certain party*, leaping beyond his limitations as an individual at the instant of his death, rendered manifest a gold chrysanthemum flower 675,000 kilometers square, surmounted and surrounded by, yes, a purple aurora, high enough in the sky to cover entirely the islands of Japan. Because the other, attacking army opened fire on their truck first, the soldiers nearby the boy were immediately massacred and he alone survived. *A certain party* had requested this of the gods on high, for it was crucial that someone, someone chosen, witness the gold chrysanthemum obliterate the heavens with its luster at the instant of his death. And, in truth, the boy did behold the appearance high in the sky, not blocking the light as would a cloud but even managing to increase the glittering radiance of the sun in the blue, midsummer sky, of a shining gold chrysanthemum against a vast background of purple light. And when the light from that flower irradiated his *Happy Days* they were instantly transformed into an unbreaking, eternal construction built of light. From that instant on, for the twenty-five years that were to be the remainder of his life, he would constantly inhabit this strong edifice of light that was his *Happy Days*. Half-standing in the cart, his sword held high in his right hand, his left hand thrust out in front of him and spread so wide that each white, fat finger was distinctly visible, *a certain party* faced his chosen son and spoke as follows, heedless of the enemy firing into him, *Have you seen what must be seen? For the next quarter-century that you will live remember always what you have seen, All has been accomplished, you have seen what must be seen, Survive and remember, that is your role, Do nothing else! All has been accomplished!* When *a certain party* finished speaking a fighter plane dived, machine guns ringing, and the head protruding from the wooden cart became a round, bright red pomegranate full of cracks, the mouth, still full of reddish darkness at the back, wrenched open by an unuttered scream.

[[When the person who has climbed onto his bed suddenly yanks his underwater goggles up to his hairline "he" is quick to shut his eyes against the painful glare, but already they have teared. I thought he might be talking that nonsense because he was delirious with fever, but his eyes are normal! The voice that has come from the foot of the bed until now speaks in the darkness above his head, and before "he" can adjust his goggles two thin, scratchy thumbs expertly wipe away the tears in the corners of his closed eyes. His face is so thin, he looks just the way he did when he was a child, it's like his face as a little boy at the end of the war when there wasn't enough to eat, yessir! In the darkness overhead from where the voice falls "he" distinguishes a single after-image, like a photo printed with a flashlight. Coal-black hair, eyes bulging from eyelids like gray grapes, narrow, egg-shaped face trimmed of flesh, expressionless, dry skin. In his imagination the image merges swiftly with the negative of the last photograph taken of ——— before his execution. Though he was only twenty-six, the brutal trial and death sentence were said to have turned the young monk's hair white. If he was in his right mind when he did all that talking, why, he's got to be challenged! says the person wedged down close to the floor again beyond the foot of his bed. *To see what must be seen*—my real father found that line in the *Tale of the Heike* when he read it in prison and sent it to relatives that were about to be bereaved, yessir! Can you imagine *a certain party* turning to a pitiful little child and speaking to him in classical Japanese? This child made that preposterous conversation up because he hoped it would excuse him from responsibility for that incident on August sixteenth, yessir! If I'd known it was going to hold his mind prisoner all those years I would never have let him set out that morning all determined like a silly fool and his bayonet a-clanking! It was a cruel business, yessir! *A certain party* did a lot of mean and low things with his little rising sun flag in his headband and his chrysanthemum crest on his back, in China and Manchuria, but the lowest thing he ever did was drag this child along on that make-believe uprising! He knew it was a *fake* that would fail, he even wanted it to fail, and he took the child along because he was afraid of the rumor after the fiasco that he never had been in earnest. He took the ridiculous, transparent, mean-and-low precaution of having ———'s grandson along with him, because he figured that would make it easier to convince people he really had been prepared to bomb the palace. And young as he was, this child must have understood that perfectly well. Because while *a certain party* and the officers were in the bank transacting business, before anything had happened, he got scared to death and jumped out of that army truck where he'd been told to wait and ran off! He must have, otherwise he'd have been killed as soon as the shooting started! Not only the driver but all the soldiers who stayed with that truck were shot to death right away! This child didn't run off *after* the shooting began, he had the feeling he was being used to give credibility to the entire *fake* uprising, and that's when he ran off. Down inside he'd been frightened right along about the blood of a traitor running in his veins, wondering when that blood would start to work in him, and when he was told he was actually on his way to bomb the palace he decided the responsibility was all his, because the blood flowing in his body led to the kind of action that turned the country's history upside-down, and that made him want to run and run as far away as he could go, even from his own body, yessir! And when *a certain party* was shot to death as they pushed his wooden wagon out of the bank it was probably this child who was more relieved than anyone! When the police who brought the news drove me to the scene of the crime later that day, that wooden box with wooden wheels like large pulleys was standing in a bombed-out lot next to the bank, all spattered with blood, and *a certain party's* stiff corpse was sticking out at an angle like a fountain pen somebody had stuck into the box, but this child wasn't watching over him, he was squatting down in the shadow of a truck with the air raid crew that had carried away the soldiers' bodies, and every once in a while he'd steal a quick look in the direction of the box, peering through the dusk. And no one had any idea he was the son of the dead man in that wooden box! He deceived everyone that day, the air raid crew, the police, the soldiers, and he's been deceiving without a minute's rest ever since. I never said a word to him about the blood flowing in his veins until now, he managed to dig that up himself and he began fearing it by himself. Neither *a certain party* or this child were serious about bombing the palace, just playing with the idea had them both so horrified they began scrambling around for a way out. There's no point in speaking ill of *a certain party* after all these years. But I still can't understand where he found the gall to tell a person who wasn't able to live anywhere on these islands just because she was the daughter of a man who had been implicated in grand treason, and who just barely managed to survive overseas by becoming the foster daughter of an agitator who was a socialist and an ultra-nationalist at the same time, *We will accomplish what your father tried and failed to do*—now if that wasn't gall I don't know what is! Especially when he wasn't even serious about it, just trying to get money out of me! At the time I didn't have the energy to find out whether the stocks had been sold or not, but assuming they hadn't and were still worth something, we would have had an easy time after the war. But *a certain party* made sure this child and I would have hard times after the war, and then he tells me *We'll accomplish what your father tried and failed to do*—that's how mean and low he was, yessir! Of course this child is just as mean and low, he's afraid there may even be an emperor in the Japanese world after death, and if the emperor *over yonder* said to him You may not have rebelled against the emperor in the world of the living, but you escaped by committing suicide, which means you weren't truly a subject, either, he's terrified he wouldn't have an answer, and that's why he won't commit suicide, but he tries to blame it on me. Which seems pretty rude, impertinent too, wouldn't you say, considering I'm ——'s daughter! And now the child can hardly wait to die of cancer, the day and hour of his death is all he can think about and it makes him so excited he can't help singing a happy song, and do you know why? Because he reckons he's finally going to be able to run away and not be responsible, yessir! YOU'RE RIGHT! YOU'RE ABSOLUTELY RIGHT! shouts the "acting executor of the will," who has been silent for some time. Do you know he's made me promise over and over again that I'll take our child and marry an American when he dies! He even went out and found an American deserter. We kept him at home for a long time as a member of the family, and a number of times he pretended to get drunk and started carrying on, trying to make me seduce the American. He hopes that if his child becomes an American citizen his own blood will be freed from both the emperor and the ghost of the name of ——. Abruptly "he" shouts in a voice like a cracked bell, his underwater goggles bouncing on the bridge of his nose, I RELIEVE YOU OF YOUR POSITION AS "ACTING EXECUTOR OF THE WILL"! Listen to him still carrying on, mean and low as he is! The voice crawls up from beyond the foot of his bed. I'll take the child back to the forest, and you come along, dear, and we'll live together. This time I'll make right sure to tell the child about his great-grandfather ——. Sooner or later the Japanese are going to change their attitude about what happened, and I intend to live to see it, yessir! THIS IS THE DREAM. THIS *MUST* BE THE DREAM! I've figured out the dream that's been making me scream and weep! "he" shouts, and bursts into tears, writhing on his bed. It is a dream, truly. When he was a child he used to have cruel dreams and sob, and he's still dreaming and weeping uselessly! The mild, flat voice from below the foot of the bed is comforting now. And here he is thirty-five years old, it's a cruel business! When he was a child he'd dream the teacher at elementary school was asking him *If the emperor ordered you to die, would you die?* and he'd sob and repeat the cruel answer in his sleep, *Yes, I would die, I would die happily!* and here he is thirty-five years old and still weeping away as if the teacher was asking him that same question, it's a cruel business, yessir!]]

VIII

[[Clamping to his head a set of newly purchased earphones in addition to the underwater goggles covered with cellophane, which "he" continues to wear as usual, "he" listens all the day long to a repeating tape recording of Fischer-Dieskau singing the Bach cantata. Already "he" rejects all overtures to contact from the outside, except those over which "he" has no conscious control, like the medical treatment applied to his body. The person who has been relieved of duty as "acting executor of the will" has ceased to exist in his consciousness. Still, there are times when "he" resumes his "history of the age," as if the tape recorder endlessly playing the Bach tape could record at the same time, or a newly-employed amanuensis were waiting at his bedside. "He" also sings his beloved song of *Happy Days*. To be sure, since the Bach cantata continues to reach him through the earphones, the melody and rhythm of the song "he" hums are frequently affected by it. If "he" understood German, the words "he" mouths would also be deranged.]]

The night a madman with beard all over his face very like *a certain party* had invaded his hospital room, he had thrown his Rotex rotary nostril clipper and cut an arabesque pattern in the fellow's beard which he supposed would permit him to track him down, but for someone as prudent as himself he had been hasty and careless. For the bearded intruder was actually no madman at all but a madwoman! Undoubtedly she had thrown away the false beard that had been clippered, and with that the only clue had been lost forever. With abnormal alertness, he had seen through the madwoman to the bearded man the minute he had discovered, in the creature's style as she spoke to him from, curiously, *below* the foot of his bed, probably squatting, something identical, though the words were different, to the voice that had shouted that night, foaming, What in god's name are you? *What? WHAT?* To repulse the old woman whose madness was plain to see in the abnormal expressionlessness of her thin, egg-shaped face beneath her white hair, he should have screamed at her, just as he had screamed back at the bearded man, I'm cancer, *cancer,* the spirit and soul of liver cancer is *ME!* and instantly have put an end to the matter.

[[Having been thus shouted at, the other party can have had little to protest. To expand upon a line by an English playwright-actor, "Just as there is abundance in the world of the living, so there is abundance in the world of the dead," so, to be sure, did the abundance of the world of the cancer-man actually exist in this world, and in the case of his own body in particular, in which cancer is proliferating at supersonic speed, his abundance is in fact cancer's! "He" doubts not that his custom-made cancer has already spread to all his lymph glands and mucous membranes, or that cancer cells cover his body layer upon layer, like a detailed road map. On the other side, cancer's side, of the pain "he" feels at present, before his transformation into cancer-man is complete, there is surely pleasure of equal value; the feeling of pressure on the surrounding organs "he" suffers as his liver enlarges, if

107

"he" became the liver itself, would undoubtedly be rich with the joy of proliferating cancer's vigor and vitality. "He" hopes somehow to sample however small a taste of that pleasure before "he" completes his transformation into cancer-man.

Covering his eyes with the cylinder-type underwater goggles and plugging his ears with the headphones, his mouth stretched open, "he" approximates the instant of death when at last the transformation will be completed. The most vital substance in his body until that instant, cancer, as death arrives, undergoes a subtle change of great interest, goes into motion placid and self-generated in the direction of decay and dissolution. It is a motion like the first bubble of methane gas rising to the surface of the water, a premonition of decay, and as "he" savors the sensation at the very core of his physical body, "he" strokes his withered arms and chest. Restlessly, hoping to verify the existence of as much skin as "he" can touch in the brief moment remaining, and as much of the wasted muscle just beneath. Nothing can move him so deeply or nourish him so richly now as the joy of experiencing the premonition of decay of his own body as the sensation of existence itself. So far as "he" is aware, his feelings toward the cancer that has overtaken more than half of his body-and-soul are his feelings toward a true brother. The instant his beloved brother has completed its enormous job, ineluctably, they will begin to decay together. Cancer, radiant and fresh compared to the body "he" has used for thirty-five years, will begin to decay in the bloom of its youth. "He" concedes that his attempt to reconstruct his own life has been defeated by the appearance of an unexpected sniper, but that no longer troubles him. Because, with cancer's destructive help, "he" has stripped away the excess flesh that was loaded on his real body over the past twenty-five years and is now already reduced all the way to his body at three in the afternoon on August sixteenth, 1945. In all that madwoman's tedious talking the only thing she said of even slight significance was that "he" had become so thin "he" had regained his face as a child at the end of the war. Lifting his voice shrilly in an imitation of a boy soprano, "he" sings *Let us sing a song of cheer again, Happy days are here again!* Admittedly, the melody is transformed, by the music resounding incessantly through the earphones, into a melody appropriate to the shout *da wischt mir die Tränen mein Heiland selbst ab,* to the prayerful shout understood by him to mean *His Majesty the Emperor, with his own hands, shall wipe my tears away.* At times, instead of *Happy days are here again,* "he" even sings *Come, Oh Death, thou brother of sleep, Komm, o Tod, du Schlafes Bruder.* Before long, without fail, cancer will eat away the useless outer layers of body-and-soul which have concealed his true essence ever since August sixteenth, 1945, and will whisper, in a voice that pierces all the way from the root of his body to his soul, *Now then, this is you, there was no need for you to have become any you other than this, Let us sing a song of cheer again, Happy days are here again!* At that moment, the clear, midsummer afternoon in 1945 will unfurl before him as a truly elastic "now" whose shape can be selected at will. Seconds before "he" completes his transformation into cancer-man, "he" will joyfully enter the vastness of that "now."]]

His bayonet clanking at his side, he crawls toward the stone steps at the bank entrance where *a certain party* waits, bullet-riddled, an army sword held high in one hand, the other outstretched to embrace him, shot in the back and dying. His eyes, filled with tears and his own blood, are already blind to all things in reality, but the colossal chrysanthemum topped with a purple aurora illuminates the darkness behind his closed lids more radiantly than any light he has ever seen. His head nothing more than a dark void now, the blood all drained away, he is no longer certain whether the person awaiting him at the top of the stone steps is *a certain party*, but if he can crawl just one yard more, digging at the hot ground with his bullet-broken hands, he will reach the feet of the person unmistakably awaiting him, whoever he may be, and his blood and his tears will be wiped away.

[[Exasperated by his refusal to remove the head-phones, a resourceful doctor plugs a microphone into the tape recorder, connects the headphones to a monitor and begins to speak through them, It's time we started being honest with one another about your condition, you must understand and cooperate. Your condition ... Having swiftly broken the connection to his consciousness, "he" is deaf to any further disturbance from the outside. Gasping in the shrill voice of a ten-year-old on the verge of death, distorting the melody in a multitude of ways, "he" continues to sing, *Let us sing a song of cheer again, Happy Days are here again!*]]

PRIZE STOCK

My kid brother and I were digging with pieces of wood in the loose earth that smelled of fat and ashes at the surface of the crematorium, the makeshift crematorium in the valley that was simply a shallow pit in a clearing in the underbrush. The valley bottom was already wrapped in dusk and fog as cold as the spring water that welled up in the woods, but the side of the hill where we lived, the little village built around a cobblestone road, was bathed in grape light. I straightened out of a crouch and weakly yawned, my mouth stretching open. My brother stood up too, gave a small yawn, and smiled at me.

Giving up on "collecting," we threw our sticks into

the thick summer underbrush and climbed the narrow path shoulder to shoulder. We had come down to the crematorium in search of remains, nicely shaped bones we could use as medals to decorate our chests, but the village children had collected them all and we came away empty-handed. I would have to beat some out of one of my friends at elementary school. I remembered peeking two days earlier, past the waists of the adults darkly grouped around the pit, at the corpse of a village woman lying on her back with her naked belly swollen like a small hill, her expression full of sadness in the light of the flames. I was afraid. I grasped my brother's slender arm and quickened my step. The odor of the corpse, like the sticky fluid certain kinds of beetles leaked when we squeezed them in our calloused fingers, seemed to revive in my nostrils.

Our village had been forced to begin cremating out of doors by an extended rainy season: early summer rains had fallen stubbornly until floods had become an everyday occurrence. When a landslide crushed the suspension bridge that was the shortest route to the *town*, the elementary school annex in our village was closed, mail delivery stopped, and our adults, when a trip was unavoidable, reached the *town* by walking the narrow, crumbly path along the mountain ridge. Transporting the dead to the crematorium in the *town* was out of the question.

But being cut off from the *town* caused our old but undeveloped homesteaders' village no very acute distress. Not only were we treated like dirty animals in the *town*, everything we required from day to day was packed into the small compounds clustered on the slope above the narrow valley. Besides, it was the beginning of summer, the children were happy school was closed.

Harelip was standing at the entrance to the village, where the cobblestone road began, cuddling a dog against his chest. With a hand on my brother's shoulder, I ran through the deep shade of the great gingko tree to peer at the dog in Harelip's arms.

"See!" Harelip shook the dog and made him snarl. "Look at him!"

The arms Harelip thrust in front of me were covered with bites matted with dog hair and blood. Bites stood out like buds on his chest, too, and his short, thick neck.

"See!" Harelip said grandly.

"You promised to go after mountain dogs with me!" I said, my chest clogged with surprise and chagrin. "You went alone!"

"I went looking for you," Harelip said quickly. "You weren't around. . . ."

"You really got bit!" I said, just touching the dog with my fingertips. Its eyes were frenzied, like a wolf's, its nostrils flared. "Did you crawl into the lair?"

"I wrapped a leather belt around my neck so he couldn't get my throat," Harelip said proudly.

In the dusking, purple hillside and the cobblestone road I distinctly saw Harelip emerging from a lair of withered grass and shrubs with a leather belt around his throat and the puppy in his arms while a mountain dog bit into him.

"As long as they don't get your throat," he said, confidence strong in his voice. "And I waited until there were only puppies inside."

"I saw them running across the valley," my brother said excitedly, "five of them."

"When?"

"Just after noon."

115

"I went after that."

"He sure is white," I said, keeping envy out of my voice.

"His mother *mated* with a wolf!" The dialect Harelip used was lewd but very real.

"You swear?" My brother spoke as if in a dream.

"He's used to me now," Harelip said, accentuating his confidence. "He won't go back to his friends."

My brother and I were silent.

"Watch!" Harelip put the dog down on the cobblestones and released him. "See!"

But instead of looking down at the dog we looked up at the sky covering the narrow valley. An unbelievably large airplane was crossing it at terrific speed. The roar churned the air into waves and briefly drowned us. Like insects trapped in oil we were unable to move in the sound.

"It's an enemy plane!" Harelip screamed. "The enemy's here!"

Looking up at the sky we shouted ourselves hoarse. "An enemy plane . . ."

But except for the clouds glowing darkly in the setting sun the sky was already empty. We turned back to Harelip's dog just as it was yowling down the gravel path away from us, its body dancing. Plunging into the underbrush alongside the path it quickly disappeared. Harelip stood there dumbfounded, his body poised for pursuit. My brother and I laughed until our blood seethed like liquor. Chagrined as he was, Harelip had to laugh, too.

We left him, and ran back to the storehouse crouching in the dusk like a giant beast. In the semidarkness inside, my father was preparing our meal on the dirt floor.

"We saw a plane!" my brother shouted at my father's back. "A great big enemy plane!"

My father grunted and did not turn around. Intending to clean it, I lifted his heavy hunting gun down from the rack on the wall and climbed the dark stairs, arm in arm with my brother.

"Too bad about that dog," I said.

"And that plane," my brother said.

We lived on the second floor of the cooperative storehouse in the middle of the village, in the small room once used for raising silkworms. When my father stretched out on his straw mats and blankets on the floor of thick planks that were beginning to rot and my brother and I lay down on the old door which was our sleeping platform, the former residence of countless silkworms that had left stains on the paper walls still reeking of their bodies and bits of rotten mulberry leaf stuck to the naked beams in the ceiling filled to repletion with human beings.

We had no furniture at all. There was the dull gleam of my father's hunting gun, not only the barrel but even the stock, as if the oiled wood were also steel that would numb your hand if you slapped it, to provide our poor quarters with a certain direction, there were dried weasel pelts hanging in bunches from the exposed beams, there were various traps. My father made his living shooting rabbits, birds, wild boar in winter when the snow was deep, and trapping weasels and delivering the dried pelts to the *town* office.

As my brother and I polished the stock with an oil rag we gazed up through the chinks in the wooden slats at the dark sky outside. As if the roar of an airplane would descend from there again. But it was rare for a plane to cross the sky above the village. When I had put the gun

117

back in the rack on the wall we lay down on the sleeping platform, huddling together, and waited, threatened by the emptiness in our stomachs, for my father to bring the pot of rice and vegetables upstairs.

My brother and I were small seeds deeply embedded in thick flesh and tough, outer skin, green seeds soft and fresh and encased in membrane that would shiver and slough away at the first exposure to light. And outside the tough, outer skin, near the sea that was visible from the roof as a thin ribbon glittering in the distance, in the city beyond the heaped, rippling mountains, the war, majestic and awkward now like a legend that had survived down the ages, was belching foul air. But to us the war was nothing more than the absence of young men in our village and the announcements the mailman sometimes delivered of soldiers killed in action. The war did not penetrate the tough outer skin and the thick flesh. Even the "enemy" planes that had begun recently to traverse the sky above the village were nothing more to us than a rare species of bird.

Near dawn I was awakened by the noise of a gigantic impact and a furious ringing in the ground. I saw my father sit up on his blanket on the floor like a beast lurking in the forest night about to spring upon his prey, his eyes bright with desire and his body tense. But instead of springing he dropped back to the floor and appeared to fall asleep again.

For a long time I waited with my ears peeled, but that ringing did not occur again. Breathing quietly the damp air that smelled of mold and small animals I waited patiently in the pale moonlight creeping through the skylight high in the storehouse roof. A long time passed, and my brother, who had been asleep, his sweaty forehead pressed against my side, began to whimper. He too had been

118

waiting for the ground to quiver and ring again, and the prolonged anticipation had been too much for him. Placing my hand on his delicate neck like a slender plant stem I shook him lightly to comfort him, and, lulled by the gentle movement of my own arm, fell asleep.

When I woke up, fecund morning light was slanting through every crack in the slat walls, and it was already hot. My father was gone. So was his gun from the wall. I shook my brother awake and went out to the cobblestone road without a shirt. The road and the stone steps were awash in the morning light. Children squinting and blinking in the glare were standing vacantly or picking fleas out of the dogs or running around and shouting, but there were no adults. My brother and I ran over to the blacksmith's shed in the shade of the lush nettle tree. In the darkness inside, the charcoal fire on the dirt floor spit no tongues of red flame, the bellows did not hiss, the blacksmith lifted no red-hot steel with his lean, sun-blackened arms. Morning and the blacksmith not in his shop—we had never known this to happen. Arm in arm, my brother and I walked back along the cobblestone road in silence. The village was empty of adults. The women were probably waiting at the back of their dark houses. Only the children were drowning in the flood of sunlight. My chest tightened with anxiety.

Harelip spotted us from where he was sprawled at the stone steps that descended to the village fountain and came running over, arms waving. He was working hard at being important, spraying fine white bubbles of sticky saliva from the split in his lip.

"Hey! Have you heard?" he shouted, slamming me on the shoulder.

"Have you?"

"Heard?" I said vaguely.

119

"That plane yesterday crashed in the hills last night. And they're looking for the enemy soldiers that were in it, the adults have all gone hunting in the hills with their guns!"

"Will they shoot the enemy soldiers?" my brother asked shrilly.

"They won't shoot, they don't have much ammunition," Harelip explained obligingly, "They aim to catch them!"

"What do you think happened to the plane?" I said.

"It got stuck in the fir trees and came apart," Harelip said quickly, his eyes flashing. "The mailman saw it, you know those trees."

I did, fir blossoms like grass tassles would be in bloom in those woods now. And at the end of summer, fir cones shaped like wild bird eggs would replace the tassles, and we would collect them to use as weapons. At dusk then and at dawn, with a sudden rude clatter, the dark brown bullets would be fired into the walls of the storehouse. . . .

"Do you know the woods I mean?"

"Sure I do. Want to go?"

Harelip smiled slyly, countless wrinkles forming around his eyes, and peered at me in silence. I was annoyed.

"If we're going to to go I'll get a shirt," I said, glaring at Harelip. "And don't try leaving ahead of me because I'll catch up with you right away!"

Harelip's whole face became a smirk and his voice was fat with satisfaction.

"Nobody's going! Kids are forbidden to go into the hills. You'd be mistaken for the foreign soldiers and shot!"

I hung my head and stared at my bare feet on the cobblestones baking in the morning sun, at the sturdy,

120

stubby toes. Disappointment seeped through me like treesap and made my skin flush hot as the innards of a freshly killed chicken.

"What do you think the enemy looks like?" my brother said.

I left Harelip and went back along the cobblestone road, my arm around my brother's shoulders. What *did* the enemy soldiers look like, in what positions were they lurking in the fields and the woods? I could feel foreign soldiers hiding in all the fields and woods that surrounded the valley, the sound of their hushed breathing about to explode into an uproar. Their sweaty skin and harsh body odor covered the valley like a season.

"I just hope they aren't dead," my brother said dreamily. "I just hope they catch them and bring them in."

In the abundant sunlight we were hungry; saliva was sticky in our throats and our stomach muscles were tight. Probably it would be dusk before my father returned, we would have to find our own food. We went down behind the storehouse to the well with the broken bucket and drank, bracing ourselves with both hands against the chilly, sweating stones jutting from the inside wall like the swollen belly of a pupa. When we had drawn water for the shallow iron pot and built a fire, we stuck our arms into the chaff heaped at the rear of the storehouse and stole some potatoes. As we washed them, the potatoes were hard as rocks in our hands.

The meal we began after our brief efforts was simple but plentiful. Eating away like a contented animal at the potato he grasped in both hands, my brother pondered a minute, then said, "Do you think the soldiers are up in the fir trees? I saw a squirrel on a fir branch!"

"It would be easy to hide in the fir because they're in bloom," I said.

121

"The squirrel hid right away, too," my brother said, smiling.

I pictured fir trees covered with blossoms like grass tassles, and the foreign soldiers lurking in the highest branches and watching my father and the others through the bunched green needles. With fir blossoms stuck to their bulky flying suits, the soldiers would look like fat squirrels ready for hibernation.

"Even if they're hiding in the trees the dogs will find them and bark," my brother said confidently.

When our stomachs were full we left the pot on the dirt floor with the remaining potatoes and a fistful of salt and sat down on the stone steps at the entrance to the storehouse. For a long time we sat there drowsily, and in the afternoon we went to bathe at the spring that fed the village fountain.

At the spring, Harelip, sprawled naked on the broadest, smoothest stone, was allowing the girls to fondle his rosy penis as if it were a small doll. Every so often, face beet-red, laughing shrilly in a voice like a screaming bird, he slapped one of the girls on her naked rear.

My brother sat down next to Harelip and raptly observed the merry ritual. I splashed water on the ugly children drowsily sunning themselves around the spring, put on my shirt without drying myself, returned to the stone steps at the storehouse entrance, leaving wet footprints on the cobblestones, and sat there without moving for a long time again, hugging my knees. Anticipation that was like madness, a heated, drunken feeling, was crackling up and down beneath my skin. Dreamily I pictured myself absorbed in the odd game to which Harelip seemed abnormally attached. But whenever the girls among the children returning naked from the spring smiled timidly at me, their hips swaying at each step they took and an unstable color like mashed peaches peeking from the folds of their meager, exposed vaginas, I rained pebbles and abuse on them and made them cringe.

I waited in the same position until a passionate sunset covered the valley, clouds the color of a forest fire wheeling in the sky, but still the adults did not return. I felt I would go mad with waiting.

The sunset had paled, a cool wind that felt good on newly burned skin had begun to blow up from the valley, and the first darkness of night had touched the shadows of things when the adults and the barking dogs finally returned to the hushed village, the village whose mind had been affected by uneasy anticipation. With the other children I ran out to greet them, and saw a large black man surrounded by adults. Fear struck me like a fist.

Surrounding the *catch* solemnly as they surrounded the wild boar they hunted in winter, their lips drawn tightly across their teeth, their backs bent forward almost sadly, the adults came walking in. The *catch*, instead of a flying suit of burnt-ocher silk and black leather flying shoes, wore a khaki jacket and pants and, on his feet, ugly, heavy-looking boots. His large, darkly glistening face was tilted up at the sky still streaked with light, and he limped as he dragged himself along. The iron chain of a boar trap was locked around both his ankles, rattling as he moved. We children fell in behind the adults, as silent as they were. The procession slowly advanced to the square in front of the school house and quietly halted. I pushed my way through the children to the front, but the old man who was our village headman loudly ordered us away; we retreated as far as the apricot trees in one corner of the square, halted there determinedly, and from beneath the trees kept watch through the thickening darkness over the adults' meeting. In the dirt floor houses that faced on the square the women hugging themselves beneath their white smocks strained irritably to catch the murmuring of the men who returned from a dangerous hunt with a *catch*. Harelip poked me sharply in the side from behind and pulled me away from the other children into the deep shadow of a camphor tree.

"He's black, you see that! I thought he would be all along." Harelip's voice trembled with excitement. "He's a real black man, you see!"

"What are they going to do with him, shoot him?"

"Shoot him!" Harelip shouted, gasping with surprise. "Shoot a real live black man!"

"Because he's the enemy," I asserted without confidence.

"Enemy! You call him an enemy!" Harelip seized my shirt and railed at me hoarsely, spraying my face with saliva through his lip.

"He's a black man, he's no enemy!"

"Look! Look at that!" It was my brother's awed voice, coming from the crowd of children. "Look!"

Harelip and I turned around and peered at the black soldier; standing a little apart from the adults observing him in consternation, his shoulders sagging heavily, he was pissing. His body was beginning to melt into the thickened evening darkness, leaving behind the khaki jacket and pants that were somehow like overalls. His head to one side, the black soldier pissed on and on, and when a cloud of sighs from the children watching rose behind him he mournfully shook his hips.

The adults surrounded the black soldier again and slowly led him off; we followed a short distance behind. The silent procession surrounding the *catch* stopped in front of the loading entrance at the side of the storehouse. There the steps down to the cellar where the best of the

autumn chestnuts were stored over the winter after the
grubs beneath their hard skin had been killed with carbon
disulfide yawned open blackly, like a hole inhabited by
animals. Still surrounding the black soldier, the adults
descended into the hole solemnly, as if a ceremony were
beginning, and the white wavering of an adult arm closed
the heavy trapdoor from inside.

Straining to catch a sound, we watched an orange
light go on inside the long, narrow skylight window that
ran between the floor of the storehouse and the ground.
We could not find the courage to peek through the
skylight. The short, anxious wait exhausted us. But no
gunshot rang out. Instead, the village headman's shadowed face appeared beneath the partly opened trapdoor
and we were yelled at and had to abandon even keeping
watch at a distance from the skylight; the children,
carrying with them expectations that would fill the night
hours with bad dreams, ran off down the cobblestone road
without a word of disappointment. Fear, awakened by
their pounding feet, pursued them from behind.

Leaving Harelip lurking in the darkness of the apricot
trees, still determined to observe the adults and the *catch*,
my brother and I went around to the front of the
storehouse and climbed, supporting ourselves against the
railing that was always damp, to our room in the attic. We
were to live in the same house as the *catch*, that was how it
was to be! No matter how hard we listened in the attic, we
would never be able to hear screaming in the cellar, but
the luxurious, hazardous, entirely unbelievable fact was
that we were sitting on a sleeping platform above the
cellar to which the black soldier had been taken. My teeth
were chattering with fear and joy, and my brother
huddling beneath the blanket was shaking as if he had
caught a cold. As we waited for my father to come home

dragging his fatigue and his heavy gun we smiled together at the wonderful good fortune that had befallen us.

Not so much to satisfy our hunger as to distract ourselves from the uproar in our chests with raising and lowering of arms and precise chewing, we were beginning to eat the cold, hardened, sweating potatoes that were left over when my father climbed the stairs. Shivering, my brother and I watched him place his hunting gun in the wooden rack on the wall and lower himself to the blanket spread on the dirt floor, but he said nothing, merely looked at the pot of potatoes we were eating. I could tell he was tired to death, and irritated. There was nothing we children could do about that.

"Is the rice gone?" he said, staring at me, the skin of his throat puffing like a sack beneath the stubble of beard.

"Yes. . . ." I said weakly.

"The barley too?" he grunted sourly.

"There's nothing!" I was angry.

"What about the airplane?" my brother said timidly. "What happened to it?"

"It burned. Almost started a forest fire."

My brother let out a sigh. "The whole thing?"

"Just the tail was left."

"The tail . . ." my brother murmured.

"Were there any others?" I asked. "Was he flying alone?"

"Two other soldiers were dead. He came down in a parachute."

"A parachute . . ." My brother was entirely lost in a dream. I summoned up my courage.

"What are you going to do with him?"

"Until we know what the town thinks, rear him."

"Rear him? Like an animal?"

126

"He's the same as an animal," my father said gravely. "He stinks like an ox."

"It would sure be nice to see him," my brother said with an eye on my father, but my father went back down the stairs in grim silence.

We sat down on the wooden frame of our sleeping platform to wait for my father to come back with borrowed rice and vegetables and cook us a pot of steaming gruel. We were too exhausted to be really hungry. And the skin all over our bodies was twitching and jumping like the genitals of a bitch in heat. We were going to rear the black soldier. I hugged myself with both arms, I wanted to throw off my clothes and shout—we were going to rear the black soldier, like an animal!

The next morning my father shook me awake without a word. Dawn was just breaking. Thick light and heavy fog were seeping through every crack in the wall boards. As I gulped my cold breakfast I gradually woke up. My father, his hunting gun on his shoulder and a lunch basket tied to his waist, watched me as I ate, waiting for me to finish, eyes dull yellow from lack of sleep. When I saw the bundle of weasel skins wrapped in a torn burlap bag at his knee I swallowed hard and thought to myself, so we are going down to the *town!* And surely we would report the black man to the authorities.

A whirlpool of words at the back of my throat was slowing the speed at which I could eat, but I saw my father's strong lower jaw covered in coarse beard moving incessantly as if he were chewing grain and I knew he was nervous and irritated from lack of sleep. Asking about the black soldier was impossible. The night before, after supper, my father had loaded his gun with new bullets and gone out to stand night watch.

My brother was sleeping with his head buried under a blanket that smelled of dank hay. When I was finished eating I moved around the room on tiptoes, careful not to wake him. Wrapping a green shirt of thick cloth around my bare shoulders, I stepped into the cloth sneakers I normally never used, shouldered the bundle that was between my father's knees, and ran down the stairs.

Low fog rolled along just above the wet cobblestones; the village, wrapped in haze, was fast asleep. The chickens were already tired and silent; the dogs did not even bark. I saw an adult with a gun leaning against the apricot tree alongside the storehouse, his head drooping. My father and the guard exchanged a few words in low voices. I stole a look at the cellar skylight yawning blackly open like a wound and I was gripped by terrific fear. The black soldier's arm reaches through the skylight and extends to seize me. I wanted to leave the village quickly. When we began walking in silence, careful not to slip on the cobblestones, the sun penetrated the layers of fog and struck at us with tough, heated light.

To reach the village road along the ridge we climbed the narrow path of red earth into the fir forest, where once again we were at the bottom of dark night. Fog that filled my mouth with a metallic taste slanted down on us in droplets large as rain, making it hard for me to breathe and wetting my hair and forming white, shiny beads on the lint of my grimy, wrinkled shirt. The spring water that seeped up through the rotten leaves so soft beneath our feet to soak our cloth shoes and to freeze our toes was not so bad; we had to be truly careful not to wound our skin against the iron stalks of ferns or to surprise the adders watchfully coiled among their stubborn roots.

When we emerged from the fir forest onto the village road, where it was brightening and the fog was burning off, I brushed the fog out of my shirt and short pants as carefully as if I were removing sticky tickseeds. The sky was clear and violently blue. The distant mountains the color of the copper ore we found in the dangerous abandoned mine in our valley was a sparkling, deep-blue sea rushing at us. And a single, whitish handful of the real sea.

All around us wild birds were singing. The upper branches of the high pines were humming in the wind. Crushed beneath my father's boot, a fieldmouse leaped from the piled leaves like a spurting gray fountain, frightening me for an instant, and ran in a frenzy into the brilliant underbrush alongside the road.

"Are we going to tell about the black man when we get to town?" I asked my father's broad back.

"Umm?" my father said. "Yes. . . ."

"Will the constable come out from town?"

"There's no telling, " my father grunted. "Until the report gets to the prefectural office there's no telling what will happen."

"Couldn't we just go on rearing him in the village? Is he dangerous? You think he is?"

My father rejected me with silence. I felt my surprise and fear of the night before, when the black soldier was led back to the village, reviving in my body. What was he doing in that cellar? The black soldier leaves the cellar, slaughters the people and the hunting dogs in the village and sets fire to the houses. I was so afraid I was trembling, I didn't want to think about it. I passed my father and ran, panting, down the long slope.

By the time we were on level road again the sun was high. The red earth exposed by small landslides on both sides of the road was raw as blood and glistening in the sun. We walked along with our foreheads bared to the fierce light. Sweat bubbled from the skin on my head, soaked through my cropped hair and ran from my forehead down my cheeks.

When we entered the *town* I pressed my shoulder against my father's high hip and marched straight past the provocations of the children in the street. If my father hadn't been there the children would have jeered at me and thrown stones. I hated the children of the *town* as I would have hated a species of beetle with a shape I could never feel comfortable with, and I disdained them. Skinny children in the noonday light flooding the town, with treacherous eyes. If only adult eyes had not been watching me from the rear of dark shops I was confident I could have knocked any one of them down.

The town office was closed for lunch. We worked the pump in the square in front of the office and drank some water, then sat down on wooden chairs beneath a window with hot sun pouring through it and waited a long time. An old official finally finished his lunch and appeared, and when he and my father had spoken together in low voices and stepped into the mayor's office I carried the weasel pelts over to the small scales lined up behind a reception window. There the skins were counted and entered in an account book with my father's name. I watched carefully as a nearsighted lady official with thick glasses wrote down the number of skins.

When this job was finished I had no idea what to do. My father was taking forever. So I went looking, my bare feet squishing down the hall like suction cups, one shoe in each hand, for my only acquaintance in the *town*, a man who frequently carried notices out to our village. We all called this one-legged man "Clerk," but he did other things as well, such as assisting the doctor when we had our physicals at the school annex in the village.

"Well if it isn't Frog!" Rising from the chair behind his desk, Clerk shouted, making me just a little angry, but I went over anyway. Since we called him "Clerk," we couldn't very well complain about his calling us, the village children, "Frog." I was happy to have found him.

"So you caught yourselves a black man!" Clerk said, rattling his false leg under the desk.

"Yes. . . ." I said, resting my hands on his desk where his lunch was wrapped in yellowed newspaper.

"That's really something!"

I wanted to nod grandly at his bloodless lips, like an adult, and talk about the black soldier, but words to explain the huge negro who had been led through the dusk to the village like captured prey I simply couldn't find.

"Will they shoot him?" I asked.

"I don't know." Clerk gestured with his chin at the mayor's office. "They're probably deciding now."

"Will they bring him to town?" I said

"You look mighty happy the schoolroom is closed," Clerk said, evading my important question. "The schoolmistress is too lazy to make the trip out there, all she does is complain. She says the village children are dirty and smelly."

I felt ashamed of the dirt creasing my neck, but I shook my head defiantly and made myself laugh. Clerk's artificial leg jutting from beneath his desk was twisted awkwardly. I liked to watch him hopping along the mountain road with his good right leg and the artifical leg and just one crutch, but here the artificial leg was weird and treacherous, like the children of the *town*.

"But what do you care, as long as school is out you have no complaints, right, Frog!" Clerk laughed, his artificial leg rattling again. "You and your pals are better off playing outside than being treated like dirt in a schoolroom!"

"They're just as dirty," I said.

It was true, the women teachers were ugly and dirty, all of them; Clerk laughed. My father had come out of the mayor's office and was calling me quietly. Clerk patted me on the shoulder and I patted him on the arm and ran out.

"Don't let the prisoner escape, Frog!" he shouted at my back.

"What did they decide to do with him?" I said to my father as we returned through the sunwashed *town*.

"You think they're going to take any responsibility!" My father spat out the words as if he were scolding me and said nothing more. Intimidated by my father's foul humor I walked along in silence, in and out of the shade of the *town's* shriveled, ugly trees. Even the trees in the *town*, like the children in the streets, were treacherous and unfamiliar.

When we came to the bridge at the edge of the *town* we sat down on the low railing and my father unwrapped our lunch in silence. Struggling to keep myself from asking questions, I extended a slightly dirty hand toward the package on his lap. Still in silence we ate our rice balls.

As we were finishing, a young girl with a neck as refreshing as a bird's came walking across the bridge. I swiftly considered my own clothes and features and decided I was finer and tougher than any child in the *town*. I stuck both feet out in front of me, my shoes on, and waited for the girl to pass. Hot blood was singing in my ears. For a brief instant the girl peered at me scowlingly, then she ran off. Suddenly my appetite was gone. I climbed down the narrow stairs at the approach to the bridge and walked to the river for a drink of water. Tall wormwood bushes clustered thickly along the bank. I kicked and tore my way through them to the river's edge, but the water was a stagnant, dirty brown. It struck me I was a miserable and meager creature.

By the time we had left the road along the ridge, cleared the fir forest, and emerged at the entrance to the village, calves stiffened and faces caked with dust and oil and sweat, evening had covered the valley entirely; in our bodies the heat of the sun lingered and the heavy fog was a relief. I left my father on his way to the village headman's house to make his report and climbed to the second floor of the storehouse. My brother was sitting on the sleeping platform, fast asleep. I reached out and shook him, feeling the fragile bones in his naked shoulder against my palm. My brother's skin contracted slightly beneath my hot hand, and from his eyes that suddenly opened fatigue and fear faded.

"How was he?" I said.

"He just slept in the cellar."

"Were you scared all by yourself?" I said gently.

My brother shook his head, his eyes serious. I opened the wooden shutters just a little and climbed onto the window sill to piss. The fog engulfed me like a living thing and swiftly stole into my nostrils. My urine jumped a great distance, spattering against the cobblestones, and when it struck the bay window that jutted from the first floor it rebounded and warmly wet the tops of my feet and my goosepimpled thighs. My brother, his head pressed against my side like a baby animal, observed intently.

We remained in that position for a while. Small yawns rose from our narrow throats, and with each yawn we cried just a few transparent, meaningless tears.

"Did Harelip get to see him?" I said to my brother as

he helped me close the wooden shutters, the slender muscles in his shoulders knotting.

"Kids get yelled at if they go to the square," he said with chagrin. "Are they coming from town to take him?"

"I don't know," I said.

Downstairs, my father and the lady from the general store came in talking in loud voices. The lady from the general store was insisting that she couldn't carry the food for the black soldier down to the cellar. That's no job for a woman, your son should be a help! I finished removing my shoes and straightened up. My brother's soft palm was pressed against my hip. Biting my lip, I waited for my father's voice.

"Come down here!" When I heard my father shout I threw my shoes under the sleeping platform and ran down the stairs.

With the butt of his hunting gun my father pointed to the basket of food the woman had left on the dirt floor. I nodded, and lifted the basket carefully. In silence we left the storehouse and walked through the chill fog. The cobblestones underfoot retained the warmth of day. At the side of the storehouse no adult was standing guard. I saw the pale light leaking through the narrow cellar window and felt fatigue break out all over my body. Yet my teeth were chattering with excitement at this first opportunity to see the black man close up.

The imposing padlock on the cellar door was dripping wet; my father unlocked it and peered inside, then carefully, his gun ready, went down alone. I squatted at the entrance, waiting, and air wet with fog fastened to the back of my neck. In front of the countless eyes hovering behind and peering at me I was ashamed of the trembling in my brown, sturdy legs.

"C'mon," said my father's muffled voice.

134

Holding the foodbasket against my chest, I went down the short steps. The *catch* was crouching in the dim light of a naked bulb. The thick chain of a boar-trap connecting his black leg and a pillar drew and locked my gaze.

Arms clasped around his knees and his chin resting even further down on his long legs, the *catch* looked up at me with bloodshot eyes, sticky eyes that wrapped themselves around me. All the blood in my body rushed toward my ears, heating my face. I turned away and looked up at my father, who was leaning against the wall with his gun pointed at the black soldier. My father motioned at me with his chin. With my eyes almost closed I stepped forward and placed the basket of food in front of the black soldier. As I stepped back, my insides shuddered with sudden fear and I had to fight my nausea down. At the basket of food the black soldier stared, my father stared, I stared. A dog barked in the distance. Beyond the narrow skylight window the dark square was hushed.

Suddenly the food basket began to interest me, I was seeing the food through the black soldier's starved eyes. Several large rice balls, dried fish with the fat broiled away, stewed vegetables, goat's milk in a cut-glass bottle. Without unfolding from his crouch, still hugging his knees, the black soldier continued to stare at the food basket for a long time until finally I began to feel hunger pangs myself. It occurred to me the black soldier might disdain the meager supper we provided, and disdain us, and refuse to touch the food. Shame assaulted me. If the black soldier showed no intention of eating, my shame would infect my father, adult's shame would drive my father to desperation and violence, the whole village would be torn apart by adults pale with shame. What a terrible idea it had been to feed the black soldier!

135

But all of a sudden he extended an unbelievably long arm, lifted the wide-mouthed bottle in thick fingers covered with bristly hair, drew it to himself, and smelled it. Then the bottle was tipped, the black soldier's thick, rubbery lips opened, large white teeth neatly aligned like parts inside a machine were exposed, and I saw milk flowing back into a vast, pink, glistening mouth. The black soldier's throat made a noise like water and air entering a drain, from the corners of his swollen lips like overripe fruit that had been bound with string the thick milk spilled, ran down his bare neck, soaked his open shirt and chest, and coagulated like fat on his tough, darkly gleaming skin, trembling there. I discovered, my own lips drying with excitement, that goat's milk was a beautiful liquid.

With a harsh clanking the black soldier returned the glass bottle to the basket. Now his original hesitation was gone. The rice balls looked like small cakes as he rolled them in his giant hands; the dried fish, head bones and all, was crushed between his gleaming teeth. Standing alongside my father with my back against the wall, buffeted by admiration, I observed the black soldier's powerful chewing. Since he was engrossed in his meal and paid no attention to us, I had the opportunity, even as I fought the pangs in my own empty stomach, to observe the adults' *catch* in suffocating detail. And what a wonderful *catch* he was!

The black soldier's short, curly hair tightened into small cowlicks here and there on his well-shaped skull, and just above his ears, which were pointed like a wolf's, turned a smoldering gray. The skin from his throat to his chest was lit from inside with a somber, purple light; every time he turned his head and supple creases appeared in his thick, oily neck, I felt my heart leap. And there was the odor of his body, pervading with the persistence of nausea rising into the throat, permeating all things like a corrosive poison, an odor that flushed my cheeks and flashed before my eyes like madness. . . . As I watched the black soldier feeding ravenously, my eyes hot and watery as though infected, the crude food in the basket was transformed into a fragrant, rich, exotic feast. If even a morsel had remained when I lifted the basket I would have seized it with fingers that trembled with secret pleasure and wolfed it down. But the black soldier finished every bit of food and then wiped the dish of vegetables clean with his fingers.

My father poked me in the side and, trembling with shame and outrage, as if I had been aroused from a lewd daydream, I walked over to the black soldier and lifted the basket. Protected by the muzzle of my father's gun I turned my back to the black soldier and was starting up the steps when I heard his low, rich cough. I stumbled, and felt fear goosepimple the skin all over my body.

At the top of the stairs to the second floor of the storehouse a dark, distorting mirror swayed in the hollow of a pillar; as I climbed the stairs a totally insignificant Japanese boy with twitching cheeks and pale, bloodless lips on which he chewed rose gradually out of the dimness. My arms hung limply and I felt almost ready to cry. I fought a beaten, tearful feeling as I opened the rain shutters that someone had closed at some point in the day.

My brother, eyes flashing, was sitting on the sleeping platform. His eyes were hot, and a little dry with fear.

"You closed the rain shutters, didn't you!" I said, sneering to hide the trembling of my own lips.

"Yes—" Ashamed of his timidness my brother lowered his eyes. "How was he?"

"He smells terrible," I said, sinking in fatigue. Truly I

was exhausted, and I felt wretched. The trip to the *town*, the black soldier's supper—after the long day's work my body was as heavy as a sponge soaked with fatigue. Taking off my shirt, which was covered with dried leaves and burrs, I bent over to wipe my dirty feet with a rag, a demonstration for my brother's sake that I had no desire to accept further questions. My brother observed me worriedly, his lips pursed. I crawled in next to him and burrowed under our blanket with its smell of sweat and small animals. My brother sat there watching me, his knees together and pressing against my shoulder, not asking any more questions. It was just as he sat when I was sick with fever, and I too, just as when I was sick with fever, longed only to sleep.

When I woke up late the next morning I heard the noise of a crowd coming from the square alongside the storehouse. My brother and father were gone. I looked up at the wall and saw that the hunting gun was not there. As I listened to the clamor and stared at the empty gun rack my heart began to pound. I sprang out of bed, grabbed my shirt, and ran down the stairs.

Adults were crowded into the square, and the dirty faces of the children looking up at them were tight with uneasiness. Apart from everyone, Harelip and my brother were squatting next to the cellar window. They've been watching! I thought to myself angrily, and was running toward them when I saw Clerk emerge, head lowered, lightly supporting himself on his crutch, from the cellar entrance. Violent, dark exhaustion and landsliding disappointment buried me. But what followed Clerk was not the dead body of the black soldier but my father, his gun on his shoulder and the barrel still in its bag, talking

138

quietly with the village headman. I breathed a sigh, and sweat hot as boiling water steamed down my sides and the insides of my thighs.

"Take a look!" Harelip shouted at me as I stood there. "Go on!"

I got down on all fours on the hot cobblestones and peered in through the narrow skylight window that was just at ground level. At the bottom of the lake of darkness the black soldier lay slumped on the floor like a domestic animal that had been pummeled senseless.

"Did they beat him?" I said to Harelip, my body trembling with anger as I straightened. "Did they beat him when he had his feet tied and couldn't move?" I shouted.

"What?" In order to repel my anger Harelip had readied himself for a fight, his face taut, his lip thrust out.

"Who?"

"The adults!" I shouted. "Did they beat him?"

"They didn't have to beat him," Harelip said regretfully. "All they did was go in and look. Just looking at him did that!"

Anger faded. I shook my head vaguely. My brother was peering at me.

"It's all right," I said to my brother.

One of the village children stepped around us and tried to look through the skylight window but Harelip kicked him in the side and he screamed. Harelip had already reserved the right to decide who should look at the black soldier through the skylight. And he was keeping a nervous watch on those who would usurp his right.

I walked over to where Clerk was talking to the adults surrounding him. As if I were a village brat with snot drying on my upper lip he ignored me completely and went right on talking, damaging my self-respect and my feeling of friendship for him. But there are times when

139

you cannot afford to nurse your own pride and self-respect. I thrust my head past the hips of the adults and listened to Clerk and the headman talking.

Clerk was saying that neither the *town* office nor the police station was able to take charge of the black prisoner. Until a report had been made to the prefectural office and a reply received, the village must keep the black soldier, was obliged to keep him. The headman objected, repeating that the village lacked the force to hold the black soldier prisoner. Moreover, delivering the dangerous prisoner under guard by the long mountain route was too much for the villagers to handle unaided. The long rainy season and the floods had made everything complicated, difficult.

But when Clerk assumed a peremptory tone, the arrogant tone of a minor bureaucrat, the adults submitted weakly. When it became clear that the village would keep the black soldier until the prefecture had settled on a policy, I left the perplexed, disgruntled adults and ran back to my brother and Harelip where they sat in front of the skylight, monopolizing it. I was filled with deep relief, anticipation, and anxiety I had contracted from the adults and which moved in me like sluggish worms.

"I told you they weren't going to kill him!" Harelip shouted triumphantly. "How can a black man be an enemy!"

"It'd be a waste," said my brother happily. The three of us peered through the skylight, cheeks bumping, and seeing the black soldier stretched out as before, his chest lifting and falling as he breathed, we sighed with satisfaction. There were some children who advanced right to the soles of our feet upturned on the ground and drying under the sun, muttering their displeasure with us, but when Harelip sprang up and shouted they scattered, screaming.

Presently we tired of watching the black soldier lying there, but we did not abandon our privileged position. Harelip allowed the children one by one, when they had promised compensation in dates, apricots, figs, persimmons or whatever, to look through the skylight for a short time. As the children stared through the window even the backs of their necks reddened with their surprise and wonder, and when they stood up they rubbed the dirt from their jaws with their palms. Leaning against the storehouse wall I looked down at the children engrossed in this first real experience of their lives while Harelip yelled at them to hurry and their small butts burned in the sun, and I felt a strange satisfaction and fullness, exhilaration. Harelip turned over on his knees a hunting dog that wandered over from the crowd of adults and began pulling ticks and crushing them between his amber nails as he shouted orders and arrogant abuse at the children. Even after the adults had left with Clerk to see him as far as the ridge road we continued our strange game. From time to time we took long looks ourselves, the children's resentful voices at our backs, but the black soldier lay sprawled there as before and gave no indication of moving. As if he had been beaten and kicked, as if merely looking at him had been enough to wound him!

That night, accompanied once again by my father with his gun, I went down into the cellar carrying a heavy pot of gruel. The black soldier looked up at us with eyes yellowed heavily along the edges with fat, then thrust his hairy fingers directly into the hot pot and ate hungrily. I was able to observe him calmly, and my father, who had stopped pointing his gun, leaned against the wall looking bored.

As I looked down at the black man with his forehead aslant above the pot, watching the trembling of his thick neck and the sudden flexing and relaxing of his muscles, I began to perceive him as a gentle animal, an obedient animal. I looked up at Harelip and my brother peering through the skylight with bated breath and flashed a sly smile at their gleaming eyes. I was growing used to the black soldier—the thought planted a seed of proud happiness that sprouted in me. But when the black soldier moved in such a way that the chain on the boar-trap rattled, fear revived in me with tremendous vigor, rushing into even the most distant blood vessels in my body and making my skin crawl.

From that day on, the job of carrying food to the black soldier, once in the morning and once at night, accompanied by my father, who no longer bothered to remove his rifle from his shoulder, was a special privilege reserved for me. When my father and I appeared at the side of the storehouse early in the morning or as evening was becoming night, the children who had been waiting in the square would release all at once a large sigh that rose spreading, like a cloud, into the sky. Like a specialist who has lost all interest in his work but retains his meticulousness on the job, I crossed the square with brows intently knit, never glancing at the children. My brother and Harelip were satisfied to walk on either side of me, so close our bodies touched, as far as the entrance to the cellar. And when my father and I went down the steps they ran back and peered through the skylight. Even if I had become entirely bored with carrying food to the black soldier, I would have continued the job simply for the pleasure of feeling at my back as I walked along that hot sigh of envy risen to resentment in all the children, Harelip included.

I did ask my father, however, for special permission for Harelip to come to the cellar once a day only, in the afternoon. This was to transfer to Harelip's shoulders part of a burden that was too heavy for me to handle alone. A small, old barrel had been placed next to one of the pillars in the cellar for the black soldier's use. In the afternoon, lifting the barrel between us by the thick, heavy rope that ran through it, Harelip and I carefully climbed the steps and walked to the communal compost heap to empty the stinking, sloshing mixture of the black soldier's shit and piss. Harelip went about his work with excessive zeal: sometimes, before we emptied the barrel into the large tank alongside the compost heap, he would stir the contents with a stick and discourse on the state of the black soldier's digestion, particularly his diarrhea, concluding, among other things, that the trouble was caused by the kernels of corn in his gruel.

When Harelip and I went down to the cellar with my father to get the small barrel and found the black soldier astride it, his pants down around his ankles and his black, shiny rear thrust out in almost exactly the attitude of a copulating dog, we had to wait behind him for a while. Harelip, listening to the furtive clinking of the chain that linked the black soldier's ankles on either side of the barrel, eyes glazed dreamily with surprise and awe, kept a tight grip on my arm.

The children came to be occupied entirely with the black soldier, he filled every smallest corner of our lives. Among the children the black soldier spread like a plague. But the adults had their work. The adults did not catch the children's plague. They could not afford to wait motionlessly for the instructions that were so slow to arrive from the town office. When even my father, who had undertaken supervision of the prisoner, began leaving the village to hunt again, the black soldier began to exist in the cellar for the sole purpose of filling the children's daily lives.

My brother and Harelip and I fell into the habit of spending the daylight hours in the cellar where the black soldier sat, our chests hammering with the excitement of breaking a rule at first but soon enough, as we grew accustomed to being there, with complete casualness, as if supervising the black soldier during the day, while the adults were away in the hills or down in the valley, was a duty we had been entrusted with and must not neglect. The peephole at the skylight, abandoned by Harelip and my brother, was passed on to the village children. Flat on their bellies on the hot, dusty ground, their throats flushed and dry with envy, the children took turns peering in at the three of us sitting around the black soldier on the dirt floor. When occasionally, in an excess of envy, a child forgot himself and tried to follow us into the cellar, he received a pommeling from Harelip for his rebellious act and had to fall to the ground with a bloody nose.

In no time at all we had only to carry the black soldier's "barrel" to the top of the cellar steps, transporting it to the compost heap in the fierce sun while under attack by its ferocious stench was a task carried out by children we haughtily appointed. The designated children, cheeks shining with pleasure, carried the barrel straight up, careful not to spill a drop of the muddy yellow liquid that seemed so precious to them. And every morning all the children, including ourselves, glanced up at the narrow road that descended through the woods from the ridge with almost a prayer that Clerk would not appear with instructions we dreaded.

The chain from the boar-trap cut into the black man's ankles, the cuts became inflamed, blood trickled onto his feet and shriveled and stuck there like dried blades of grass. We worried constantly about the pinkish infection in the wounds. When he straddled the barrel the pain was so bad it made the black soldier bare his teeth like a laughing child. After looking deep into one another's eyes for a long time and talking together, we resolved to remove the boar-trap. The black soldier, like a dull black beast, his eyes always wet with a thick liquid that might have been tears or mucous, sat in silence hugging his knees on the cellar floor—what harm could he do us when we removed the trap? He was only a single head of black man!

When Harelip tightly grasped the key I brought from my father's tool bag, leaned over so far his shoulder was touching the black soldier's knees, and unlocked the trap, the black soldier suddenly rose with a groan and stamped his feet. Weeping with fear, Harelip threw the trap against the wall and ran up the steps; my brother and I, not even able to stand up, huddled together. The fear of the black soldier that had suddenly revived in us took our breaths away. But instead of dropping upon us like an eagle, the black soldier sat back down just where he was and hugged his knees and gazed with his wet, filmy eyes at the trap lying against the wall. When Harelip returned, head hanging with shame, my brother and I greeted him with kind smiles. The black soldier was as gentle as a domestic animal. . . .

Late that night my father came to lock the giant padlock on the cellar door and saw that the black soldier's ankles had been freed, yet he did not admonish me. Gentle as cattle—the thought, like air itself, had crept into the lungs of everyone in the village, children and adults alike.

The next morning my brother and Harelip and I took breakfast to the black soldier and found him puttering with the boar trap. When Harelip had thrown the trap against the wall the mechanism that snapped it shut had broken. The black soldier was examining the broken part with the same expert assurance as the trap-mender who came to the village every spring. And then abruptly he lifted his darkly glistening forehead and indicated with motions what he wanted. I looked at Harelip, unable to contain the joy that seemed to slacken my cheeks. The black soldier had communicated with us, just as our livestock communicated so had the black soldier!

We ran to the village headman's house, shouldered the tool box that was part of common village property, and carried it back to the cellar. It contained things that could have been used as weapons but we did not hesitate to entrust it to the black soldier. We could not believe that this black man like a domestic animal once had been a soldier fighting in the war, the fact rejected the imagination. The black soldier looked at the tool box, then gazed into our eyes. We watched him with joy that made us flush and shiver.

"He's like a person!" Harelip said to me softly, and as I poked my brother in the rear I was so proud and pleased I felt my body twist with laughter. Sighs of wonder from the children billowed through the skylight like fog.

We took the breakfast basket back, and when we finished our own breakfast and returned to the cellar the black soldier had taken a wrench and a small hammer from the tool box and had placed them neatly on a burlap bag on the floor. We sat next to him and he looked at us, then his large, yellowed teeth were bared and his cheeks slackened and we were jolted by the discovery that he could also smile. We understood then that we had been joined to him by a sudden, deep, passionate bond that was almost "human."

Afternoon lengthened, the lady from the blacksmith's dragged Harelip off with angry shouts and our butts began to ache from sitting directly on the dirt floor, but still the black soldier worked on the trap, his fingers soiled with old, dusty grease, the spring making a soft metallic click as he cocked and tried it again and again.

Not bored, I watched his pink palm indent where the teeth of the trap pressed into it and watched the oily grime twist into strands on his thick, sweaty neck. These things produced in me a not unpleasant nausea, a faint repulsion connected to desire. Puffing out his cheeks as if he were softly singing inside his broad mouth, the black soldier worked on intently. My brother, leaning on my knees, observed his fingers moving with eyes that shone with admiration. Flies swarmed around us, and their buzzing entangled the heat and echoed with it deep inside my ears.

When the trap bit into the braided rope with a noticeably sharper, sturdier snap, the black soldier placed it carefully on the floor and smiled at me and my brother through the dull, heavy liquid in his eyes. Beads of sweat trembled on the dark polish of his forehead. For truly a long time we peered, still smiling, just as we did with the goats and the hunting dogs, into the black soldier's gentle eyes. It was hot. We immersed ourselves in the heat, as if it were a shared pleasure connecting us and the black soldier, and continued smiling back and forth. . . .

One morning Clerk was carried in covered in mud and bleeding from his chin. He had stumbled in the woods

147

and fallen from a low cliff, and he had been found, unable to move, by a man from the village on his way to work in the hills. As he received treatment at the village headman's house Clerk stared in dismay at his artificial leg, which had bent where the thick, stiff leather was secured with a metal band and could not be properly reattached. He made no effort to communicate instructions from the *town*. The adults grew irritated; we wished Clerk had lain at the foot of the cliff undiscovered and had starved to death, assuming he had come to take the black soldier away. But he had come to explain that instructions from the prefecture still had not arrived. We regained our happiness, our energy, our sympathy for Clerk. And we took his artificial leg, and the toolbox, to the cellar.

Lying on the sweating cellar floor, the black soldier was singing in a soft, thick voice, a song that gripped us with its raw power, a song concealing regret and screams that threatened to overwhelm us. We showed him the damaged artificial leg. He stood up, peered at the leg for a minute, then swiftly fell to work. Cries of delight burst from the children peeping through the skylight, and the three of us, Harelip and my brother and I, also laughed at the top of our lungs.

When Clerk came to the cellar at dusk the artificial leg was completely restored. He fitted it onto his stump of a thigh and stood up, and we again raised a shout of happiness. Clerk bounded up the stairs and went into the square to try the fit of the leg. We pulled the black soldier to his feet by both arms and, without the slightest hesitation, as if it were an established habit already, took him into the square with us.

The black soldier filled his broad nostrils with the young, buoyant, summer-evening air, his first air above ground since he had been taken prisoner, and observed

Clerk closely as he tried his leg. All went well. Clerk came running over, took from his pocket a cigarette made of knotweed leaves, a lopsided cigarette that smelled something like a brush fire and smarted fiercely if the smoke got in your eyes, lit it, and handed it to the tall black soldier. The black soldier inhaled it and doubled over coughing violently and clutching his throat. Clerk, embarrassed, smiled a doleful smile, but we children laughed out loud. The black soldier straightened, wiped his tears with a giant palm, took from the pocket of the linen pants hugging his powerful hips a dark, shiny pipe and held it out to Clerk.

Clerk accepted the gift, the black soldier nodded his satisfaction, and the evening sun flooded them in grape light. We shouted until our throats began to hurt and milled around them, laughing as though touched by madness.

We began taking the black soldier out of the cellar frequently, for walks along the cobblestone road. The adults said nothing. When they encountered the black soldier surrounded by us children they merely looked away and circled around him, just as they stepped into the grass to avoid the bull from the headman's house when it came along the road.

Even when the children were all being kept busy working at home and could not visit the black soldier in his underground quarters, no one, adults or children, was surprised to see him napping in the shade of a tree in the square or walking slowly back and forth along the road. Like the hunting dogs and the children and the trees, the black soldier was becoming a component of village life.

On days when at dawn my father returned carrying at

149

his side a long, narrow trap made of hammered wooden slats and a fat weasel with an unbelievably long body thrashing around inside it, my brother and I had to spend the whole morning on the dirt floor of the storehouse, helping with the skinning. On those days we hoped from the bottom of our hearts that the black soldier would come to watch us work. When he did appear we would kneel on either side of my father as he grasped the bloodstained skinning knife with bits of fat stuck to the handle, and, scarcely breathing, would wish the rebellious, nimble weasel a complete and proper death and a deft skinning, for our guest's sake. A last instant of revenge in its final throes, as the weasel's neck was wrung it farted a horrible, terrific smell, and when the skin was laid back with a soft tearing noise at the dully gleaming tip of my father's knife there remained only muscle with a pearly luster encasing a small body so exposed it was lewd. My brother and I, careful not to let the guts spill out, carried the body to the communal compost heap to throw it away, and when we returned, wiping our soiled fingers on broad leaves, the weasel skin was already turned inside out and being nailed to a plank, fat membranes and thin capillaries glistening in the sun. The black soldier, producing what sounded like birdcalls through his pursed lips, was peering at the folds of the skin being cleaned of fat between my father's thick fingers so it would dry more easily. And when the fur had dried as stiff as claws on the plank and was criss-crossed with stains the color of blood like railroad lines across a map and the black soldier saw and admired it, how proud we were of my father's "technique." There were times when even my father, as he blew water on the fur, turned to the black soldier with friendly eyes. At such times my brother and the black soldier and my father and I were united, as if in a single

150

family, around my father's weasel-curing technique.

The black soldier also liked to watch the blacksmith at work. From time to time, especially when Harelip was helping forge something like a hoe, his half-naked body glowing in the fire, we would surround the black soldier and walk over to the blacksmith's shed. When the blacksmith lifted with hands covered in charcoal dust a piece of red-hot steel and plunged it into water, the black soldier would raise a cry of admiration like a scream, and the children would point and laugh. The blacksmith, flattered, frequently repeated this dangerous demonstration of his skill.

Even the women stopped being afraid of the black soldier. At times he received food directly from their hands.

It was the height of summer, and still no instructions arrived from the prefectural office. There was a rumor that the prefectural capitol had been bombed, but that had no effect on our village. Air hotter than the flames that burned a city hung over our village all the day long. And the space around the black soldier began to fill up with an odor that made our heads swim when we sat with him in the airless cellar, a strong, fatty odor like the stink of the weasel meat rotting on the compost heap. We joked about it constantly and laughed until our tears flowed, but when the black soldier began to sweat he stank so badly we could not bear to be at his side.

One hot afternoon Harelip proposed that we take him to the village spring; appalled at ourselves for not having had the thought earlier, we climbed the cellar steps tugging at the black soldier's grimy hands. The children gathered in the square surrounded us with whoops of excitement as we ran down the cobblestone road baking in the sun.

When we were as naked as birds and had stripped the black soldier's clothes we plunged into the spring all together, splashing one another and shouting. We were enraptured with our new idea. The naked black soldier was so large that the water barely reached his hips even when he went to the deepest part of the spring; when we splashed him he would raise a scream like a chicken whose neck was being wrung and plunge his head underwater and remain submerged until he shot up shouting and spouting water from his mouth. Wet and reflecting the strong sunlight, his nakedness shone like the body of a black horse, full and beautiful. We clamored around him splashing and shouting, and by and by the girls left the shade of the oak trees where they had been hesitating and came racing into the spring and hurriedly submerged their own small nakedness. Harelip caught one of the girls and began his lewd ritual, and we brought the black soldier over and from the best position showed him Harelip receiving his pleasure. The sun flooded all of our hard bodies, the water seethed and sparkled. Harelip, bright red and laughing, raised a shout each time he slapped the girl's spray-wet, shining buttocks with his open palm. We roared with laughter, and the girl cried.

Suddenly we discovered that the black soldier possessed a magnificent, heroic, unbelievably beautiful penis. We crowded around him bumping naked hips, pointing and teasing, and the black soldier gripped his penis and planted his feet apart fiercely like a goat about to copulate and bellowed. We laughed until we cried and splashed the black soldier's penis. Then Harelip dashed off naked as he was, and when he returned leading a large nanny-goat from the courtyard at the general store we applauded his idea. The black soldier opened his pink mouth and shouted, then danced out of the water and bore down upon the frightened, bleating goat. We laughed as though mad, Harelip strained to keep the goat's head down, and the black soldier labored mightily, his black, rugged penis glistening in the sun, but it simply would not work the way it did with a billy-goat.

We laughed until we could no longer support ourselves on our legs, so hard that when finally we fell exhausted to the ground, sadness stole into our soft heads. To us the black soldier was a rare and wonderful domestic animal, an animal of genius. How can I describe how much we loved him, or the blazing sun above our wet, heavy skin that distant, splendid summer afternoon, the deep shadows on the cobblestones, the smell of the children and the black soldier, the voices hoarse with happiness, how can I convey the repletion and rhythm of it all?

To us it seemed that the summer that bared those tough, resplendent muscles, the summer that suddenly and unexpectedly geysered like an oil well, spewing happiness and drenching us in black, heavy oil, would continue forever and never end.

Later in the day of our archaic bathing in the spring an evening downpour rudely locked the valley in fog, and the rain continued to fall late into the night. The next morning, Harelip and my brother and I kept close to the storehouse wall with the black soldier's food, to avoid the rain that was still falling. After breakfast, the black soldier, hugging his knees, softly sang a song in the dark cellar. Cooling our outstretched fingers in the rainspray sifting through the skylight, we were washed away by the expanse of the black soldier's voice and the sealike solemnity of his song. When the song was finished there was no more spray coming through the skylight. Taking the black soldier's arm, we led him smiling into the square. The fog had swiftly cleared from the valley; the trees had absorbed so much rainwater that their foliage was plump and swollen as baby chicks. When the wind blew, the trees trembled in fits, scattering wet leaves and drops of rainwater and causing small, momentary rainbows from which cicadas darted. In the heat beginning to revive and the tempest of shrill cicadas we sat down on the flat stone at the cellar entrance and for a long time breathed the air that smelled of wet bark.

Scarcely moving, we sat there until, in the afternoon, Clerk, carrying his rain gear, descended the road from the woods and went into the headman's house. We stood up then, leaned against an old, dripping apricot tree, and waited for Clerk to burst from the darkness of the house to wave a signal. But Clerk did not appear; instead, the alarm bell on the roof of the headman's barn began to clang, summoning the adults out working in the valley and the woods, and women and children from the rain-wet houses appeared on the cobblestone road. I looked back at the black soldier and saw that the smile was gone from his face. Anxiety suddenly born in me tightened my chest. Leaving the black soldier behind, my brother and Harelip and I ran to the headman's house.

Clerk was standing in silence on the dirt floor in the entranceway; inside, the village headman sat crosslegged on the wooden floor, lost in thought. As we waited impatiently for the adults to gather, we struggled to maintain an expectation that was beginning to feel somehow hopeless. From the fields in the valley and from the woods, dressed in their work clothes, their cheeks puffy with discontent, the adults, including my father, who stepped into the entranceway with several small birds lashed to the barrel of his gun, gradually returned.

The minute the meeting began Clerk floored the children with an explanation in dialect to the effect that the authorities had decided the black soldier was to be turned over to the prefecture. Originally the army was to have come for him, Clerk continued, but as a result of an apparent misunderstanding and general confusion within the army itself, the village had been ordered to escort the black soldier as far as the *town*. The adults would have to suffer only the minor inconvenience of bringing the black soldier in. But we were submerged in astonishment and disappointment; turn over the black soldier and what would remain in the village? Summer would become an empty husk, a shed skin!

I had to warn the black soldier. Slipping past the adults I ran back to where he was sitting in the square in front of the storehouse. Slowly lifting his dull eyeballs he looked up at me halted in front of him and gasping for breath. I was able to convey nothing to him. I could only stare at him while sadness and irritation shook me. Still hugging his knees, the black soldier was trying to peer into my eyes. His lips as full as the belly of a pregnant river fish slowly opened and shiny white saliva submerged his gums. Looking back, I saw the adults leave the dark entranceway of the headman's house with Clerk in the lead and move toward the storehouse.

I shook the black soldier's shoulder as he sat there, and shouted at him in dialect. I was so agitated I felt I would swoon. What could I do, he merely allowed himself to be shaken by my arm in silence and peered around him, craning his thick neck. I released his shoulder and hung my head.

Suddenly the black soldier rose, soaring in front of me like a tree, and seized my upper arm and pulled me tight up against himself and raced down the cellar steps. In the cellar, dumbfounded, I was transfixed for a brief moment by the flexing of the black soldier's taut thighs and the contraction of his buttocks as he moved around swiftly. Lowering the trap door, he secured it by passing the chain on the boar-trap he had repaired through the ring on the door and fastening it around the metal support protruding from the wall. Then he came back down the steps, his hands clasped and his head drooping, and I looked at his fatty, bloodshot eyes that appeared to have been packed with mud, his expressionless eyes, and realized abruptly that he was once again, as when the adults had taken him prisoner, a black beast that rejected understanding, a dangerously poisonous substance. I looked up at the giant black soldier, looked at the chain wrapped around the trap door, looked down at my own small, bare feet. A wave of fear and amazement broke over my vital organs and eddied around them. Darting away from the black soldier I pressed my back against the wall. The black soldier stood where he was in the middle of the cellar, his head drooping. I bit my lip and tried to withstand the trembling in my legs.

The adults gathered above the trap door and began to tug at it, gently at first and then abruptly with a great cackling as of chickens being pursued. But the thick oak door that had been so useful for locking the black soldier securely in the cellar was locking the adults out now, and the children, the trees, the valley.

A few adults peered frantically through the skylight and were immediately replaced by others, bumping foreheads in the scramble. There was a sudden change in their behavior. At first they shouted. Then they fell silent, and a threatening gun barrel was inserted through the skylight. Like an agile beast the black soldier leaped at me and hugged me tightly to himself, using me as a shield against the rifle, and as I moaned in pain and writhed in his arms I comprehended the cruel truth. I was a prisoner, and a hostage. The black soldier had transformed into the *enemy*, and my side was clamoring beyond the trap door. Anger, and humiliation, and the irritating sadness of betrayal raced through my body like flames, scorching me. And most of all, fear, swelling and eddying in me, clogging my throat and making me sob. In the black soldier's rude arms, aflame with anger, I wept tears. The black soldier had taken me prisoner. . . .

The gun barrel was withdrawn, the clamor increased, and then a long discussion began on the other side of the skylight. Without releasing his numbing grip on my arm the black soldier went into a corner where there was no danger of a sniper's bullet and sat down in silence. He pulled me in close to himself, and, just as I had often done when we had been friends, I kneeled with my bare knees within the circle of his body odor. The adults continued to talk for a long time. Now and then my father peered in through the skylight and nodded to his son who had been taken hostage, and each time, I cried. Dusk rose like a tide, first in the cellar and then in the square beyond the skylight. When it got dark the adults began going home several at a time, shouting a few words of encouragement to me as they left. For a long time after that I heard my father walking back and forth beyond the skylight, and then suddenly he was gone and there was no further indication of life aboveground. Night filled the cellar.

The black soldier released my arm and peered at me as though pained by the thought of the warm, everyday familiarity that had flowed between us until that morning.

Trembling with anger, I looked away and remained with my eyes on the floor, my shoulders stubbornly arched, until the black soldier turned his back on me and cradled his head between his knees. I was alone; like a weasel caught in a trap I was abandoned, helpless, sunk in despair. In the darkness the black soldier did not move.

Standing, I went over to the steps and touched the boar-trap, but it was cold and hard and repelled my fingers and the bud of a shapeless hope. I did not know what to do. I could not believe the trap that had captured me; I was a baby field rabbit who weakens and dies as it stares in disbelief at the metal claws biting into its wounded foot. The fact that I had trusted the black soldier as a friend, my incredible foolishness, was an agony to me. But how could I have doubted that black, stinking giant who never did anything but smile! Even now I could not believe that the man whose teeth were chattering in the darkness in front of me was that dumb black man with the large penis.

I was trembling with chill, and my teeth chattered. My stomach had begun to hurt. I squatted, pressing my stomach, and I encountered sudden dismay: I was going to have diarrhea, the strained nerves throughout my body had brought it on. But I could not relieve myself in front of the black soldier. I clenched my teeth and endured, cold sweat beading my forehead. I endured my distress for such a long time that the effort to endure filled the space that had been occupied by fear.

But finally I resigned myself, walked over to the barrel we had laughed and hooted to see the black soldier straddle, and dropped my pants. My exposed, white buttocks felt weak and defenseless, it seemed to me I could feel humiliation dyeing my throat, my esophagus, even the walls of my stomach pitch black. When I was finished I stood up and returned to the corner. I was beaten and I submitted, sinking to the bottom of despair. Pressing my grimy forehead against the cellar wall, warm with the heat of the ground above, I cried for a long time, stifling my sobs as best I could. The night was long. In the woods mountain dogs in a pack were barking. The air grew chill. Fatigue possessed me heavily and I slumped to the floor and slept.

When I woke up, my arm was again in the numbing grip of the black soldier's hand. Fog and adult voices were blowing in through the skylight. I could also hear the creaking of Clerk's artificial leg as he paced back and forth. Before long the thud of a heavy mallet hammering the trapdoor merged with the other noises. The heavy blows resounded in my empty stomach and made my chest ache.

Suddenly the black soldier was shouting, and then he seized me by the shoulder and pulled me to my feet and dragged me into the middle of the cellar into full view of the adults on the other side of the skylight. I could not understand why he did this. The eyes at the skylight peered in at my shame that dangled there by its ears like a shot rabbit. Had my brother's moist eyes been among them I would have bitten off my tongue in shame. But only adult eyes were clustered at the window, peering in at me.

The noise and tempo of the mallet heightened, and the black soldier screamed and grasped my throat from behind in his large hand. His nails bit into the soft skin and the pressure on my Adam's apple made it impossible to breathe. I flailed with my hands and feet and threw back my head and moaned. How bitter it was to be

159

humiliated in front of the adults! I twisted my body, trying to escape the body of the black soldier glued to my back, and kicked his shins, but his thick, hairy arms were hard and heavy. And his shrill screams rose above my moans. The adults' faces withdrew, and I imagined the black soldier had intimidated them into racing to put a stop to the smashing of the trapdoor. The black soldier stopped screaming and the pressure like a boulder against my throat eased. My love for the adults and my feeling of closeness revived.

But the pounding on the trapdoor grew louder. The adults' faces reappeared at the skylight, and the black soldier, screaming, tightened his fingers around my throat. My head was pulled back and my opened lips uttered a shrill, feeble sound I could do nothing about, like the scream of a small animal. Even the adults had abandoned me. Unmoved by the sight of the black soldier choking me to death they continued to batter the door. When they had broken in they would find me with my neck wrung like a weasel's, my hands and feet stiffened. Burning with hatred, despairing, I writhed and wept and listened to the sound of the mallet, my head wrenched back, moaning without shame.

The sound of countless wheels revolving rang in my ears and blood from my nose ran down my cheeks. Then the trapdoor splintered, muddy bare feet with bristly hair covering even the backs of the toes piled in, and ugly adults inflamed to madness filled the cellar. Screaming, the black soldier clasped me to himself and sank slowly down the wall toward the floor. My back and buttocks tight against his sweating, sticky body, I felt a current hot as rage flowing between us. And like a cat that has been surprised in the act of copulation, in spite of my shame, I

160

laid my hostility bare. It was hostility toward the adults crowded together at the bottom of the steps observing my humiliation, hostility toward the black soldier squeezing my throat in this thick hand, pressing his nails into the soft skin and making it bleed, hostility toward all things mixing together as it twisted upward in me. The black soldier was howling. The noise numbed my eardrums, there in the cellar at the height of summer I was slipping into an absence of all sensation replete as if with pleasure. The black soldier's ragged breathing covered the back of my neck.

From the midst of the bunched adults my father stepped forward dangling a hatchet from his hand. I saw that his eyes were blazing with rage and feverish as a dog's. The black soldier's nails bit into my neck and I moaned. My father bore down on us, and seeing the hatchet being raised I closed my eyes. The black soldier seized my left wrist and lifted it to protect his head. The entire cellar erupted in a scream and I heard the smashing of my left hand and the black soldier's skull. On the oily, shining skin of his arm beneath my jaw thick blood coagulated in shivering drops. The adults surged toward us and I felt the black soldier's arm slacken and pain sear my body.

Inside a sticky black bag my hot eyelids, my burning throat, my searing hand began to knit me and give me shape. But I could not pierce the sticky membrane and break free of the bag. Like a lamb prematurely born I was wrapped in a bag that stuck to my fingers. I could not move my body. It was night, and near me the adults were talking. Then it was morning, and I felt light against my eyelids. From time to time a heavy hand pressed my forehead and I moaned and tried to shake it off but my head would not move.

The first time I succeeded in opening my eyes it was morning again. I was lying on my own sleeping platform in the storehouse. In front of the rain shutters Harelip and my brother were watching me. I opened my eyes all the way, and moved my lips. Harelip and my brother raced down the stairs shouting, and my father and the lady from the general store came up. My stomach was crying for food, but when my father's hand placed a pitcher of goat's milk to my lips nausea shook me and I clamped my mouth shut, yelling, and dribbled the milk on my throat and chest. All adults were unbearable to me, including my father. Adults who bore down on me with teeth bared, brandishing a hatchet, they were uncanny, beyond my understanding, provoking nausea. I continued to yell until my father and the others left the room.

A while later my brother's arm quietly touched my body. In silence, my eyes closed, I listened to his soft voice telling me how he and the others had helped gather firewood for cremating the black soldier, how Clerk had brought an order forbidding the cremation, how the adults, in order to retard the process of decay, had carried the black soldier's corpse into the abandoned mine in the valley and were building a fence to keep mountain dogs away.

In an awed voice my brother told me repeatedly that he had thought I was dead. For two days I had lain here and eaten nothing and so he had thought I was dead. With my brother's hand on me I entered sleep that lured me as irresistibly as death.

I woke up in the afternoon and saw for the first time

162

that my smashed hand was wrapped in cloth. For a long time I lay as I was, not moving, and looking at the arm on my chest, so swollen I could not believe it was mine. There was no one in the room. An unpleasant odor crept through the window. I understood what the odor meant but felt no sadness.

The room had darkened and the air turned chill when I sat up on the sleeping platform. After a long hesitation I tied the ends of the bandage together and put it over my head as a sling, then leaned against the open window and looked down upon the *village*. The odor fountaining furiously from the black soldier's heavy corpse blanketed the cobblestone road and the buildings and the valley supporting them, an inaudible scream from the corpse that encircled us and expanded limitlessly overhead as in a nightmare. It was dusking. The sky, a teary gray with a touch of orange enfolded in it, hovered just above the valley, narrowing it.

Every so often adults would hurry down toward the valley in silence, chests thrown out. Every time they appeared I sensed them making me feel nauseous and afraid and withdrew inside the window. It was as if while I had been in bed the adults had been transformed into entirely inhuman monsters. And my body was as dull and heavy as if it had been packed with wet sand.

Trembling with chill, I bit into my parched lips and watched the cobblestones in the road, in pale golden shadow to begin with, fluidly expand, then turn breathtaking grape, contours continuing to swell until finally they submerged, disappearing, in a weak, purple, opaque light. Now and then salty tears wet my cracked lips and made them sting.

From time to time children's shouts reached me from

163

the back of the storehouse through the odor of the black soldier's corpse. Taking each trembling step with caution, as after a long illness, I went down the dark stairs and walked along the deserted cobblestone road toward the shouting.

The children were gathered on the overgrown slope that descended to the small river at the valley bottom, their dogs racing around them and barking. In the thick underbrush along the river below, the adults were still constructing a sturdy fence to keep wild dogs away from the abandoned mine. The sound of stakes being driven echoed up from the valley. The adults worked in silence, the children ran madly in circles on the slope, shrieking gaily.

I leaned against the trunk of an old paulownia tree and watched the children playing. They were sliding down the grassy slope, using the tail of the black soldier's fallen plane as a sled. Straddling the sharp-edged, wonderfully buoyant sled they went skimming down the slope like young beasts. When the sled seemed in danger of hitting one of the black rocks that jutted from the grass here and there, the rider kicked the ground with his bare feet and changed the sled's direction. By the time one of the children dragged the sled back up the hill, the grass that had been crushed beneath it on the way down was slowly straightening, obscuring the bold voyager's wake. The children and the sled were that light. The children sledded down screaming, the dogs pursued them barking, the children dragged the sled up again. An irrepressible spirit of movement like the fiery dust that precedes a sorcerer crackled and darted among them.

Harelip left the group of children and ran up the slope toward me. Leaning against the trunk of an evergreen oak that resembled a deer leg, a tussled stem of grass between his teeth, he peered into my face. I looked away, pretending to be absorbed in the sledding. Harelip peered closely at my arm in the sling and snorted.

"It smells," he said. "Your smashed hand stinks."

Harelip's eyes were lusting for battle and his feet were planted apart in readiness for my attack; I glared back at him but did not leap at his throat.

"That's not me," I said in a feeble, hoarse voice. "That's the nigger's smell."

Harelip stood there appalled, observing me. I turned away, biting my lip, and looked down at the simmering of the short, fine grass burying his bare ankles. Harelip shrugged his shoulders with undisguised contempt and spit forcefully, then ran shouting back to his friends with the sled.

I was no longer a child—the thought filled me like a revelation. Bloody fights with Harelip, hunting small birds by moonlight, sledding, wild puppies, these things were for children. And that variety of connection to the world had nothing to do with me.

Exhausted and shaking with chill I sat down on the ground that retained the midday warmth. When I lowered myself the lush summer grass hid the silent work of the adults at the valley bottom, but the children playing with the sled suddenly loomed in front of me like darkly silhouetted woodland gods. And amidst these young Pans wheeling in circles with their dogs like victims fleeing before a flood, the night air gradually deepened in color, gathered itself, and became pure.

"Hey Frog, feeling better?"

A dry, hot hand pressed my head from behind but I did not turn or try to stand. Without turning away from

165

the children playing on the slope I glanced with eyes only at Clerk's black artificial limb planted firmly alongside my own bare legs. Even Clerk, simply by standing at my side, made my throat go dry.

"Aren't you going to take a turn, Frog? I thought it must have been your idea!"

I was stubbornly silent. When Clerk sat down with a rattling of his leg he took from his jacket pocket the pipe the black soldier had presented him and filled it with his tobacco. A strong smell that nettled the soft membranes in my nose and ignited animal sentiments, the aroma of a brush fire, enclosed me and Clerk in the same pale blue haze.

"When a war starts smashing kids' fingers it's going too far," Clerk said.

I breathed deeply, and was silent. The war, a long, bloody battle on a huge scale, must still have been going on. The war that like a flood washing away flocks of sheep and trimmed lawns in some distant country was never in the world supposed to have reached our village. But it had come, to mash my fingers and hand to a pulp, my father swinging a hatchet, his body drunk on the blood of war. And suddenly our village was enveloped in the war, and in the tumult I could not breathe.

"But it can't go on much longer," Clerk said gravely, as if he were talking to an adult. "The army is in such a state you can't get a message through, nobody knows what to do."

The sound of hammers continued. Now the odor of the black soldier's body had settled over the entire valley like the luxuriant lower branches of a giant, invisible tree.

"They're still hard at work," Clerk said, listening to the thudding of the hammers. "Your father and the others don't know what to do either, so they're taking their sweet time with those stakes!"

In silence we listened to the heavy thudding that reached us in intervals in the children's shouting and laughter. Presently Clerk began with practiced fingers to detach his artificial leg. I watched him.

"Hey!" he shouted to the children. "Bring that sled over here."

Laughing and shouting, the children dragged the sled up. When Clerk hopped over on one leg and pushed through the children surrounding the sled I picked up his leg and ran down the slope. It was heavy; managing it with one hand was difficult and irritating.

The dew beginning to form in the lush grass wet my bare legs and dry leaves stuck to them and itched. At the bottom of the slope I stood waiting, holding the artificial leg. It was already night. Only the children's voices at the top of the slope shook the thickening membrane of dark, nearly opaque air.

A burst of louder shouts and laughter and a soft skimming through the grass, but no sled cleaved the sticky air to appear before me. I thought I heard the dull thud of an impact and stood as I was, peering into the dark air. After a long silence I finally saw the airplane tail sliding toward me down the slope, riderless, spinning as it came. I threw the artificial leg into the grass and ran up the dark slope. Alongside a rock jutting blackly from the grass and wet with dew, both hands limply open, Clerk lay on his back grinning. I leaned over and saw that thick, dark blood was running from the nose and ears of his grinning face. The noise the children made as they came running down the slope rose above the wind blowing up from the valley.

To avoid being surrounded by the children I abandoned Clerk's corpse and stood up on the slope. I had rapidly become familiar with sudden death and the expressions of the dead, sad at times and grinning at times, just as the adults were familiar with them. Clerk would be cremated with the firewood gathered to cremate the black soldier. Glancing up with tears in my eyes at the narrowed sky still white with twilight, I went down the grassy slope to look for my brother.

TEACH US TO OUTGROW OUR MADNESS

In the winter of 196—, an outlandishly fat man came close to being thrown to a polar bear bathing in a filthy pool below him and had the experience of very nearly going mad. As a result, the fat man was released from the fetters of an old obsession, but the minute he found himself free a miserable loneliness rose in him and withered his already slender spirit. Thereupon he resolved, for no logical reason (he was given to fits of sudden agitation), to cast off still another heavy restraint; he vowed to free himself entirely and let the sky tilt if need be, and when he had taken his oath and a reckless courage was boiling in his body, still scaly and stinking of rotten sardines from the splash of the rock which had been thrown into the pool finally in his place, he telephoned his mother in the middle of the night and said to her,

——You give me back the manuscript you stole from me, I'm fed up, do you hear! I've known all along what you were up to!

The fat man knew his mother was standing at the other end of the line eight hundred miles away with the old-fashioned receiver in her hand. He even concluded unscientifically that he could hear the whisper of breathing into the other phone as distinctly as he did because no one was near the circuits due to the lateness of the hour, and since this happened to be his mother's breathing, the fat man felt his chest constrict. As a matter of fact, what he was hearing through the receiver he had pressed against his ear, delicate out of all proportion to the massiveness of his head, was his own breath.

——If you won't give me back what's mine, that's all right too! the fat man shouted in growing anger, having realized his small mistake. I'll write another biography of Father that's even more revealing, I'll tell the whole world how the man went mad and shut himself up all those years and then let out a roar one day and died where he sat in his chair. And you can interfere all you like, it won't do you any good! Again the fat man stopped and listened for a reaction at the other end of the line, careful this time to cover the phone with his thick hand. When he heard the receiver being replaced, calmly and for that reason the more adamantly, he went pale as a young girl and returned trembling to his bed, curled up in a ball, pulled the covers over his head despite the stench of the pool, which made him gag, and sobbed in rage. It wasn't only his mother, the loneliness of the freedom he had acquired that morning at the zoo had quite intimidated him, and so he cried in the stinking darkness beneath the covers where he could be certain he was unobserved. It was rage, and terror, and his overwhelming sense of isolation that made the fat man cry, as if the polar bear immersed to its shoulders in brown, icy water had gripped his bulky head in its freezing jaws. Before long the fat man's tears had wet the sheets all around him, so he rolled over, curled up again, and continued to sob. He was able to enjoy this particular freedom, minor but not to be despised, because for several years he had been sleeping alone in the double bed he once had shared with his wife.

While the fat man cried himself to sleep that night, his mother, in the village of his birth, was steeling herself for a final battle against her son. Thus the fat man had no reason to weep, at least not out of the frustration of having had his challenge ignored yet another time. As a child, whenever he began to question her about his father's self-confinement and sudden death, his mother had closed the road to communication by pretending to go mad. It reached a point where the fat man would affect madness himself before his mother had a chance, smashing everything in reach and even tumbling backwards off the stone wall at the edge of the garden and down the briary slope. But even at times like these, his sense of victory was tiny and essentially futile: he never managed to make contact. Ever since, for close to twenty years, the tension of a showdown between two gunmen on a movie set had sustained itself between them—who would be first to affect madness and so to win an occult victory?

But late that night, the situation began to change. The very next morning the fat man's mother, resolved on new battle regulations, took to the printer in a neighboring town an announcement she had drafted during the night and had it mailed, registered mail, to the fat man's brothers and sisters, their husbands and wives, and all the family relatives. The announcement which arrived care of the fat man's wife and marked Personal in red ink, but of a nature which obliged her to show it to her husband, read as follows:

> *Our flirty whore has lost his mind, but it should be known his madness is not hereditary. It pains me to inform you that, while abroad, he contracted the Chinese chancres. In order to avoid infection, it is hoped you will abstain from further commerce with him.*

> Signed

> *winter, 196—*

> *But how much gloomier*
> *The garden*
> *Seen from the orphanage toilet—*
> *Age thirty-four!*

> —Uchida Hyakken

Unfortunately, the significance of this text was clearest to the only member of the family who depended on language for a living, the fat man himself. With her pun on his age (he was thirty-four) his mother had tried to shame him, and by adding the verse about the orphanage toilet (he wasn't clear if it was really by the poet Hyakken) she had even insinuated that he was not her real son: the announcement was the product of its author's overriding hatred, a vexatious hatred which no one in the family was equipped so adequately to feel as the fat man himself.

One thing was certain, there was no doubting the blood bond between them: like the fat man himself and like his son, her grandson, his mother was fatter than fat. The fat man was confident his wife would not suspect him of carrying a disease he had brought home from the Occident; even so, when he considered that the local printer must have read the announcement and when he pictured it being delivered into the hands of all his friends and relatives, he submerged in a terrible gloom. The effect of which was to impress on him the importance, not to his son perhaps but certainly to his own well-being, of the heavy bond of restraints which (so he had believed) had united himself and the child formerly. The trouble was, ever since his harrowing experience at the zoo, the fat man had doubted the very existence of these restraints and even suspected that his own desire to create and maintain them had led him to repeated feats of self-deception. Besides, once gained, his freedom was like an adhesive tape which could not be peeled away from his hand or heart.

He could not return to what had been. Until that day when it seemed he would be thrown to the polar bear and he was on the verge of losing his mind, the fat man had wandered around, sprawled on the floor, and eaten all his meals together with his son, allowing nothing to separate them. And this permitted him a perfectly concrete sense of the child as primarily a heavy and troublesome restraint which menaced, even as it regulated, his daily life. In truth, he enjoyed thinking of himself as a passive victim quietly enduring a bondage imposed by his son.

The fat man had always liked children; in college he had qualified for three kinds of teaching licenses. And as the time approached for his own child to be born he was unable to sit still for the spasms of anxiety and expectation which rippled through his body. Later, looking back, he had the feeling he had been counting on the birth of his child as a first step toward a new life for himself which would be out of the shadow of his dead father. But when the moment finally arrived and the fat man, painfully thin in those days, nervously questioned the doctor who emerged from the delivery room, he was told in an even voice that his child had been born with a grave defect.

——Even if we operate I'm afraid the infant will either die or be an idiot, one or the other.

That instant, something inside the fat man irreparably broke. And the baby who was either to die or to be an idiot quickly elbowed out the breakage, as cancer destroys and then replaces normal cells. In arranging for the operation the fat man dashed around so frantically that his own in those days still meager body might well have broken down. His nervous system was like a chaos of numbness and hypersensitivity, an inflamed wound which had begun to heal but only in spots: fearfully he would touch places in himself and feel no pain at all; a moment later, when relief had lowered his guard, a scorching pain would make him rattle.

The deadline for registering the new infant arrived, and the fat man went to the ward office. But until the girl at the desk asked what it was to be, he hadn't even considered a name for his son. At the time the operation was in progress, his baby was in the process of being required to decide whether he would die or be an idiot, one or the other. Could such an existence be given a name?

The fat man (let it be repeated that at the time, exhausted, he was thinner than ever in his life) took the registration form nonetheless and, recalling from the Latin vocabulary he had learned at college a word which should have related both to death and idiocy, wrote down the character for "forest" and named his son Mori. Then he took the form into the bathroom, sat down in one of the stalls, and began to giggle uncontrollably. This ignoble seizure was due in part to the state of the fat man's nerves at the time. And yet even as a child there had been something inside him, something fundamental, which now and then impelled him to frivolous derision of his own and others' lives. And this was something he was obliged to recognize in himself when his son finally left the hospital and came to live at home. Mori!—every time he called the child by name it seemed to him that he could hear, in the profound darkness in his head, his own lewd and unrepentant laughter mocking the entirety of his life. So he proposed giving his son a nickname and using it at home, though he had difficulty satisfying his wife with a reason. It was in this way that the fat man, borrowing the name of the misanthropic donkey in Winnie the Pooh, came to call his son Eeyore.

He moreover concluded, with renewed conviction, that his relationship with his own father, who had died suddenly when he was a child, must be the source of the somehow mistaken, insincere, unbalanced quality he had to recognize in himself, and he undertook somehow to recreate a whole image of the man, whom he remembered only vaguely. This produced a new repetition of collisions with his mother, who had never spoken about his father's self-confinement and death and had combatted him for years by pretending to go mad whenever he questioned her. Not only did she refuse to cooperate; during a stay at his home while he was traveling abroad she had stolen his notes and incomplete manuscript for a biography of his father and had retained them to this day. For all he knew, she had already burned the manuscript, but since the thought alone made him want to kill his mother, he had no choice but not to think it.

And yet the fat man was dependent on his mother to a degree extraordinary for an adult of his age, another truth he was obliged to recognize. Drunk one night on the whiskey he relied on instead of sleeping pills, he was toying with a clay dog he had brought all the way from Mexico when he discovered a hole beneath the creature's tail and blew into it hard, as if he were playing on a flute. Unexpectedly, a cloud of fine black dust billowed out of the hole and plastered his eyes. The fat man supposed he had gone blind, and in his distraction and his fear he called out to his mother: Mother, oh, Mother, help me, please! If I should go blind and lose my mind the way Father did, what will become of my son? Teach me, mother, how we can all outgrow our madness!

For no good reason, the fat man had been seized by the suspicion that his mother soon would age and die without having disclosed the explanation she had kept secret all these years, not only for his father's self-confinement and death but the freakish something which underlay it and must also account for his own instability and for the existence of his idiot son, an existence which, inasmuch as it presented itself in palpable form, he assumed he could never detach from himself.

The fat man's loneliness that night as he slept in the bed too large for even his bloated body has already been described, but the truth is that still another circumstance can be included as having contributed to it. That the fat man spent all his time in the company of his fat son Mori, called Eeyore, was known to most of the citizens in the neighborhood. What even the most curious of them did not know was that, until the decisive day when he was nearly thrown to a polar bear, the fat man had never failed to sleep with one arm extended toward his son's crib, which he had installed at the head of his bed. In fact, his wife had quit his bed and secluded herself in another part of the house not so much because of strife between them as a desire of her own not to interfere with this intimacy between father and son. It had always been the fat man's intention that he was acting on a wholesome parental impulse—if his son should awaken in the middle of the night he would always be able to touch his father's fleshy hand in the darkness above his head. But now, when he examined them in light of the breakage which had resulted in himself when hoodlums had lifted him by his head and ankles and swung him back and forth as if to hurl him to the polar bear eyeing him curiously from the pool below, the fat man could not help discovering, in even these details of his life, a certain incongruity, as if a few grains of sand had sifted into his socks. Wasn't it possible that he had slept with his arm outstretched so that the hand with which he groped in the darkness when uneasy dreams threatened him awake at night might encounter at once the comforting warmth of his son's hand? Once he had recognized the objection being raised inside himself, the details of their life together, which to him had always seemed to represent his bondage to his son, one by one disclosed new faces which added to his confusion. Yet the very simplest details of their life together troubled him only rarely with this disharmony, and in this the fat man took solace as he grew more and more absorbed, feeling very much alone, in the battle with his mother. The fact was, even after his experience at the zoo, that he continued to enact certain of the daily rituals he shared with his son.

Rain or shine, not figuratively but in fact, the fat man and his son bicycled once a day to a Chinese restaurant and ordered pork noodles in broth and Pepsi-Cola. In the days before his son was quite so fat, the fat man would sit him in a light metal seat which he attached to the handlebars. And how often he had been obliged to fight with policemen who held that the metal seat was illegal, not to mention riding double on a bike! The fat man had always protested earnestly, because he had believed his own claim. Now, when he looked back from his new point of view, he had to wonder if he really had believed what he had argued so vehemently, that his son was retarded (precisely because he so loathed the word itself he always used it as a weapon against the police) and that the only pleasure available to him, his only consolation, was climbing into a metal seat attached to the handlebars illegally and bicycling in search of pork noodles in broth and Pepsi-Cola. Sooner or later his son would tire of sitting on a bicycle halted precariously in the middle of the street and would begin to groan in displeasure, whereupon the fat man himself would raise his own hoarse voice in the manner of a groan and increase the fervor of his argument, with the result that the dispute generally ended with the policeman giving way. Then, as if he had been long a victim of police oppression with regard to some matter of grave importance, the fat man would announce to his son, staring at the road ahead with utter indifference to his father's feverish whisper:

——Eeyore, we really showed that cop! We won, boy, that

makes eighteen wins in a row! and pedal off triumphantly toward the Chinese restaurant.

Inside, while they waited for their pork noodles in broth, Eeyore drank his Pepsi-Cola and the fat man raptly watched him drinking it. As prepared at the restaurant they frequented, the dish amounted to some noodles in broth garnished with mushrooms and some spinach and a piece of meat from a pork bone fried in a thin batter. When it was finally brought to their table, the fat man would empty two-thirds of the noodles and some of the mushrooms and spinach into a small bowl which he placed in front of his son, carefully watch the boy eating until the food had cooled, and only then begin to eat the pork himself, probing with his tongue for the gristle between the batter and the meat and then disposing of the halved, white spheres, after examining them minutely, in an ashtray out of Eeyore's reach. Finally, he would eat his share of the noodles, timing himself so the two of them would finish together. Then, as he rode them home on his bike with his face flushed from the steaming noodles and burning in the wind, he would ask repeatedly,

——Eeyore, the pork noodles and the Pepsi-Cola were good? and when his son answered,

——Eeyore, the pork noodles and Pepsi-Cola were good! he would judge that complete communication had been achieved between them and would feel happy. Often he believed sincerely that of all the food he had ever eaten, that day's pork noodles was the most delicious.

One of the major causes of the fat man's corpulence and his son's must have been those pork noodles in broth. From time to time his wife cautioned him about this, but he prevailed in arguments at home with the same reasoning he used against the police. When his son's buttocks eventually grew too fat to fit into the metal seat, the fat man hunted up a special bicycle with a ridiculously long saddle, and propped Eeyore up in front of him when they rode off for their daily meal.

The fat man had concluded that this bicycle trip in quest of pork noodles and Pepsi-Cola was a procedure to enable his idiot son to feel, in the core of his body, the pleasure of eating. However, after his experience above the polar bears' pool, it no longer made him profoundly happy to separate the gristle from the pork rib with his tongue and inspect the shiny hemispheres; and the joy of appetite in Eeyore, eating noodles in silence at his side as always, communicated to the core of his own body as but a feeble tremor. He wondered sometimes if Eeyore's craving for pork noodles and Pepsi might not be a groundless illusion of his own, if his son had grown so fat because, pathetically, he had been eating mechanically whatever had been placed in front of him. One day when doubts like these had ruined the fat man's appetite and he had left the restaurant without even finishing his pork rib, the Chinese cook, who until then had never emerged from the kitchen, caught up with them on a bicycle which glistened with grease and inquired in a frighteningly emphatic accent whether anything was wrong with the food that day. The fat man, already so deflated that he lacked even the courage to ignore the cook, passed the question on to Eeyore and then shared the Chinaman's relief when his son intoned his answer in the usual way:

——Eeyore, the pork noodles in broth and Pepsi-Cola were good!

By accumulating numerous procedures of this kind between himself and his son, the fat man had structured a

182

life unique to themselves. And that the structure demanded his bondage to his idiot son long had been his secret belief. But when he reconsidered now, with his experience above the polar bears' pool behind him, he began to see that the maintenance of this extraordinary structure had been most ardently desired by himself.

Until his son began to peel from his consciousness like a scab, the fat man was convinced that he experienced directly whatever physical pain his son was feeling. When he read somewhere that the male celatius, a deep-sea fish common to Danish waters, lived its life attached like a wart to the larger body of the female, he dreamed that he was the female fish suspended deep in the sea with his son embedded in his body like the smaller male, a dream so sweet that waking up was cruel.

In the beginning no one would believe, even when they saw it happening, that the fat man suffered the same pain as his son. But in time even his most skeptical wife came to accept this as fact. It didn't begin the minute the child was born; several years had passed when the fat man suddenly awoke to it one day. Until then, for example when his son underwent brain surgery as an infant, although the fat man caused the doctors to wonder about him queasily when he pressed them to extract from his own body for his son's transfusions a quantity of blood not simply excessive but medically unthinkable, he did not experience faintness while his son was under anesthesia, nor did he share any physical pain. The conduit of pain between the fat man and his fat son was connected unmistakably (or so it seemed, for even now the fat man found it difficult to establish whether the pain he once had felt was real or sham, and had been made to realize that in general nothing was so difficult to recreate as pain

KENZABURO ŌE

remaining only as a memory) when Eeyore scalded his
foot in the summer of his third year.

When his son began to raise not simple screams as
much as rash shouts of protest, the fat man was sprawled
on his living room couch, reading a magazine; and
although behind his eyelids, where his tears were beginning to well, he could see with surrealistic clarity, as if he
were watching a film in slow motion, the spectacle of the
pan filled with boiling water tilting up and tipping over, he
did not rise and dash into the kitchen in aid of his son. He
lay as he was submerged in a feebleness like the disem-
bodiment that accompanies a high fever, and chorused his
son's shouts with a thick moaning of his own. Yet even
then it couldn't have been said that he had achieved a firm
hold on physical pain. He strapped his son's heavy,
thrashing body into a rusty baby carriage which he
dragged out of his shed and somehow managed to secure
the scalded foot. And although he groaned heavily all the
way to the distant clinic as he slowly pushed the carriage
past the strangers halted in the street to watch his eery
progress, he could not have said with certainty that he was
actually feeling Eeyore's pain in his own flesh.

However, as he bore down against the explosive
thrashing of his son's small projectile of a body so the
doctor could bare and treat the blistered foot, the following question coalesced in the fat man's mind: could any
conscious state be so full of fright and hurt as perceiving
pain and not its cause, and perceiving pain only, because
an idiot infant's murky brain could not begin to grasp the
logic of a situation in which pain persisted and was
apparently to go unsoothed and, as if that were not
enough, a stranger stepped in officiously to inflict still
another pain while even Father cooperated? That instant,

184

the fat man began through clenched teeth to express cries of pain himself which so resembled his son's screams that they merged with them indistinguishably and could not have shocked the doctor or the nurses. His leg had actually begun to throb (he believed!) with the pain of a burn.

By the time the wound had been bandaged, the fat man himself, at the side of his pale, limp son was too exhausted to speak. His wife, who had been in the examination room helping to hold the patient down, went home with Eeyore in a taxi, leaving the fat man to return alone down the narrow street which paralleled the railroad tracks, the rope he had used to secure his son coiled inside the empty carriage. As he walked along the fat man wondered why his wife had wrested Eeyore away from him and raced away in a taxicab. If he had put his son back in the carriage and they had returned together down this same street, had she been afraid he might have launched himself and the carriage between the used ties which had been newly erected to fence off the tracks and attempted to escape the pain which now gripped them both by throwing himself and the child beneath the filthy wheels of the commuter express? Possibly, for even if his cries had not reached the ears of the doctor and the nurses, merging with his son's screams, to his wife they must have been clearly audible; for in pinning his son's shoulders she had leaned so far over the table toward him that her head had nearly touched his own. Although he handled the empty carriage roughly, the fat man made his way down the street with excessive care, as though he were favoring a leg which had been just treated for a burn, and if he had to skip over a small puddle he produced an earnest cry of pain.

From that day on, insofar as the fat man was aware,

whatever pain his son was feeling communicated to him through their clasped hands and never failed to produce in his own body a tremor of pain in unison. If the fat man was able to attach positive significance to this phenomenon of pain shared, it was because he managed to believe that his own understanding of the pain resonating sympathetically in himself, for example as resulting from blistered and dead skin being peeled away from a burn with a tweezers, would flow backward like light through his son's hand, which he held in his own, and impart a certain order to the chaos of fear and pain in the child's dark, dulled mind. The fat man began to function as a window in his son's mind, permitting the light from the outside to penetrate to the dark interior which trembled with pain not adequately understood. And so long as Eeyore did not step forward to repudiate his function, there was no reason the fat man should have doubted it. Since now he was able to proclaim to himself that he was accepting painful bondage to his son happily, his new role even permitted him the consolation of feeling like an innocent victim.

Shortly after Eeyore's fourth birthday, the fat man took him for an eye examination at a certain university hospital. No matter who the eye specialist, examining an idiot child who never spoke at all except to babble something of little relevance in a severely limited vocabulary, or to utter noises in response to pain or simple pleasure, would certainly prove a difficult, vexatious task. And this young patient was not only fat and heavy, and therefore difficult to hold, he was abnormally strong in his arms and legs, so that once fear had risen in him he was as impossible to manage as a frightened animal.

The fat man's wife, having noticed right away something distinctively abnormal about Eeyore's sight, and having speculated in a variety of amateur ways on the possible connections to his retardation, long had wanted a specialist to examine his eyes. But at every clinic he had visited, the fat man had been turned away. Finally, he went to see the brain surgeon who had enabled the child whose alternatives were death or idiocy to escape at least from death, and managed to obtain a letter of introduction to the department of opthalmology in the same university hospital.

The family went to the hospital together, but at first his wife left the fat man in the waiting room and went upstairs alone with Eeyore. Half an hour later, dragging her heavy, shrieking son and obviously exhausted, she staggered back. The examination had scarcely begun, and already the doctor, the nurses, even his wife was prostrate, while Eeyore himself presented a picture of such cruel abuse that the other patients were looking on in dismay. The fat man, furious to see his son in such a state, and menaced, understood why his wife had left him in the waiting room and gone upstairs alone with Eeyore. There was no longer room for doubt that a thorough examination of a child's eyes was an uninterrupted ordeal, rife with some kind of grotesque and virulent terror.

Eeyore was still producing at the back of his throat something like the echo of a feeble scream when the fat man dropped to his knees on the dirty floor and embraced his pudgy body. The hand which Eeyore wound around his neck was moist with the sweat of fear, like the pads on the foot of a cat that had tasted danger. And the touch of his hand infused the fat man with the essence of his son's entire experience during the thirty minutes past (so he believed at the time). Every hollow and rise of the fat man's body was possessed by an aching numbness that followed thirty long minutes in the spiney clamps of medical instruments he had never actually seen: had not Eeyore quieted gradually in his arms until now he was only whimpering, he might have raised a terrific scream and begun writhing on the floor himself.

Unique in his household for her excessive leanness, the fat man's provident wife had taken the precaution of stopping downstairs in hopes of preventing the two of them, himself and his son, from behaving in just this lunatic way.

——They must have been horrible to him, the fat man moaned, sighing hoarsely. What the hell did they think he is, the bastards!

——It was Eeyore who was horrible: he kept kicking the doctors and the nurses away, one after the other, and he broke all kinds of things, said the fat man's wife. It wasn't that she always tried for fairness or objectivity so much as that she refused to participate in the fat man's paranoia. The fat man listened to her sighing now, mournfully angry at her violent son, and felt that he was included in her attack.

——No, there must have been something wrong basically, otherwise Eeyore wouldn't have been so wild. Think how gentle he always is! And you said the examination had just begun—then how did Eeyore know there was something so bad in store for him that he had to fight that way? There has to be something fundamentally wrong, I mean with the eye department here, and you just missed it, that's all, the fat man said rapidly, forestalling his wife's almost certainly accurate rebuttal and beginning to believe, because he was insisting it, that there was indeed something wrong with the hospital. He even established arbitrary grounds for the judgment: his son, who had finished rubbing the back of his neck with his sweaty palm and was simply moaning softly at his side, had communicated it to him telepathically.

——I'm going to take Eeyore back up there. We may not be able to get a diagnosis, but at least I'll see what they're doing wrong, the fat man rasped, his round face an angry red. Otherwise it will be the same business all over again, no matter how many times you come back, and Eeyore's experience here will haunt him like the memory of an awful nightmare without ever making any sense to him!

——It won't take Eeyore long to forget about it—he's nearly forgotten already.

——That's nonsense, Eeyore won't forget. Do you know that he's been crying a lot in the middle of the night recently? It's frightening enough just that Eeyore's frightened, can you stand to think of him having nightmares he can't make any sense of?

With this the fat man decisively silenced his wife, who did not sleep in her son's room at night. He then swung Eeyore on to his shoulders with the same emphaticness and marched up the stairs toward the examination room, the dirt from the floor still on his coat. Being able to parade the truth this way, that the existence essential to his pudgy son was not his mother but himself, inspired the fat man with a courage close to gallantry. At the same time, the prospect of the cruel ordeal the two of them might have to undergo left him pale and dizzy, and at each breathless step he climbed his head flashed hot and his body shook with chill.

——Eeyore! we have to keep a sharp watch, you and I, to see they don't put anything over on us, said the fat man, lifting his voice in an appeal to the warm and heavy presence on his shoulders which sometimes felt, to his confusion, more like his guardian spirit than his ward.

——Eeyore, if we can finish this up together, we'll go out for some pork noodles and Pepsi-Cola!

——Eeyore, the pork noodles and Pepsi-Cola were good! his fat son lazily replied, satisfied to be riding on his father's shoulder and seemingly liberated from the memory of his experience a while ago.

This seemed to testify to the accuracy of his wife's prediction, and if the fat man had not been spurred by his son's voice he would certainly have lost his courage at the entrance to the examination room and returned meekly as he had come. For not only was a young nurse bolting the door which she had just closed, with the unmistakable intention of locking further patients out, the clock having struck noon, but when she turned and saw the child riding on the fat man's shoulders a look of panic and protest came over her face, as if she were re-encountering a ghost she had finally managed to be rid of, and she scurried behind the door to hide. The fat man, counting on the elitism of a university hospital, announced unbidden and as pretentiously as possible that he had been referred by a certain Professor of Medicine, and named the brain surgeon. The nurse didn't answer him directly; it was unlikely she even considered chasing away by herself the large, fat man who had planted himself in front of the office without even lowering his son from his shoulders. Instead, leaving the door half open, she ran back inside to a dark corner which was curtained off at the rear of the room and began some kind of an appeal.

For just a minute, the fat man hesitated. Then he stepped over the lowered bolt and strode to the back of the room, where he encountered a shrill voice protesting behind the curtain in what sounded like uncontainable anger.

——No, no, no! Absolutely not! It would take every man in the building to hold down that little blimp. What's that? He's here already? I don't care if he is, the answer is No!

This was a point for the fat man's side. With calm to spare, he slowly lowered Eeyore to the floor. Then he thrust his large head inside the curtain and discovered a doctor so diminutive that he looked in his surgical gown like a child dressed up in grownup clothes, arching backward in the dimness right under his nose a tiny head that recalled a praying mantis as he shouted at the disconcerted nurse. The fat man took a long, brazen look, then said with stunning politeness,

——I was referred here by Professor of Medicine X. Could we possibly try again, perhaps I can help?

So the examination began. How can you refuse when the patient's enormous parent interrupts you with that deadly politeness in the middle of shrieking at your nurse? seemed to be the question smouldering in the praying mantis's head as, peevishly ignoring the fat man, he began his examination by shining a pencil light in Eeyore's eyes. It was to increase the efficiency of this tiny bulb that half the room was kept in shrouded darkness. The fat man crouched uncomfortably in the narrow space behind the swivel chair, his arms locked around Eeyore's chest. It made him proud to think that the boy was sitting in the chair at all, although his body was straining backward and continued to shudder, because it was himself, who invariably stayed with his son through the night, who was holding him around the chest. Thirty minutes ago, not realizing that Eeyore's fear of the dark could not be overcome unless it was directed through the conduit between father and son, his wife and the doctor and these nurses must have driven the boy to the desperation of a small animal at bay in this same stage of the examination. But this time, he was able to think with satisfaction, the fat man had observed himself that the darkness in this room was not particularly frightening, and the essence of his judgment had been transmitted to Eeyore through the pressure of his hands and was lowering one by one the danger flags flapping in the boy's dim mind.

Even so, Eeyore was afraid of the pencil light itself and refused to look in the direction the doctor desired, straight into its tiny beam. By tossing his head from side to side and watching out of the corner of his eye, he continued to evade the agitated pursuit of the pencil light in the little doctor's hand. Presently, the young nurse stepped in to help, probably hoping to redeem herself with the doctor. *Garuk! Garuk!* The fat man heard an odious noise and felt Eeyore's body contract with anxiety, and when he looked up in reproof he saw a hair-raising rubber frog, coated with phosphorescent paint which made it gleam in the dark, dancing back and forth in the nurse's hand and croaking horribly, *garuk, garuk, garuk,* as she attempted to attract the patient's attention. The fat man, more in response to the formidable protest rising from his own bowels than to stop the nurse for his son's sake, was about to utter something angrily when Eeyore succumbed to total panic, began to rotate around the axis of his father's arms, and kicked to the floor not only the doctor's pencil light and the rubber frog in the nurse's hand but a variety of objects on a small table diagonally in front of him. Even as he gave vent to a moan of rage in secret chorus with his son the fat man saw in a flash that Eeyore had brought clattering to the floor, in addition to several large books, a bowl of rice and fried eel which seemed to be the doctor's lunch. And from the abnormally rapid pitch of the examination after this, it was impossible to avoid the impression that the little doctor was indeed provoking his intractable patient, and out of anger which derived at least in part from hunger unappeased. This permitted them—the composite of his son and himself—to sample the pleasure of retaliation. At the same time, it was the basis for a very grave fear. Here was a doctor tired and hungry after a full morning of appointments, and now his lunch was in ruins, yet he lacked the courage openly to revile this idiot boy and his corpulent father who flaunted a letter of introduction from Professor of Medicine X— how could the fat man be sure the little man wouldn't work some subtle vengeance on his son's eyes? This new terror was accompanied by regret; the fat man withered.

The doctor loudly assembled his entire staff, and when the young patient had been stretched out on a bare, black leather bed, he gave triumphant instructions that all hands were to help to hold the boy down (the fat man just managed to appropriate for himself the task of securing Eeyore's head between his arms and pinning his chest beneath the weight of his whole body), and then jumped ahead to the second, unquestionably more complicated, stage of the examination, though it was clear that the first test had not been completed.

With Eeyore secured so firmly to the bed from head to foot that his only freedom was the screaming which wrenched open his mouth and bared his yellow teeth (it was impossible to train Eeyore to brush his teeth: he was terrified of opening his mouth under coercion from no matter who it came; even if you managed to work the toothbrush between his closed lips, he would act as if it hurt or sometimes tickled him and simply clamp down), the nurse placed at the head of his bed a slender aluminum rod bent into an oblong diamond so as to fashion a kind of forceps. The fat man had only to estimate that the slender, tapered apex of this instrument would be introduced beneath the eyelid and then opened to bare the eyeball for a throbbing pain to spread like fire from his own eyes to the central nerve of his brain. Ignoring him and his panic, the doctor squeezed two kinds of drops into Eeyore's eyes, which, though tightly closed, continued to spill tears like signals of the boy's protest. Eeyore renewed his screaming and the fat man shuddered violently. Only then would the doctor say, by way of information:

——This anesthetizes his eyes, so he won't feel any pain.

When the fat man heard this, the silver shimmer of pain connecting his eyes and the marrow of his brain flickered out. But Eeyore continued to moan, as if he were being strangled to death. The fat man, rubbing the tears out of his own eyes with the back of his hand, just managed to see the doctor insert the slender instrument under Eeyore's eyelid while the boy's moaning surged even higher and then completely bare the eyeball only inches away from him. It was truly a large sphere, egg-white in color, and what it felt like to the fat man was the earth itself, the entire world of man. At its center was a brown circle, softly blurred, from which the pupil, lighted with a poor, dull light, blankly and feebly gazed. What it expressed was dumbness and fear and pain, and it was working hard to focus on something, laboring to resolve the blurred whatever-it-was that kept cruelly bringing back the pain. With this eye the fat man identified all of himself. He was not in pain because of the drug, but there was a numbed sense of terror, of discord, in his heart, and this he had to battle as he gazed up helplessly at the crowd of faces bearing down on him. He nearly began to moan along with his son. But he could not help noticing that the brown blur of the eye conveying only dumbness and fear and pain was including his own face in its scrutiny of the crowd of Eeyore's unknown tormentors. A jagged fissure opened between himself and his son. And the fat man forced the first finger of his right hand between Eeyore's yellow, gnashing teeth (not until after his experience above the polar bears' pool would he recognize that he had done this because he was afraid of that fissure, afraid that if he saw to the bottom of it he would have to confront what certainly would have revealed itself there in its true form, the self-deception impregnating his conscious formulation Eeyore = the fat man), saw wasted blood begin to spurt in the same volume as the tears his son continued to weep, heard the sound of teeth grinding bone and, clamping his eyes shut, began to scream in chorus with his son.

When the fat man had received emergency treatment and descended to the waiting room, his wife reported to him, with Eeyore sitting at her side, still pale and limp but calm again, the little doctor's diagnosis. Eeyore's eyes, as with mice, had different fields of vision; like mice again, he was color blind; furthermore, he could not clearly resolve objects farther away than three feet, a condition impossible to correct at present, because, according to the doctor, the child had no desire to see objects in the distance clearly.

——That must be why Eeyore nearly rubs his face against the screen when he watches commercials on TV! The fat man's wife valued the practice of maintaining the will in good health at all times, and she spoke with emphasis in her attempt to raise the fat man from his gloom, as if she had discovered even in this hopeless diagnosis an analysis of benefit to herself.

——There are children with normal vision who rub the TV screen with their noses, too, the fat man protested apprehensively. That little doctor didn't do much of anything, you know, except frighten Eeyore and hurt him and make him cry. In which part of the examination is he supposed to have discovered all that calamity?

——I think it's true that Eeyore doesn't see distant objects clearly and doesn't want to, said the fat man's wife in a voice that was beginning honestly to reveal her own despondency. When I took him to the zoo, he didn't get the least bit excited about the real animals, and you know how he loves the animal pictures in this books—he just looked at the railings or the ground in front of him. Aren't most of the cages at the zoo more than three feet away?

The fat man resolved to take his son to the zoo. With his own eyes and ears for antennae and their clasped hands for a coil, he would broadcast live on their personal band a day at the zoo for Eeyore's sake.

And so it came about one morning in the winter of 196— that the fat man and his fat son set out for the zoo together. Eeyore's mother, anxious about the effect of the cold on his asthma, had bundled him into clothing until he couldn't have worn another scrap; and the fat man himself, who preferred the two of them to be dressed as nearly alike as possible, had outfitted him on their way to the station in a woolen stocking cap identical to the one he had worn out of the house. The result was that, even to his father, the boy looked like an Eskimo child just arrived from the Pole. This meant without question that in other eyes they must have appeared, not a robust, but simply corpulent, Eskimo father and son. Bundled up like a pair of sausages, they stepped onto the train with their hands clasped tightly and, sweat beading the bridges of their noses and all the skin beneath their clothing, a flush on their moon faces where they were visible between their stocking caps and the high collars of their overcoats, enjoyed its lulling vibrations.

Eeyore loved the thrill, which was why he liked bicycles, of entrusting himself to a sensation of precarious motion. Bu the thrill had to be insulated by the secure feeling that his own never very stable body was being protected by another, ideally his fat father's. Even when they took a cab, one of Eeyore's delights, if the fat man tried to remain inside to pay the fare after Eeyore and his mother had stepped into the street, the boy would disintegrate in a manner terrible to see. If ever he got lost from his father in a train, he would probably go mad. For the fat man, riding the train with his son who was so dependent on him, in the face of the strangers all around them, was a frank and unlimited satisfaction. And since, compared to the feelings he normally identified in the course of his life from day to day, this satisfaction was so pure and so dominant, he knew it did not have its source within himself, but was in fact the happiness rising like mist in his son's turbid, baffled mind, reaching him through their clasped hands and being clarified in his own consciousness. Moreover, by identifying his own satisfaction in this way, he was in turn introducing in Eeyore a new happiness, this time with focus and direction—such was the fat man's logic.

The doctor had suggested that Eeyore lacked the vision to see distinctly at a distance and apparently he was right, for Eeyore, unlike other children, was never fascinated by the scenery hurtling by outside. He took his enjoyment purely in the train's vibration and acceleration, in the sensation of motion. And when they pulled into a station, the opening and closing of the automatic door became the focus of his pleasure. Naturally, Eeyore had to observe this from less than three feet away, so the fat man and his son always stood at the pole in front of the door, even when there were empty seats.

Today, Eeyore was busily concerned with the fit of his new cap. And since his standard was not the cap's appearance but how it felt against his skin, it was not until, after a long series of adjustments, he finally pulled it down over his ears and even his eyelids that he discovered the final sense of stability and comfort. The fat man followed suit, and felt indeed that a stocking cap could not possibly be worn in greater comfort. At the station where they had to change trains, as they walked along the underground passage and climbed up and down stairs, the fat man often was aware of eyes mocking them as an outlandish pair. But far from feeling cowed, when he saw their squat, bulky image reflected in a show window in the underground arcade, he stopped and shouted hotly, as if they had the place all to themselves,

——Eeyore, look! A fat Eskimo father and son; we look really sharp!

Eeyore's hand functioned as a wall against other people, turning the fat man, who had to take tranquilizers when he went out alone, into such an extrovert. Holding his son's hand liberated him, allowing him to feel even in a crowd that they were all alone together and protected by a screen. Much to his father's relief, as Eeyore shuffled along cautiously, staring down at his feet as if to determine with his poor eyes whether the checkerboard pattern of the passage continued on a level or rose into a staircase, he repeated civilly,

——Eeyore, we look really sharp!

With the mediation of their hands, which were moist with sweat though it was before noon on a winter day, the fat man and his son were in a state of optimum communication when they reached the zoo at ten-thirty, so the fat man imagined to his satisfaction, exalted by the prospect of the experience still wholly in front of them. So when they approached the special enclosure called the Children's Zoo, where it was possible to fondle baby goats and lambs and little pigs and ageing geese and turkeys, and saw that it was too crowded with children on a school excursion to permit a sluggish little boy like Eeyore to work his way inside, they were not particularly disappointed. It was the fat man's wife who had wanted Eeyore to get within three feet of the animals in the first place, so he could observe and touch them. But the fat man had something different in mind. He intended to defy the eye doctor's diagnosis by functioning as Eeyore's eyes; he would focus sharply on the beasts in the distance and transmit their image to Eeyore through the coil of their clasped hands, whereupon his son's own vision, responding to this signal, would begin gradually to resolve its object. It was the realization of this procedure so like a dream that had brought the fat man to the zoo. Accordingly, after one look at the children brandishing bags of popcorn and paper cups of mudfish as they clamored with excitement in their eyes around the pitiful, down-sized animals in the special enclosure, the fat man turned away from the Children's Zoo and led Eeyore toward the larger, fiercer animal cages.

——Tell me, Eeyore! who comes to the zoo to see wild animals as friendly as cows! We're here to see the bears and the elephants and especially the lions, wouldn't you say, Eeyore? We're here to see the guys who would be our worst enemies if they weren't in cages! To this felt opinion the fat man's son did not respond directly, but as they passed the lion cages, like an animal cub born and abandoned in the heart of the jungle scenting the presence of dangerous beasts, he seemed to grow wary, and the fat man thrilled to the feeling that he had been attended and understood.

——Look, Eeyore, a tiger! You see the great big guy with deep black and yellow stripes and a few patches of white, you see him moving over there? Well, that's a tiger, Eeyore is watching a tiger! said the fat man

——Eeyore is watching a tiger, his son parroted, detecting the presence of something with a sense of smell which was certainly too acute and tightening his grip on his father's hand while with one poorly focused eye, his flushed moon-face consequently a-tilt, he continued to gaze vacantly at the spot where the bars sank into the concrete floor of the cage.

——Eeyore, look up at the sky. You see the black, bushy monster on the round, brown thing; that's an orangutan, Eeyore's watching a big ape!

Without letting go his hand the fat man stepped behind his son and with his free arm tilted back the boy's head and held it against his thigh. Eeyore, required to look obliquely upward, squinted into the glare of the clear winter sky, screwing his face into a scowl of delicate wrinkles which made him look all the more like an Eskimo child. Perhaps it wasn't a scowl at all but a smile of recognition, perhaps he had verified the orangutan squatting uneasily on an old car tire with the blue sky at his back, the fat man couldn't be sure.

——Eeyore's watching a big ape, the fat little boy intoned, his vocal cords communicating their tremor directly to his father's hand cupped around his chin.

The fat man maintained his grip on Eeyore's head, gambling that the orangutan would go into action. It had rained until dawn and there was still a rough wind up high, which gave the blue of the sky a hard brilliance rare for Tokyo. And the orangutan itself was as giant and as black as it could be, its outlines etched vividly into the sky at its back. Furthermore, as the fat man knew from a zoology magazine, this was a lethargic orangutan, for it happened to be afflicted with melancholia so severely that it needed daily stimulants just to stay alive. So this particular orangutan had all the requisites for a suitable object of Eeyore's vision. But unfortunately it appeared that the monkey's melancholia was indeed profound, for though it frequently peered down with suspicious eyes at the pair waiting so forbearingly in front of its cage, it gave no indication that it was even preparing to move. Eventually the brilliance of the sky began to tire even the fat man's eyes, until he was seeing the monkey as a kind of black halo. He finally led his son gloomily away from the orangutan's cage. He could feel himself beginning to tire already, and he was afraid the feeling might reach his son through the conduit of their clasped hands. Dreamily he considered the quantity of drugs the orangutan would consume in a day, and was badly shaken to remember that he had forgotten to take his own tranquilizers before leaving the house that morning.

But far from giving up, the fat man renewed his determination to function as a pipeline of vision connecting his son's brain with the dangerous beasts in the zoo. Possibly he was spurring himself lest he communicate to his son—echoing his father mechanically as he directed his vague, misfocused gaze not at the animals so much as the sparse grass growing between the cages and the railings, or the refuse lying there, or the fat pigeons pecking at the refuse with their silly, blunted beaks—a mood developing in himself of submission to that eye doctor who had performed all manner of cruelties in his soiled, baggy gown, the smoked meat of his insect's face twitching with tension, only to deliver his disheartening diagnosis. He was also resisting the deeprooted disgust which threatened to stain the twilight of his son's spirit along with his own head. The truth was that the odor of countless animal bodies and their excrement had nauseated the fat man and given him the beginnings of a migraine headache from the moment before they had entered the zoo. An abnormally sensitive nose was certainly one of the attributes which testified to the blood bond between them. Nonetheless, in defiance of every one of these baleful portents, the fat man continued to wander around the zoo, gripping his son's hand even tighter, addressing him with more spirit.

——Don't forget, Eeyore, that seeing means grasping something with your imagination. Even if you were equipped with normal optic nerves you wouldn't see a thing unless you felt like starting up your imagination about the animals here. Because the characters we're running into here at the zoo are a different story from the animals we're used to seeing every day that don't require any imagination at all to grasp. Take those hard, brown boards with all the sharp ridges that are jammed up in that muddy water over there. Eeyore! how would anybody without an imagination know those boards were crocodiles? Or those two sheets of yellow metal slowly swaying back and forth down there next to that mound of straw and dung, how would you know that was the head and part of the back of a rhinoceros? Eeyore! you got a good look at that large, gray, tree-stump of a thing, well that happened to be one of an elephant's ankles, but it's perfectly natural that looking at it didn't give you much of an impression that you'd seen an elephant—tell me, Eeyore, why should a little boy in an island country in Asia be born with an imagination for African elephants? Now if you should be asked when we get home whether you saw an elephant, just forget about that ridiculous hunk of tree-strump and think of the nice, accessible elephants like cartoons that you see in your picture books. And then go ahead and say, Eeyore saw an elephant! Not that the gray tree-stump back there isn't the real thing, it is, that's what they mean by a real elephant. But none of the normal children crowding this zoo is using genuine imagination to construct a real elephant from what he observes about that tree-stump; no, he's just replacing what he sees with the cartoon elephants in his head, so no one has any reason to be disappointed because you weren't so impressed when you encountered a real elephant!

While the fat man continued in this vein, speaking sometimes to himself and sometimes to his son, they made their way gradually up a sloping walk and wandered into a narrow passage which had been built to look like a rock canyon. The fat man talked on, but he was aware of a precarious balance being maintained at the outer edge of his consciousness, now directed inwardly and sealed, by jubilation at having escaped the crowds, and anxiety of a kind that somehow tightened his chest. And all of a

sudden there sprang up from the ground, where they had
been sitting in a circle, a group of men dressed like
laborers, shouting incomprehensibly, and the fat man
discovered that he and his son had been surrounded. Even
as panic mushroomed in the fat man, he wrested his
consciousness away from Eeyore, where it wanted to
remain, and cast it outward—not only had they left the
crowds behind, they had wandered into a cul-de-sac like a
small, stifling valley. It was the back of the polar bears'
enclosure; far below, on the other side of a cliff of natural
stones piled up to look like mountain rock, was a steep
ice-wall for the bears to roam and a pool for them to sport
in. To someone looking up from the other side, this place
would seem to be the peak of a high and unknown
mountain beyond an ice-wall and a sea: the fat man and
his son had wandered behind the set of a glacial mountain.
This secret passageway was probably used by the keepers
to gain entrance to the artificial Antarctic below when they
wanted to feed the bears or to clean the pool and the icy
slope, though it was hard to believe, judging from the
stench, that much cleaning was done. Now that the fat
man had his bearings, the stench emanating from the back
of the zoo, the animals' side, a very nearly antihuman
stench, was assaulting his body like an army of ants.

But who were these men? What were they doing
squatting at the back of this passageway? And why had
they surrounded the fat man and his son with such fierce
hostility for simply wandering in on them? The fat man
quickly concluded that they were young laborers who had
hidden themselves back here to gamble. From the private
room of his one-sided dialogue with Eeyore in which it
had been locked, he had only to expand his consciousness
outward to discover at once the signs of an interrupted

game, so openly had they been playing. In the course of a dialogue entirely personal to themselves, a dialogue which turned about the axis of their clasped hands, the fat man and his son had already invaded too deeply their den, in animal terms, their territory, to avoid a confrontation with the gamblers.

Still gripping his son's hand, the fat man began to back off, at a loss for the words he needed on the spur of the moment. But one of the men was already in position behind him, and another was pommeling him even while he attempted the move. A severe interrogation began, while several pairs of rough arms poked and pushed the fat man around. Are you a cop? An informer? Were you doing all that talking into a hidden mike so all your copper friends could hear you? As he was kicked and punched around, the fat man tried to explain, but what he said only angered the men. You were blabbing a mile a minute just now, and serious too, that's the way you talk to a kid like this? The fat man protested that his son was nearly blind in addition to being retarded, so that he had to explain their surroundings in detail or nothing made any sense. But how could a little idiot make sense of all those big words, and this kid really is an idiot, look at him, he don't look as if he understands a word we're saying! The fat man started to say that they communicated through their clasped hands, then simply closed his punched and swollen mouth with a feeling of futility. How could he hope to make these hoodlums understand the unique relationship he shared with his son! Instead of trying, he drew Eeyore protectively to himself, started to, when suddenly his hand had been wrenched away from the boy's hot, sweaty hand and he had been seized by the wrists and the ankles and hoisted into the air by several of the men, who continued to shower him with threats as they began to swing him back and forth as if to hurl him down to the polar bears. The fat man saw himself being swung back and forth as passively as a sack of flour at this outrageous height, saw clearly, if intermittently, the revolving sky and ground, the distant city, trees, and, directly beneath him, now at the hellishly deep bottom of a sheer drop, the polar bears' enclosure and pool. His panic and reflexive fear were buried under an avalanche of despair more grotesque and fundamental; he began to scream in a voice which was unfamiliar even to his own ears, screams that seemed to him must move all the animals in the zoo to begin howling in response. As he was swung out over the pool on the hoodlums' arms and reeled in and cast out again (the vigor of this seemed to anticipate hurling him all the way down to the polar bear submerged to its muddy yellow shoulders in the pool below), the fat man perceived, with the vividness of a mandala in which, like revelation itself, time and space are intermingled in a variety of ways, the despair gripping him as a compound of the following three sentiments: a) Even if these hoodlums understood that I'm not an informer, they could easily throw me to the polar bear for the sake of a little fun, just to protract their excitement. The fact is, they're capable of that; b) I'll either be devoured by a polar bear whose anger will be justified because its territory really will have been invaded, or I'll be wounded and drown in that filthy water, too weak to swim. Even if I escape all that, I'll probably go mad in thirty seconds or so—if it was madness that drove my father to confine himself for all those years until he died, how can I escape madness myself when his blood runs in me? c) Eeyore has always had to go through me to reach his only window of understanding on the outside world; when madness converts the passageway itself into a ruined maze, he'll have to back up into a state of idiocy even darker than before, he'll become a kind of abused animal cub and never recover; in other words, two people are about to be destroyed.

The tangle of these emotions confronted the fat man with a bottomless darkness of grief and futile rage and he allowed himself to tumble screaming and shouting into its depths and as he tumbled, screaming into the darkness, he saw his own eye, an eye laid bare, the pupil which filled its brown, blurred center expressing fear and pain only: an animal eye. There was a heavy splash, the fat man was soaked in filthy spray, the claws and heavy paws of maddened, headlong polar bears rasped and thudded around him. But it was a piece of rock broken from the cliff which had been dropped, the fat man was still aloft in the hoodlums' arms. He was becoming a single, colossal eye being lofted into the air, the egg-white sphere was the entirety of the world he had lived, the entirety of himself, and within its softly blurred, brown center, fear and pain and the stupor of madness were whirling around and around in a tangle like the pattern inside a colored glass bead. The fat man no longer had the presence of mind to trouble himself about his son. No longer was he even the fat man. He was an egg-white eye, a one-hundred-and-seventy-pound, enormous eye. . . .

Night had fallen on the zoo when the fat man completed his gradual return from a giant eye to himself (he assumed from the savage odor of his skin and clothing, which was like a dirty finger probing in his chest, that he had actually fallen into the pool, and learned only later that he had been splashed by a rock), and began to enquire frantically about his son, who, for all he knew, having become a kind of animal cub, was already dead of frenzy. But the veterinarian (!) taking care of him at first insisted there had been no talk about a small boy, and then tried to use the subject to make the fat man remember what had happened to himself. According to this animal doctor, he had been discovered after closing time when the zoo was being cleaned, weeping in a public toilet in roughly the opposite direction from the polar bears' enclosure, and for several hours thereafter had only mumbled deliriously about his son. The fat man insisted he had no memory of his movements during the nine or so hours of his madness. Then he grabbed the veterinarian and begged him to find the little boy either dead of frenzy already or soon to be dead. Presently an employee came in to the office where the fat man had been stretched out on a cot (there were several kinds of stuffed animals in evidence), and reported that he had himself taken a stray child to the police. His panic unabated, the fat man went to the police station and there re-encountered Eeyore. His fat son had just finished a late supper with some young policemen and was thanking them individually:

——Eeyore, the pork noodles in broth and Pepsi-Cola were good! Asked for proof that he was the child's guardian, the fat man finally had to telephone his wife and then wait in the police station until she arrived to take them home.

It was in this manner that a cruel freedom was enforced on the fat man. It came his way just four years and two months after the abnormal birth of Mori, his son.

The fat man's this-time conscious battle for yet another freedom did elicit a printed notice from his

208

mother, but beyond that the front did not advance; for she would not respond further, and continued to ignore her son's repeated letters and phone calls. She refused to accept the letters, and would not come to the phone when he called.

Late one night after several weeks of this, the fat man renewed his determination and once again telephoned his mother. The village operator took the phone call in standard, formal Japanese, but when she came back on the line after a minute of silence, she addressed the fat man directly by name (since he was the only Tokyo resident to place long-distance calls to this little valley, the operator knew from whom and to whom the call came as soon as she heard the number being called, and would probably eavesdrop, something which occurred to the fat man but which he was too distracted to pursue), and then apologized to him in excessively familiar dialect which conveyed her sympathy and confusion:

——There's no answer again tonight, no matter how many times I ring. She (meaning the fat man's mother, living alone in the family house) never goes anywhere, and it's the middle of the night besides—she doesn't come to the phone on purpose every time you call! That isn't right, you want me to hop over on my bike and wake her up?

So the fat man asked this special favor of the operator and before long the phone was answered. Not that his mother said anything, merely lifted the receiver and held it in silence. As soon as he had cleared his mind of the friendly operator, who had probably hurried back to the switchboard on her bicycle (professional duty!) and was listening in, the fat man began a somehow persuasive, somehow threatening speech to his silent mother:

——Who did you think was going to believe the lies in that announcement? And sending it to my wife's relatives!

Mother, if I'm crazy from a disease I picked up abroad and if the baby was born abnormal as a result, then the baby's mother has to be infected too, isn't that so? But you sent your announcement directly to my wife, the baby's mother, Mother! Now that's all I need to tell me that you don't even believe yourself what you insinuated about my disease and my madness. . . . Or have you gone into that old act about being mad yourself? Well that routine is too old, you won't fool anybody that way. And let me tell you something, if you can pretend to be mad well enough to fool someone again then you're not pretending anymore, you really have gone mad! . . . Mother, why won't you speak? You're hiding my notes because you're afraid if I publish something about Father every one who knows the family will think he was mad, and that his blood runs in all the children, and that my son is the living proof of that, isn't that so? And you're afraid of the humiliation that would be to my brothers and sisters, isn't that so? But don't you realize that pretending to be crazy and advertising that an evil disease has made me mad is going to result in something even worse? . . . Mother, I haven't made up my mind that Father died of madness, I just want to know what really happened. My older brothers were in the army and the others were just kids, so I'm the only one of the children who remembers Father letting out a scream all of a sudden and then dying in that storehouse he'd locked himself in, that's why I want to know what that was all about. You ask why it's only me, only me of all the children who keeps worrying about Father's last years and death, I'll tell you why, Mother, because I really have to know. You used to say to me when you brushed me aside, "The other boys have important things on their minds, and you ask questions like that!" but to me it is important to know what really happened. . . . Mother, if I don't find out, I have a feeling that sooner or later I'll confine myself in a storehouse of my own, and one day I'll scream all of a sudden and the next morning my wife will be telling Eeyore just what you once told me and nothing more, "Your father has passed away, you mustn't cry or spit or make big or little business thoughtlessly, especially when you're facing West!" . . . Mother, you must remember a lot about Father. . . . Didn't you ask my wife not to take "sonny boy" seriously if he started glorifying his father's behavior during his last years? My father happens to have spent his last years sitting in a storehouse without moving, with his eyes and ears covered—didn't you tell my wife not to believe for a minute that he'd done that as a protest against the times, because he wanted to deny the reality of a world in which Japan was making war on the China he revered? Didn't you tell her it was simply madness that made him do what he did? Didn't you even say that Father had been as fat as a pig when he died because he'd been stuffing himself with everything he could lay hands on without moving anything but his mouth, and then insinuate that he had hidden himself in that storehouse because he was ashamed of being the only fat man around at a time when food was so scarce? You tell my wife all that and you won't talk to me at all, you even steal the notes I've made about things I've managed to remember by myself, how can you do that Mother? . . . That morning my wife had the illusion I was about to hang myself, you told her my father was never in earnest; that he knew everything he did was fake, because he told himself he was not in earnest whenever he began something, but he didn't notice the effect it was actually having on him however little at a time, wasn't conscious of it, and that it

was too late when he did notice. Tell me, Mother, what is
it my father did that was not in earnest? What was too
late? . . . Mother, if you intend to continue ignoring me, I
have some thoughts of my own: I'll sit down in a dark
room just as Father did, with sunglasses on and plugs in
my ears, and I'll show you what fat can really be, I'm
already a tub of lard, you know, and when I eventually let
out my big scream and die, what do you intend to do,
Mother, console my wife by telling her again that "sonny
boy" and his father noticed whatever it is they noticed too
late? Do you intend to say Foolishness! again, and play the
Grand Lady? . . . I've only learned this recently, but it
seems my son can get along without me, as an idiot in an
idiot's way, and that means I'm free now, I'm as good as
liberated from my son, so from now on I can concentrate
exclusively on my Father; I'm free to sit myself in a
barber's chair in a dark storehouse until the day I die just
as Father did. . . . Mother, why do you keep repudiating
me with silence? I keep telling you, I only want to get at
the truth about my Father's last years. . . . I don't really
care about writing his biography, even if I do write
something I'll promise never to have it published if that's
what you want, do you still refuse to talk to me? . . . If you
won't be convinced that I'm telling the truth when I say I
only want to know what really happened, then let me tell
you something, Mother, I can write up a biography of
Father that chronicles his madness and ends in suicide any
time I want, and I can have it published, too. And if I did
that, you could spend every penny of your estate on paper
and printing and mailing announcements, and people in
numbers you couldn't possibly match would believe what
I had to say and not you! What I'm telling you is that I
don't care so much about getting back my manuscript, I

just want to hear the truth from you, because I have to have it, Mother, I need it. . . . Believe me, there'd be no problem if it were the manuscript I needed, I can probably recite it for you right now, listen: "My father began his retreat from the world because . . ."

Quietly, but firmly, the phone was hung up. The fat man returned, pale with cold and despair, to his bed, pulled the covers over his head and for a long time lay trembling. And he wept furtively, as he had wept that night after his experience above the polar bears' enclosure. He remembered how long it had been since he had actually heard his mother's voice. This last time it was through his wife that he had finally managed to learn what she had said about his dead father. When it came to talk of his father in particular, he couldn't even recall when last he had heard his mother's voice. When she spoke to his wife, she had apparently referred to his father as "the man." The Man. The fat man was reminded of a line from a wartime poem by an English poet, actually it resided in him always, as if it were his prayer. Like the Pure Land hymns which had resided in his grandmother until the day she died, it was part of his body and his spirit. And the poem itself happened to be a prayer spoken at the height of the very battle in which his father had lost his Chinese friends one after the other. The voice of Man: "O, teach us to outgrow our madness." If that voice is the voice of the Man, then "our madness" means the Man's and mine, the fat man told himself for the first time. In the past, whenever he whispered the poem to himself as though in prayer, "our madness" had always meant his own and his son Eeyore's. But now he was positive that only himself and *the Man* were included. The Man had deposited his massive body in the barber chair he had installed in a dark

213

storehouse, covered his eyes and ears, and tirelessly prayed, "Teach us to outgrow our madness, mine and his!" The Man's madness is my madness, the fat man insisted stubbornly to himself, his son already banished beyond the borders of his consciousness. But what right did his mother have to obstruct the passageway leading from himself toward the Man's madness? The fat man wasn't weeping any more, but he was still trembling so that the sheets rustled, not with cold but rage alone.

Once he had adjusted his perspective in this way, the fat man no longer equated himself and Eeyore, even when he considered the hoodlums' attack above the polar bears' pool. He was even able to feel, precisely because it had liberated him from bondage to his son, that the experience had been beneficial. What kept his already ignited anger aflame was his knowledge that his own mother had so long prevented him, in danger even now of being hurled to a polar bear of madness, from discovering the true meaning of that appeal to which *the Man* may have been so close to hearing an answer at the end of his life, "Teach us to outgrow our madness."

The fat man finally fell asleep, but his fury survived even in his dream: his hot hand was clutched in the hand of a hippopotamus of a man sitting with his back to him in a barber chair in a dark storehouse, and fury flowed back and forth between them as rapidly as an electric current. But no matter how long he waited, the fuming giant continued to stare into the darkness and would not turn around to face the fat child who was himself.

When the fat man woke up, he readied himself for a final assault on his mother and swore to begin a new chronicle of the Man's madness in his last years and to

214

undertake an investigation into outgrowing "our madness," *the Man's* and his own. But once again he was beaten to the offensive. During the night, while he had been weeping and raging and having dreams, his mother had been so prudent as to contrive a strategy of her own, and by dawn had even drafted a new announcement in which she broke a silence of twenty years and spoke of her dead husband. Only two days after his phone call, the notes and incomplete manuscript for the biography in which he had attempted to reconstruct an entire image of his dead father arrived at the fat man's house, registered mail, special delivery. That same week, delayed by only the number of days it had taken the printer to fill the order but unquestionably written the same night as the fat man's call, a new announcement also arrived, addressed to the fat man's wife, registered mail, special delivery:

> *Recently it was my duty to inform you that my third son had lost his mind. I must now announce that I was mistaken in this, and ask you kindly to forget it. Apropos this season of the year, I am reminded that my late husband, having had an acquaintance with the officers involved in a certain coup d'état, was led upon its failure to the dreadful conclusion that no course of action remained but the assassination of his Imperial Majesty. It was the horror of this which moved him to confine himself in a storehouse, where he remained until his death.*
>
> *The cause of death, let me conclude, was heart failure; the death certificate is on file at the county office. Begging to inform you of the above, I remain,*
>
> *Sincerely yours,*
Signed

215

winter, 196—

But who will save the people?
I close my eyes and think:
A world without conspirators!

—*Choku*

Although she had not appeared much moved by the first announcement, this one jolted the fat man's wife surprisingly. For most of an evening she read it over to herself and only then, having reached no conclusions of her own, informed the fat man that it had arrived and showed it to him. Only when the fat man had read it over to himself and was simply standing in silence with the announcement in his hand did she speak up and disclose the substance of her agitation:

——You remember your mother asked me not to take you seriously if you started glorifying your father's last years? Do you think she decided to bring all this to light because you've finally made her begin to hate you with your attacks on her? Do you think your mother has made up her mind to renounce you, and this is her way of saying, imitate your father all you want, nothing you do is her responsibility any more?

Since the shock which the fat man had received himself came from an entirely different aspect of the announcement, he could only pursue his own distress in silence. The minute he read it he had sensed that this blow, like the blow he had received through Eeyore, was aimed at something fundamental in himself and could be neither countered nor returned. For several days he tried to discredit his mother's account of his father by checking it against what he remembered from his childhood and what he had heard. But among all the details he had collected in order to write the biography, he could find nothing which mortally contradicted the announcement.

His grandmother had said more than once that his father had been attacked by an assassin with a Japanese sword, and that he had managed to escape harm by sitting perfectly still in the dark storehouse without offering any resistance. The assassin was probably one of the band which had been associated with his father through the junior officers in the revolt. And he must have been a man with no more stomach than his father for an actual uprising or for individual action in the next stage of the revolt. He had tracked down a craven like himself to the place where he was living in self-confinement, and brandished his Japanese sword and threatened emptily, but that was all he had ever intended to do.

Then there was the drama commemorating a certain coup d'état, one of the fat man's reveries since his youth, in which the widows of the junior officers who had been involved, old women now and incarcerated in a rest home, playing themselves as young wives thirty-five years earlier, attacked with drawn daggers a man seated with his back to them in a barber chair, "the highest Authority to have abandoned the insurgents; or—a private citizen who sympathized politically, provided funds, and was generally in league with the junior officers until the day of the revolt, finally betrayed them, dropped out of the uprising, and spent what remained of his life hiding in a storehouse in his country village." The idea undoubtedly had its distant source in things the fat man had been told as a child, probably in such a way as to hint even that long ago at the contents of his mother's announcement. At any rate, he must have known vaguely that there was some

217

connection between his father and that attempted coup, for he had spoken about it to his wife. It was on a stormy night some time ago, and he had been relating a perfectly normal memory which had renewed itself in him, of his father telling him as a child, on another stormy night, that life was like a family emerging from the darkness, coming together for a brief time around a lighted candle, and then disappearing one by one into their own darkness once again.

For a week, the fat man studied his mother's announcement and pored over the notes and fragments of manuscript which he had written for his dead father's biography. And then early one morning (he hadn't been to sleep at all; that entire week he had slept only four or five hours a night and, except for quick meals, had remained in his study) he went into the garden in back of his house and incinerated a sheaf of pages which contained every word he had written about his father. He also burned a picture card which had been thumbtacked above his desk ever since he had brought it back from New York, of a sculpture, a plaster-of-Paris man who resembled his father as he fancied him, about to straddle a plaster-of-Paris bicycle. He then informed his wife, who was out of bed now and getting breakfast ready, that he had changed his mind about a plan which until then he had opposed. It was a plan to get eyeglasses for Eeyore and to place him in an institution for retarded children. The fat man knew that his wife had gone back to that eye doctor without his permission and persuaded him to prescribe a special pair of glasses, probably by groveling in front of the little man, which she was secretly training Eeyore to wear. The fat man had been severed from his son already, they were free of one another. And now he had confirmed that, in

218

the same way, he had been severed from his dead father and was free. His father had not gone mad, and even if he had, insofar as there was a clear reason for his madness, it was something altogether different from his own. Gradually he had been giving up his habit of bicycling off with Eeyore to eat pork noodles in broth; and although, as he approached the age at which his father had begun his self-confinement, his tastes had inclined toward fatty things such as pigs' feet Korean style, he was losing once again almost all positive desire for food.

The fat man began taking a sauna bath once a week and sweating his corpulence away. And one bright spring morning he had come out of the sauna and was taking his shower when he discovered a swarthy stranger who was nonetheless of tremendous concern to him standing right in front of his eyes. Perhaps his confusion had to do with the steam fogging the mirror—there was no question that he was looking at himself.

The man peered closely at the figure standing alone in the mirror and identified several portents of madness. Now he had neither a father nor a son with whom to share the madness closing in on him. He had only the freedom to confront it by himself.

The man decided not to write a biography of his dead father. Instead, he sent repeated letters to *the Man*, whose existence nowhere was evident now, "Teach us to outgrow our madness," and jotted down a few lines which always opened with the words "I begin my retreat from the world because ..." And as if he intended these notes to be discovered after his death, he locked them in a drawer and never showed them to anyone.

AGHWEE THE SKY MONSTER

Alone in my room, I wear a piratical black patch over my right eye. The eye may look all right, but the truth is I have scarcely any sight in it. I say scarcely, it isn't totally blind. Consequently, when I look at this world with both eyes I see two worlds perfectly superimposed, a vague and shadowy world on top of one that's bright and vivid. I can be walking down a paved street when a sense of peril and unbalance will stop me like a rat just scurried out of a sewer, dead in my tracks. Or I'll discover a film of unhappiness and fatigue on the face of a cheerful friend and clog the flow of an easy chat with my stutter. I suppose I'll get used to this eventually. If I don't, I intend to wear my patch not only in my room when I'm alone but on the street and with my friends. Strangers may pass with condescending smiles—what an old-fashioned joke!—but I'm old enough not to be annoyed by every little thing.

The story I intend to tell is about my first experience earning money; I began with my right eye because the memory of that experience ten years ago revived in me abruptly and quite out of context when violence was done to my eye last spring. Remembering, I should add, I was freed from the hatred uncoiling in my heart and beginning to fetter me. At the very end I'll talk about the accident itself.

Ten years ago I had twenty-twenty vision. Now one of my eyes is ruined. *Time* shifted, launched itself from the springboard of an eyeball squashed by a stone. When I first met that sentimental madman I had only a child's understanding of *time*. I was yet to have the cruel awareness of *time* drilling its eyes into my back and *time* lying in wait ahead.

Ten years ago I was eighteen, five feet six, one hundred and ten pounds, had just entered college and was looking for a part-time job. Although I still had trouble reading French, I wanted a cloth-bound edition in two volumes of *L'Âme Enchanté*. It was a Moscow edition, with not only a foreword but footnotes and even the colophon in Russian and wispy lines like bits of thread connecting the letters of the French text. A curious edition to be sure, but sturdier and more elegant than the French, and much cheaper. At the time I discovered it in a bookstore specializing in East European publications I had no interest in Romain Rolland, yet I went immediately into action to make the volumes mine. In those days I often

224

succumbed to some weird passion and it never bothered me, I had the feeling there was nothing to worry about so long as I was sufficiently obsessed.

As I had just entered college and wasn't registered at the employment center, I looked for work by making the rounds of people I knew. Finally my uncle introduced me to a banker who came up with an offer. "Did you happen to see a movie called *Harvey?*" he asked. I said yes, and tried for a smile of moderate but unmistakable dedication, appropriate for someone about to be employed for the first time. *Harvey* was that Jimmy Stewart film about a man living with an imaginary rabbit as big as a bear; it had made me laugh so hard I thought I would die. "Recently, my son has been having the same sort of delusions about living with a monster." The banker didn't return my smile. "He's stopped working and stays in his room. I'd like him to get out from time to time but of course he'd need a— companion. Would you be interested?"

I knew quite a bit about the banker's son. He was a young composer whose avant-garde music had won prizes in France and Italy and who was generally included in the photo roundups in the weekly magazines, the kind of article they always called "Japan's Artists of Tomorrow." I had never heard his major works, but I had seen several films he had written the music for. There was one about the adventures of a juvenile delinquent that had a short, lyrical theme played on the harmonica. It was beautiful. Watching the picture, I remember feeling vaguely troubled by the idea of an adult nearly thirty years old (in fact, the composer was twenty-eight when he hired me, my present age), working out a theme for the harmonica, I suppose because my own harmonica had become my little brother's property when I had entered elementary school.

225

And possibly because I knew more about the composer, whose name was D, than just public facts; I knew he had created a scandal. Generally I have nothing but contempt for scandals, but I knew that the composer's infant child had died, that he had gotten divorced as a result, and that he was rumored to be involved with a certain movie actress. I hadn't known that he was in the grips of something like the rabbit in Jimmy Stewart's movie, or that he had stopped working and secluded himself in his room. How serious was his condition, I wondered, was it a case of nervous breakdown, or was he clearly schizo-phrenic?

"I'm not certain I know just what you mean by companion," I said, reeling in my smile. "Naturally, I'd like to be of service if I can." This time, concealing my curiosity and apprehension I tried to lend my voice and expression as much sympathy as possible without seeming forward. It was only a part-time job, but it was the first chance of employment I had had and I was determined to do my accommodating best.

"When my son decides he wants to go somewhere in Tokyo, you go along—just that. There's a nurse at the house and she has no trouble handling him, so you don't have to worry about violence." The banker made me feel like a soldier whose cowardice had been discovered. I blushed and said, trying to recover lost ground, "I'm fond of music, and I respect composers more than anyone, so I look forward to accompanying D and talking with him."

"All he thinks about these days is this thing in his head, and apparently that's all he talks about!" The banker's brusqueness made my face even redder. "You can go out to see him tomorrow," he said.

"At—your house?"

226

"That's right, did you think he was in an asylum?" From the banker's tone of voice I could only suppose that he was at bottom a nasty man.

"If I should get the job," I said with my eyes on the floor, "I'll drop by again to thank you." I could easily have cried.

"No, he'll be hiring you (All right then, I resolved defiantly, I'll call D my employer), so that won't be necessary. All I care about is that he doesn't get into any trouble outside that might develop into a scandal. . . . There's his career to think about. Naturally, what he does reflects on me—"

So that was it! I thought, so I was to be a moral sentinel guarding the banker's family against a second contamination by the poisons of scandal. Of course I didn't say a thing, I only nodded dependably, anxious to warm the banker's chilly heart with the heat of reliance on me. I didn't even ask the most pressing question, something truly difficult to ask: This monster haunting your son, sir, is it a rabbit like Harvey, nearly six feet tall? A creature covered in bristly hair like an Abominable Snowman? What kind of a monster is it? In the end I remained silent and consoled myself with the thought that I might be able to pry the secret out of the nurse if I made friends with her.

Then I left the executive's office, and as I walked along the corridor grinding my teeth in humiliation as if I were Julien Sorel after a meeting with someone important I became self-conscious to the tips of my fingers and tried assessing my attitude and its effectiveness. When I got out of college I chose not to seek nine-to-five employment, and I do believe the memory of my dialogue with that disagreeable banker played a large part in my decision.

227

Even so, when classes were over the next day I took a train out to the residential suburb where the composer lived. As I passed through the gate of that castle of a house, I remember a roaring of terrific beasts, as at a zoo in the middle of the night. I was dismayed, I cowered, what if those were the screams of my employer? A good thing it didn't occur to me then that those savage screams might have been coming from the monster haunting D like Jimmy Stewart's rabbit. Whatever they were, it was so clear that the screaming had rattled me that the maid showing me the way was indiscreet enough to break into a laugh. Then I discovered someone else laughing, voicelessly, in the dimness beyond a window in an annex in the garden. It was the man who was supposed to employ me; he was laughing like a face in a movie without a sound track. And boiling all around him was that howling of wild beasts. I listened closely and realized that several of the same animals were shrieking in concert. And in voices too shrill to be of this world. Abandoned by the maid at the entrance to the annex, I decided the screaming must be part of the composer's tape collection, regained my courage, straightened up and opened the door.

Inside, the annex reminded me of a kindergarten. There were no partitions in the large room, only two pianos, an electric organ, several tape recorders, a record player, something we had called a "mixer" when I was in the high-school radio club—there was hardly room to step. A dog asleep on the floor, for example, turned out to be a tuba of reddish brass. It was just as I had imagined a composer's studio; I even had the illusion I had seen the place before. His father had said D had stopped working and secluded himself in his room, could he have been mistaken?

The composer was just bending to switch off the tape recorder. Enveloped in a chaos that was not without its own order, he moved his hands swiftly and in an instant those beastly screams were sucked into a dark hole of silence. Then he straightened and turned to me with a truly tranquil smile.

Having glanced around the room and seen that the nurse was not present I was a little wary, but the composer gave me no reason in the world to expect that he was about to get violent.

"My father told me about you. Come in, there's room over there," he said in a low, resonant voice.

I took off my shoes and stepped up onto the rug without putting on slippers. Then I looked around for a place to sit, but except for a round stool in front of the piano and the organ, there wasn't a bit of furniture in the room, not even a cushion. So I brought my feet together between a pair of bongo drums and some empty tape boxes and there I stood uncomfortably. The composer stood there too, arms hanging at his sides. I wondered if he ever sat down. He didn't ask me to be seated either, just stood there silent and smiling.

"Could those have been monkey voices?" I said, trying to crack a silence that threatened to set more quickly than any cement.

"Rhinoceros—they sounded that way because I speeded the machine up. And I had the volume way up, too. At least I think they're rhinoceros—rhino is what I asked for when I had this tape made—of course I can't really be sure. But now that you're here, I'll be able to go to the zoo myself."

"I may take that to mean that I'm employed?"

"Of course! I didn't have you come out here to test

you. How can a lunatic test a normal person?" The man who was to be my employer said this objectively and almost as if he were embarrassed. Which made me feel disgusted with the obsequiousness of what I had said—I may take that to mean that I'm employed? I had sounded like a shopkeeper! The composer was different from his businessman father and I should have been more direct with him.

"I wish you wouldn't call yourself a lunatic. It's awkward for me." Trying to be frank was one thing, but what a brainless remark! But the composer met me half way, "All right, if that's how you feel. I suppose that would make work easier."

Work is a vague word, but, at least during those few months when I was visiting him once a week, the composer didn't get even as close to work as going to the zoo to record a genuine rhino for himself. All he did was wander around Tokyo in various conveyances or on foot and visit a variety of places. When he mentioned work, he must therefore have had me in mind. And I worked quite a lot; I even went on a mission for him all the way to Kyoto.

"Then when should I begin?" I said.

"Right away if it suits you. Now."

"That suits me fine."

"I'll have to get ready—would you wait outside?"

Head lowered cautiously, as though he were walking in a swamp, my employer picked his way to the back of the room past musical instruments and sound equipment and piles of manuscript to a black wooden door which he opened and then closed behind him. I got a quick look at a woman in a nurse's uniform, a woman in her early forties with a longish face and heavy shadows on her cheeks that might have been wrinkles or maybe scars. She seemed to encircle the composer with her right arm as she ushered him inside, while with her left hand she closed the door. If this was part of the routine, I would never have a chance to talk with the nurse before I went out with my employer. Standing in front of the closed door, in the darkest part of that dim room, I shuffled into my shoes and felt my anxiety about this job of mine increase. The composer had smiled the whole time and when I had prompted him he had replied. But he hadn't volunteered much. Should I have been more reserved? Since outside might have meant two things and since I was determined that everything should be perfect on my first job, I decided to wait just inside the main gate, from where I could see the annex in the garden.

D was a small, thin man, but with a head that seemed larger than most. To make the bony cliff of his forehead look a little less forbidding he combed his pale, well-washed, and fluffy hair down over his brow. His mouth and jaw were small, and his teeth were horribly irregular. And yet, probably due to the color of his deeply recessed eyes, there was a static correctness about his face that went well with a tranquil smile. As for the overall impression, there was something canine about the man. He wore flannel trousers and a sweater with stripes like fleas. His shoulders were a little stooped, his arms outlandishly long.

When he came out of the back door of the annex, my employer was wearing a blue wool cardigan over his other sweater and a pair of white tennis shoes. He reminded me of a grade-school music teacher. In one hand he held a black scarf, and as if he were puzzling whether to wrap it around his neck, there was perplexity in his grin to me as I waited at the gate. For as long as I knew D, except at the very end when he was lying in a hospital bed, he was always dressed this way. I remember his outfit so well because I was always struck by something comical about an adult man wearing a cardigan around his shoulders, as if he were a woman in disguise. Its shapelessness and nondescript color made that sweater perfect for him. As the composer pigeon-toed toward me past the shrubbery, he absently lifted the hand that held the scarf and signaled me with it. Then he wrapped the scarf resolutely around his neck. It was already four in the afternoon and fairly cold out-of-doors.

D went through the gate, and as I was following him (our relationship was already that of employer and employee) I had the feeling I was being watched and turned around: behind the same window through which I had discovered my employer, that forty-year-old nurse with the scarred—or were they wrinkled?—cheeks was watching us the way a soldier remaining behind might see a deserter off, her lips clamped shut like a turtle's. I resolved to get her alone as soon as I could to question her about D's condition. What was wrong with the woman, anyway? Here she was taking care of a young man with a nervous condition, maybe a madman, yet when her charge went out she had nothing to say to his companion! Wasn't that professional negligence? Wasn't she at least obliged to fill in the new man on the job? Or was my employer a patient so gentle and harmless that nothing had to be said?

When he got to the sidewalk D shuttered open his tired-looking eyes in their deep sockets and glanced swiftly up and down the deserted, residential street. I didn't know whether it was an indication of madness or what—sudden action without any continuity seemed to be a habit of his. The composer looked up at the clear, end-of-autumn sky, blinking rapidly. Though they were sunken, there was something remarkably expressive about his deep brown eyes. Then he stopped blinking and his eyes seemed to focus, as though he were searching the sky. I stood obliquely behind him, watching, and what impressed me most vividly was the movement of his Adam's apple, which was large as any fist. I wondered if he had been destined to become a large man; perhaps something had impeded his growth in infancy and now only his head from the neck up bespoke the giant he was meant to be.

Lowering his gaze from the sky, my employer found and held my puzzled eyes with his own and said casually, but with a gravity that made objection impossible, "On a clear day you can see things floating up there very well. He's up there with them, and frequently he comes down to me when I go outdoors."

Instantly I felt threatened. Looking away from my employer, I wondered how to survive this first ordeal that had confronted me so quickly. Should I pretend to believe in "him," or would that be a mistake? Was I dealing with a raving madman, or was the composer just a poker-faced humorist trying to have some fun with me? As I stood there in distress, he extended me a helping hand: "I know you can't see the figures floating in the sky, and I know you wouldn't be aware of him even if he were right here at my side. All I ask is that you don't act amazed when he comes down to earth, even if I talk to him. Because you'd upset him if you were to break out laughing all of a sudden or tried to shut me up. And if you happen to notice when we're talking that I want some support from you, I'd appreciate it if you'd chime right in and say something, you know, affirmative. You see, I'm explaining Tokyo to him as if it were a paradise. It might seem a lunatic paradise to you, but maybe you could think of it as a satire and be affirmative anyway, at least when he's down here with me."

I listened carefully and thought I could make out at least the contours of what my employer expected of me. Then was he a rabbit as big as a man after all, nesting in the sky? But that wasn't what I asked; I permitted myself to ask only: "How will I know when he's down here with you?"

"Just by watching me; he only comes down when I'm outside."

"How about when you're in a car?"

"In a car or a train, as long as I'm next to an open window he's likely to show up. There have been times when he's appeared when I was in the house, just standing next to an open window."

"And . . . right now?" I asked uncomfortably. I must have sounded like the class dunce who simply cannot grasp the multiplication principle.

"Right now it's just you and me," my employer said graciously. "Why don't we ride in to Shinjuku today; I haven't been on a train in a long time."

We walked to the station, and all the way I kept an eye peeled for a sign that something had appeared at my employer's side. But before I knew it we were on the train and, so far as I could tell, nothing had materialized. One thing I did notice: the composer ignored the people who passed us on the street even when they greeted him. As if he himself did not exist, as if the people who approached with hellos and how-are-yous were registering an illusion which they mistook for him, my employer utterly ignored all overtures to contact.

The same thing happened at the ticket window; D

declined to relate to other people. Handing me one thousand yen he told me to buy tickets, and then refused to take his own even when I held it out to him. I had to stop at the gate and have both our tickets punched while D swept through the turnstile onto the platform with the freedom of the invisible man. Even on the train, he behaved as if the other passengers were no more aware of him than of the atmosphere; huddling in a seat in the farthest corner of the car, he rode in silence with his eyes closed. I stood in front of him and watched in growing apprehension for whatever it was to float in through the open window and settle at his side. Naturally, I didn't believe in the monster's existence. It was just that I was determined not to miss the instant when D's delusions took hold of him; I felt I owed him that much in return for the money he was paying me. But, as it happened, he sat like some small animal playing dead all the way to Shinjuku Station, so I could only surmise that he hadn't had a visit from the sky. Of course, supposition was all it was: as long as other people were around us, my employer remained a sullen oyster of silence. But I learned soon enough that my guess had been correct. Because when the moment came it was more than apparent (from D's reaction, I mean) that something was visiting him.

We had left the station and were walking down the street. It was that time of day a little before evening when not many people are out, yet we ran across a small crowd gathered on a corner. We stopped to look; surrounded by the crowd, an old man was turning around and around in the street without a glance at anyone. A dignified-looking old man, he was spinning in a frenzy, clutching a brief-case and an umbrella to his breast, mussing his gray, pomaded hair a little as he stamped his feet and barked like a seal. The faces in the watching crowd were lusterless and dry in the evening chill that was stealing into the air; the old man's face alone was flushed, and sweating, and seemed about to steam.

Suddenly I noticed that D, who should have been standing at my side, had taken a few steps back and had thrown one arm around the shoulders of an invisible something roughly his own height. Now he was peering affectionately into the space slightly above the empty circle of his arm. The crowd was too intent on the old man to be concerned with D's performance, but I was terrified. Slowly the composer turned to me, as if he wanted to introduce me to a friend. I didn't know how to respond; all I could do was panic and blush. It was like forgetting your silly lines in the junior high school play. The composer continued to stare at me, and now there was annoyance in his eyes. He was seeking an explanation for that intent old man turning singlemindedly in the street for the benefit of his visitor from the sky. A paradisical explanation! But all I could do was wonder stupidly whether the old man might have been afflicted with Saint Vitus' dance.

When I sadly shook my head in silence, the light of inquiry went out of my employer's eyes. As if he were taking leave of a friend, he dropped his arm. Then he slowly shifted his gaze skyward until his head was all the way back and his large Adam's apple stood out in bold relief. The phantom had soared back into the sky and I was ashamed; I hadn't been equal to my job. As I stood there with my head hanging, the composer stepped up to me and indicated that my first day of work was at an end: "We can go home, now. He's come down today already, and you must be pretty tired." I did feel exhausted after all that tension.

We rode back in a taxi with the windows rolled up, and as soon as I'd been paid for the day, I left. But I didn't go straight to the station; I waited behind a telephone pole diagonally across from the house. Dusk deepened, the sky turned the color of a rose, and just as the promise of night was becoming fact, the nurse, in a short-skirted, one-piece dress of a color indistinct in the dimness, appeared through the main gate pushing a brand-new bicycle in front of her. Before she could get on the bicycle, I ran over to her. Without her nurse's uniform, she was just an ordinary little woman in her early forties; vanished from her face was the mystery I had discovered through the annex window. And my appearance had unsettled her. She couldn't climb on the bike and pedal away, but neither would she stand still; she had begun to walk the bike along when I demanded that she explain our mutual employer's condition. She resisted, peevishly, but I had a good grip on the bicycle seat and so in the end she gave in. When she began to talk, her formidable lower jaw snapped shut at each break in the sentence; she was absolutely a talking turtle.

"He says it's a fat baby in a white cotton nightgown. Big as a kangaroo, he says. It's supposed to be afraid of dogs and policemen and it comes down out of the sky. He says its name is Aghwee! Let me tell you something, if you happen to be around when that spook gets hold of him, you'd better just play dumb, you can't afford to get involved. Don't forget, you're dealing with a looney! And another thing, don't you take him anyplace funny, even if he wants to go. On top of everything else, a little gonorrhea is all we need around here!"

I blushed and let go of the bicycle seat. The nurse, jangling her bell, pedaled away into the darkness as fast as

237

KENZABURO ŌE

she could go with legs as round and thin as handlebars. Ah, a fat baby in a white cotton nightgown, big as a kangaroo!

When I showed up at the house the following week, the composer fixed me with those clear brown eyes of his and rattled me by saying, though not especially in reproof, "I hear you waited for the nurse and asked her about my visitor from the sky. You really take your work seriously."

That afternoon we took the same train in the opposite direction, into the country for half an hour to an amusement park on the banks of the Tama river. We tried all kinds of rides and, luckily for me, the baby as big as a kangaroo dropped out of the sky to visit D when he was up by himself in the Sky Sloop, wooden boxes shaped like boats that were hoisted slowly into the air on the blades of a kind of windmill. From a bench on the ground, I watched the composer talking with an imaginary passenger at his side. And until his visitor had climbed back into the sky, D refused to come down; again and again a signal from him sent me running to buy him another ticket.

Another incident that made an impression on me that day occurred as we were crossing the amusement park toward the exit, when D accidentally stepped in some wet cement. When he saw that his foot had left an imprint he became abnormally irritated, and until I had negotiated with the workmen, paid them something for their pains and had the footprint troweled away, he stubbornly refused to move from the spot. This was the only time the composer ever revealed to me the least violence in his nature. On the way home on the train, I suppose because

238

he regretted having barked at me, he excused himself in this way: "I'm not living in present time anymore, at least not consciously. Do you know the rule that governs trips into the past in a time machine? For example, a man who travels back ten thousand years in time doesn't dare do anything in that world that might remain behind him. Because he doesn't exist in time ten thousand years ago, and if he left anything behind him there the result would be a warp, infinitely slight maybe but still a warp, in all of history from then until now, ten thousand years of it. That's the way the rule goes, and since I'm not living in present time, I mustn't do anything here in this world that might remain or leave an imprint."

"But why have you stopped living in present time?" I asked, and my employer sealed himself up like a golf ball and ignored me. I regretted my loose tongue; I had finally exceeded the limits permitted me, because I was too concerned with D's problem. Maybe the nurse was right; playing dumb was the only way, and I couldn't afford to get involved. I resolved not to.

We walked around Tokyo a number of times after that, and my new policy was a success. But the day came when the composer's problems began to involve me whether I liked it or not. One afternoon we got into a cab together and, for the first time since I had taken the job, D mentioned a specific destination, a swank apartment house designed like a hotel in Daikan Yama. When we arrived, D waited in the coffee shop in the basement while I went up the elevator alone to pick up a package that was waiting for me. I was to be given the package by D's former wife, who was living alone in the apartment now.

I knocked on a door that made me think of the cell blocks at Sing Sing (I was always going to the movies in those days; I have the feeling about ninety-five percent of what I knew came directly from the movies) and it was opened by a short woman with a pudgy red face on top of a neck that was just as pudgy and as round as a cylinder. She ordered me to take my shoes off and step inside, and pointed to a sofa near the window where I was to sit. This must be the way high society receives a stranger, I remember thinking at the time. For me, the son of a poor farmer, refusing her invitation and asking for the package at the door would have taken the courage to defy Japanese high society, the courage of that butcher who threatened Louis XIV. I did as I was told, and stepped for the first time in my life into a studio apartment in the American style.

The composer's former wife poured me some beer. She seemed somewhat older than D, and although she gestured grandly and intoned when she spoke, she was too round and overweight to achieve dignity. She was wearing a dress of some heavy cloth with the hem of the skirt unraveled in the manner of a squaw costume, and her necklace of diamonds set in gold looked like the work of an Inca craftsman (now that I think about it, these observations, too, smell distinctly of the movies). Her window overlooked the streets of Shibuya, but the light pouring through it into the room seemed to bother her terrifically; she was continually shifting in her chair, showing me legs as round and bloodshot as her neck, while she questioned me in the voice of a prosecutor. I suppose I was her only source of information about her former husband. Sipping my black, bitter beer as if it were hot coffee, I answered her as best I could, but my knowledge of D was scant and inaccurate and I couldn't satisfy her. Then she started asking about D's actress girl friend, whether she came to see him and things like that, and there was nothing I could say. Annoyed, I thought to myself, what business was it of hers, didn't she have any woman's pride?

"Does D still see that Phantom?"

"Yes, it's a baby the size of a kangaroo in a white cotton nightgown and he says its name is Aghwee, the nurse was telling me about it," I said enthusiastically, glad to encounter a question I could do justice to. "It's usually floating in the sky, but sometimes it flies down to D's side."

"Aghwee, you say. Then it must be the ghost of our dead baby. You know why he calls it Aghwee? Because our baby spoke only once while it was alive and that was what it said—Aghwee. That's a pretty mushy way to name the ghost that's haunting you, don't you think?" The woman spoke derisively; an ugly, corrosive odor reached me from her mouth. "Our baby was born with a lump on the back of its head that made it look as if it had two heads. The doctor diagnosed it as a brain hernia. When D heard the news he decided to protect himself and me from a catastrophe, so he got together with the doctor and they killed the baby—I think they only gave it sugar water instead of milk no matter how loud it screamed. My husband killed the baby because he didn't want us to be saddled with a child who could only function as a vegetable, which is what the doctor had predicted! So he was acting out of fantastic egotism more than anything else. But then there was an autopsy and the lump turned out to be a benign tumor. That's when D began seeing ghosts; you see he'd lost the courage he needed to sustain his egotism, so he declined to live his own life, just as he had declined to let the baby go on living. Not that he committed suicide, he just fled from reality into a world of phantoms. But once your hands are all bloody with a baby's murder, you can't get them clean again just by running from reality, anybody knows that. So here he is, hands as filthy as ever and carrying on about Aghwee."

The cruelness of her criticism was hard to bear, for my employer's sake. So I turned to her, redder in the face than ever with the excitement of her own loquacity , and struck a blow for D. "Where were you while all this was going on? You were the mother, weren't you?"

"I had a Caesarean, and for a week afterwards I was in a coma with a high fever. It was all over when I woke up," said D's former wife, leaving my gauntlet on the floor. Then she stood up and moved toward the kitchen. "I guess you'll have some more beer?"

"No, thank you, I've had enough. Would you please give me the package I'm supposed to take to D?"

"Of course, just let me gargle. I have to gargle every ten minutes, for pyorrhea—you must have noticed the smell?"

D's former wife put a brass key into a business envelope and handed it to me. Standing behind me while I tied my shoes, she asked what school I went to and then said proudly: "I hear there's not even one subscriber to the T——Times in the dormitories there. You may be interested to know that my father will own that paper soon."

I let silence speak for my contempt.

I was about to get into the elevator when doubt knifed through me as though my chest were made of butter. I had to think. I let the elevator go and decided to use the stairs. If his former wife had described D's state of mind correctly, how could I be sure he wouldn't commit suicide with a pinch of cyanide or something taken from a box this key unlocked? All the way down the stairs I wondered what to do, and then I was standing in front of

D's table and still hadn't arrived at a conclusion. The composer sat there with his eyes tightly shut, his tea untouched on the table. I suppose it wouldn't do for him to be seen drinking materials from this time now that he had stopped living in it and had become a traveler from another.

"I saw her," I began, resolved all of a sudden to lie, "and we were talking all this time but she wouldn't give me anything."

My employer looked up at me placidly and said nothing, though doubt clouded his puppy eyes in their deep sockets. All the way back in the cab I sat in silence at his side, secretly perturbed. I wasn't sure whether he had seen through my lie. In my shirt pocket the key was heavy.

But I only kept it for a week. For one thing, the idea of D's suicide began to seem silly; for another, I was worried he might ask his wife about the key. So I put it in a different envelope and mailed it to him special delivery. The next day I went out to the house a little worried and found my employer in the open space in front of the annex, burning a pile of scores in manuscript. They must have been his own compositions: that key had unlocked the composer's music.

We didn't go out that day. Instead I helped D incinerate his whole opus. We had burned everything and had dug a hole and I was burying the ashes when suddenly D began to whisper. The phantom had dropped out of the sky. And until it left I continued working, slowly burying those ashes. That afternoon Aghwee (and there was no denying it was a mushy name) the monster from the sky remained at my employer's side for fully twenty minutes.

From that day on, since I either stepped to one side or

dropped behind whenever the baby phantom appeared, the composer must have realized that I was complying with only the first of his original instructions, not to act amazed, while his request that I back him up with something affirmative was consistently ignored. Yet he seemed satisfied, and so my job was made easier. I couldn't believe D was the kind of person to create a disturbance in the street; in fact his father's warning began to seem ridiculous, our tours of Tokyo together continued so uneventfully. I had already purchased the Moscow edition of *L'Âme Enchanté* I wanted, but I no longer had any intention of giving up such a wonderful job. My employer and I went everywhere together. D wanted to visit all the concert halls where works of his had been performed and all the schools he had ever been to. We would make special trips to places he had once enjoyed himself—bars, movie theaters, indoor swimming pools—and then we would turn back without going inside. And the composer had a passion for all of Tokyo's many forms of public transportation: I'm sure we rode the entire metropolitan subway system. Since the monster baby couldn't descend from the sky while we were underground, I could enjoy the subway in peace of mind. Naturally, I tensed whenever we encountered dogs or officers of the law, remembering what the nurse had told me, but those encounters never coincided with an appearance by Aghwee. I discovered that I was loving my job. Not loving my employer or his phantom baby the size of a kangaroo. Simply loving my job.

One day the composer approached me about making a trip for him. He would pay traveling expenses, and my daily wage would be doubled; since I would have to stay overnight in a hotel and wouldn't be back until the second day, I would actually be earning four times what I usually made. Not only that, the purpose of the trip was to meet D's former girlfriend the movie actress in D's place. I accepted eagerly, I was delighted. And so began that comic and pathetic journey.

D gave me the name of the hotel the actress had mentioned in a recent letter and the date she was expecting him to arrive. Then he had me learn a message to the girl: my employer was no longer living in present time; he was like a traveler who had arrived here in a time machine from a world ten thousand years in the future. Accordingly, he couldn't permit himself to create a new existence with his own signature on it through such acts as writing letters.

I memorized the message, and then it was late at night and I was sitting opposite a movie actress in the basement bar of a hotel in Kyoto, with a chance first to explain why D hadn't come himself, next to persuade his mistress of his conception of time, and finally to deliver his message. I concluded: "D would like you to be careful not to confuse his recent divorce with another divorce he once promised you he would get; and since he isn't living in present time anymore, he says it's only natural that he won't be seeing you again." I felt my face color; for the first time I had the sensation that I had a truly difficult job.

"Is that what D-boy says? And what do you say? How do you feel about all this that you'd run an errand all the way to Kyoto?"

"Frankly, I think D is being mushy."

"That's the way he is—I'd say he's being pretty mushy with you, too, asking this kind of favor!"

"I'm employed; I get paid by the day for what I do."

"What are you drinking there? Have some brandy."

I did. Until then I'd been drinking the same dark beer D's former wife had given me, with an egg in it to thin it down. By some queer carom of a psychological billiard, I'd been influenced by a memory from D's former wife's apartment while waiting to meet his mistress. The actress had been drinking brandy all along. It was the first imported brandy I'd ever had.

"And what's all this about D-boy seeing a ghost, a baby as big as a kangaroo? What did you call it, Raghbee?"

"Aghwee! The baby only spoke once before it died and that was what it said."

"And D thought it was telling him its name? Isn't that darling! If that baby had been normal, it was all decided that D was going to get a divorce and marry me. The day the baby was born we were in bed together in a hotel room and there was a phone call and then we knew something awful had happened. D jumped out of bed and went straight to the hospital. Not a word from him since—". The actress gulped her brandy down, filled her glass to the brim from the bottle of Hennessy on the table as if she were pouring fruit juice, and drained her glass again.

Our table was hidden from the bar by a display case full of cigarettes. Hanging on the wall above my shoulder was a large color poster with the actress's picture on it, a beer advertisement. The face in the poster glittered like gold, no less than the beer. The girl sitting opposite me was not quite so dazzling, there was even a depression in her forehead, just below the hairline, that looked deep enough to contain an adult thumb. But it was precisely the fault that made her more appealing than her picture.

She couldn't get the baby off her mind.

"Look, wouldn't it be terrifying to die without memories or experiences because you'd never done anything human while you were alive? That's how it would be if you died as an infant—wouldn't that be terrifying?"

"Not to the baby, I don't imagine," I said deferentially.

"But think about the world after death!" The actress's logic was full of leaps.

"The world after death?"

"If there is such a thing, the souls of the dead must live there with their memories for all eternity. But what about the soul of a baby who never knew anything and never had any experiences? I mean what memories can it have?"

At a loss, I drank my brandy in silence.

"I'm terribly afraid of death so I'm always thinking about it—you don't have to be disgusted with yourself because you don't have a quick answer for me. But you know what I think? The minute that baby died, I think D-boy decided not to create any new memories for himself, as if he had died, too, and that's why he stopped living, you know, positively, in present time. And I bet he calls that baby ghost down to earth all over Tokyo so he can create new memories for it!"

At the time I thought she must be right. This tipsy movie actress with a dent in her forehead big enough for a thumb is quite an original psychologist, I thought to myself. And much more D's type, I thought, than the pudgy, tomato-faced daughter of a newspaper baron. All of a sudden I realized that, even here in Kyoto with hundreds of miles between us, I, the model of a faithful employee, was thinking exclusively about D. No, there was something else, too, there was D's phantom. I realized that the baby whose appearance I waited for nervously every time my employer and I went out together hadn't been off my mind for a minute.

It was time for the bar to close and I didn't have a room. I'd managed to get as old as I was without ever staying in a hotel and I knew nothing about reservations. Luckily, the actress was known at the hotel, and a word from her got me a room. We went up in the elevator together, and I started to get off at my floor when she suggested we have one last drink and invited me to her room. It was from that point that memories of the evening get comic and pathetic. When she had seated me in a chair, the actress returned to the door and looked up and down the hall, then went through a whole series of nervous motions, flounced on the bed as if to test the springs, turned lights on and switched them off, ran a little water in the tub. Then she poured me the brandy she had promised and, sipping a Coca-Cola, she told me about another man who had courted her during her affair with D, and finally going to bed with him, and D slapping her so hard the teeth rattled in her mouth. Then she asked if I thought today's college students went in for "heavy petting"? It depended on the student, I said—suddenly the actress had become a mother scolding a child for staying up too late and was telling me to find my own room and go to sleep. I said good night, went downstairs, and fell asleep immediately. I woke up at dawn with a fire in my throat.

The most comic and pathetic part was still to come. I understood the minute I opened my eyes that the actress had invited me to her room intending to seduce a college student who was wild for heavy petting. And with that understanding came rage and abject desire. I hadn't slept

248

with a woman yet, but this humiliation demanded that I retaliate. I was drunk on what must have been my first Hennessy VSOP, and I was out of my head with the kind of poisonous desire that goes with being eighteen. It was only five o'clock in the morning and there was no sign of life in the halls. Like a panther wild with rage I sped to her door on padded feet. It was ajar. I stepped inside and found her seated at the dresser mirror with her back to me. Creeping up directly behind her (to this day I wonder what I was trying to do), I lunged at her neck with both hands. The actress whirled around with a broad smile on her face, rising as she turned, and then she had my hands in her own and was pumping them happily up and down as if she were welcoming a guest and sing-songing, "Good morning! Good morning! Good morning!" Before I knew it I had been seated in a chair and we were sharing her toast and morning coffee and reading the newspaper together. After a while the movie actress said in a tone of voice she might have used to discuss the weather: "You were trying to rape me just now, weren't you!" She went back to her makeup and I got out of there, fled downstairs to my own room and burrowed back into bed, trembling as though I had malaria. I was afraid that a report of this incident might reach D, but the subject of the movie actress never came up again. I continued to enjoy my job.

Winter had come. Our plan that afternoon was to bicycle through D's residential neighborhood and the surrounding fields. I was on a rusty old bike and my employer had borrowed the nurse's shiny new one. Gradually we expanded the radius of a circle around D's house, riding into a new housing development and coasting down hills in the direction of the fields. We were sweating, relishing the sensation of liberation, more and more exhilarated. I say "we" and include D because that afternoon it was evident that he was in high spirits, too. He was even whistling a theme from a Bach sonata for flute and harpsichord called Siciliana. I happened to know that because when I was in high school I had played flute. I never learned to play well but I did develop a habit of thrusting out my upper lip the way a tapir does. Naturally, I had friends who insisted my buck teeth were to blame. But the fact is, flutists frequently look like tapirs.

As we pedaled down the street, I picked up the tune and began to whistle along with D. Siciliana is a sustained and elegant theme, but I was out of breath from pedaling and my whistle kept lapsing into airy sibilance. Yet D's phrasing was perfect, absolutely legato. I stopped whistling then, ashamed to go on, and the composer glanced over at me with his lips still pursed in a whistle like a carp puckering up to breathe and smiled his tranquil smile. Granted there was a difference in the bikes, it was still unnatural and pathetic that an eighteen-year-old student, skinny maybe, but tall, should begin to tire and run short of breath before a twenty-eight-year-old composer who was a little man and sick besides. Unjust is what it was, and infuriating. My mood clouded instantly and I felt disgusted with the whole job. So I stood up on the pedals all of a sudden and sped away as furiously as a bicycle racer. I even turned down a narrow gravel path between two vegetable fields purposely. When I looked back a minute later, my employer was hunched over the handle bars, his large, round head nodding above his narrow shoulders, churning the gravel beneath his wheels in hot pursuit of me. I coasted to a stop, propped a foot on the barbed wire fence that bordered the field and waited for D to catch up. I was already ashamed of my childishness.

His head still bobbing, my employer was approaching fast. And then I knew the phantom was with him. D was racing his bike down the extreme left of the gravel path, his face twisted to the right so that he was almost looking over his right shoulder, and the reason his head appeared to bob was that he was whispering encouragement to something running, or maybe flying, alongside the bicycle. Like a marathon coach pacing one of his runners. Ah, I thought, he's doing that on the premise that Aghwee is neck and neck with his speeding bike. The monster as large as a kangaroo, the fat, funny baby in a white cotton nightgown was bounding—like a kangaroo!—down that gravel path. I shuddered, then I kicked the barbed wire fence and slowly pedaled away, waiting for my employer and the monster in his imagination to catch up.

Don't think I had let myself begin to believe in Aghwee's existence. I had taken the nurse's advice, sworn not to lose sight of the anchor on my common sense as in those slightly solemn slapstick comedies where, for example, the keeper of the mad house goes mad; consciously derisive, I was thinking to myself that the neurotic composer was putting on a show with his bicycle just to follow up a lie he had told me once, and what a lot of trouble to go to! In other words, I was keeping a clinical distance between myself and D's phantom monster. Even so, there occurred a strange alteration in my state of mind.

It began this way: D had finally caught up and was biking along a few feet behind me when, as unexpectedly as a cloudburst, and as inescapably, we were enveloped by the belling of a pack of hounds. I looked up and saw them racing toward me down the gravel path, young adult

251

Dobermans that stood two feet high, more than ten of them. Running breathlessly behind the pack, the thin black leather leashes grasped in one hand, was a man in overalls, chasing the dogs perhaps, or maybe they were dragging him along. Jet-black Dobermans, sleek as wet seals, with just a dusting of dry chocolate on their chests and jowls and pumping haunches. And down on us they howled, filling the gravel path, keening for the attack at such a forward tilt they looked about to topple on their foaming snouts. There was a meadow on the other side of the field; the man in overalls must have been training the beasts there and now he was on his way home with them.

Trembling with fear, I got off my bike and helplessly surveyed the field on the other side of the fence. The barbed wire came up to my chest. I might have had a chance myself but I would never have been able to boost the little composer to safety on the other side. The poisons of terror were beginning to numb my head, but for one lucid instant I could see the catastrophe that was bound to occur in a few seconds. As the Dobermans neared, D would sense that Aghwee was being attacked by a pack of the animals it most feared. He would probably hear the baby's frightened crying. And certainly he would meet the dogs head-on, in defense of his baby. Then the Dobermans would rip him to pieces. Or he would try to escape with the baby and make a reckless leap to clear the fence and be just as cruelly torn. I was rocked by the pity of what I knew must happen. And while I stood there dumbly without a plan, those giant black-and-chocolate devils were closing in on us, snapping in the air with awful jaws, so close by now that I could hear their alabaster claws clicking on the gravel. Suddenly I knew I could do

252

nothing for D and his baby, and with that knowledge I went limp, unresisting as a pervert when he is seized in the subway, and was swallowed whole in the darkness of my fear. I backed off the gravel path until the barbed wire was a fire in my back, pulled my bike in front of me as if it were a wall, and shut my eyes tight. An animal stench battered me, together with the howling of the dogs and the pounding of their feet, and I could feel tears seeping past my eyelids. I abandoned myself to a wave of fear and it swept me away. . . .

On my shoulder was a hand gentle as the essence of all gentleness; it felt like Aghwee touching me. But I knew it was my employer; he had let those fiendish dogs pass and no catastrophe of fear had befallen him. I continued crying anyway, with my eyes closed and my shoulders heaving. I was too old to cry in front of other people, I suppose the shock of fright had induced some kind of infantile regression in me. When I stopped crying, we walked our bikes past that barbed wire fence like prisoners in a concentration camp, in silence, our heads hanging, to the meadow beyond the field where strangers were playing ball and exercising dogs (D wasn't occupied with Aghwee anymore, the baby must have left while I was crying). We laid our bikes down and then sprawled on the grass ourselves. My tears had flooded away my pretensions and my rebelliousness and the perverse suspicion in my heart. And D was no longer wary of me. I lay back on the grass and clasped my hands beneath my head, curiously light and dry after all that crying. Then I closed my eyes and listened quietly while D peered down at me with his chin in his hand and spoke to me of Aghwee's world.

253

"Do you know a poem called 'Shame' by Chuya Nakahara? Listen to the second verse:

> The mournful sky
> High where branches tangle
> Teems with dead baby souls;
> I blinked and saw
> above the distant fields
> fleece knit into a dream
> of mastodons.

"That's one aspect of the world of the dead baby I see. There are some Blake engravings, too, especially one called 'Christ Refusing the Banquet Offered by Satan'—have you ever seen it? And there's another, 'The Morning Stars Singing Together.' In both there are figures in the sky who have the same reality about them as the people on the ground, and whenever I look at them I'm sure Blake was hinting at an aspect of this other world. I once saw a Dali painting that was close, too, full of opaque beings floating in the sky about a hundred yards above the ground and glowing with an ivory white light. Now that's exactly the world I see. And you know what those glowing things are that fill the sky? Beings we've lost from our lives down here on earth, and now they float up there in the sky about a hundred yards above the ground, quietly glowing like amoebas under a microscope. And sometimes they descend the way our Aghwee does (my employer said it and I didn't protest, which doesn't mean I acquiesced). But it takes a sacrifice worthy of them to acquire the eyes to see them floating there and the ears to detect them when they descend to earth, and yet there are moments when suddenly we're endowed with that ability without any sacrifice or even effort on our part. I think that's what happened to you a few minutes ago."

Without any sacrifice or even effort on my part, just a few tears of expiation, my employer seemed to have wanted to say. The truth was I had shed tears out of fear and helplessness and a kind of vague terror about my future (my first job, an experiment in a kind of microcosm of life, was guarding this mad composer, and since I had failed to do that adequately, it was predictable that situations I couldn't cope with would recur as one of the patterns of my life), but instead of interrupting with a protest, I continued to listen docilely.

"You're still young, probably you haven't lost sight of anything in this world that you can never forget, that's so dear to you you're aware of its absence all the time. Probably the sky a hundred yards or so above your head is still nothing more than sky to you. But all that means is that the storehouse happens to be empty at the moment. Or have you lost anything that was really important to you?"

The composer paused for my answer, and I found myself remembering his former mistress, that movie actress with a dent in her forehead as big as an adult thumb. Naturally, no crucial loss of mine could have had anything to do with her, all that crying had eroded my head and a sentimental honey was seeping into the crevices.

"Well, have you?" For the first time since we had met, my employer was insistent. "Have you lost anything that was important to you?"

Suddenly I had to say something silly to cover my embarrassment.

"I lost a cat," I tried.

"A Siamese or what?"

"Just an ordinary cat with orange stripes; he disappeared about a week ago."

"If it's only been a week he might come back. Isn't it the season for them to wander?"

"That's what I thought, too, but now I know he won't be back."

"Why?"

"He was a tough tom with his own territory staked out. This morning I saw a weak-looking cat walking up and down his block and it wasn't even on its guard—my cat won't be coming back." When I'd stopped talking I realized I'd told a story intended for laughs in a voice that was hoarse with sadness.

"Then there's a cat floating in your sky," my employer said solemnly.

Through closed eyes I pictured an opaque cat as large as an ad balloon, glowing with an ivory-white light as it floated through the sky. It was a comical flight all right, but it also made me wistful.

"The figures floating in your sky begin to increase at an accelerating rate. That's why I haven't been living in present time ever since that incident with the baby, so I could stop that spreading. Since I'm not living in our time, I can't discover anything new, but I don't lose sight of anything, either—the state of my sky never changes." There was profound relief in the composer's voice.

But was my own sky really empty except for one bloated cat with orange stripes? I opened my eyes and started to look up at the clear, now almost evening sky, when dread made me close my eyes again. Dread of myself, for what if I had seen a glowing herd of numberless beings I had lost from time down here on earth!

We lay on the grass in that meadow for quite a while, ringed by the passive affinity two people have for one another when the same gloom is gripping them. And gradually I began to get my perspective back. I reproached myself: how unlike the eighteen-year-old pragmatist I really was to have let myself be influenced by a mad composer! I'm not suggesting my equilibrium was perfectly restored. The day I succumbed to that strange panic, I drew closer than ever to the sentiments of my employer and to that glowing herd in the sky one hundred yards above the ground. To an extent, what you might call the aftereffects remained with me.

And then the final day came. It was Christmas Eve. I'm certain about the date because D gave me a wristwatch with a little apology about being a day early. And I remember that a powdery snow fell for about an hour just after lunch. We went down to the Ginza together but it was already getting crowded, so we decided to walk out to Tokyo harbor. D wanted to see a Chilean freighter that was supposed to have docked that day. I was eager to go, too; I pictured a ship with snow blanketing her decks. We had left the Ginza crowds and were just passing the Kabuki Theater when D looked up at the dark and still snowy sky. And Aghwee descended to his side. As usual, I walked a few steps behind the composer and his phantom. We came to a wide intersection. D and the baby had just stepped off the curb when the light changed. D stopped, and a fleet of trucks as bulky as elephants heaved into motion with their Christmas freight. That was when it happened. Suddenly D cried out and thrust both arms in front of him as if he were trying to rescue something; then

257

he leaped in among those trucks and was struck to the ground. I watched stupidly from the curb.

"That was suicide; he just killed himself!" said a shaky voice at my side.

But I had no time to wonder whether it might have been suicide. In a minute that intersection had become backstage at a circus, jammed with milling trucks like elephants, and I was kneeling at D's side, holding his bloody body in my arms and trembling like a dog. I didn't know what to do, a policeman had dashed up and then disappeared on the run again.

D wasn't dead; it was more awful than that. He was dying, lying there in the filthy wet that had been a light snow, oozing blood and something like tree-sap. The dark and snowy pattern of the sky ripped open and the stately light of a Spanish pieta made my employer's blood glisten like silly fat. By that time a crowd had gathered, snatches of "Jingle Bells" wheeled above our heads like panic-stricken pigeons, and I knelt at D's side listening hard for nothing in particular and hearing screaming in the distance. But the crowd just stood there silently in the cold, as if indifferent to the screams. I have never listened so hard on a street corner again, nor again heard screams like that.

An ambulance finally arrived and my employer was lifted inside unconscious. He was caked with blood and mud, and shock seemed to have withered his body. In his white tennis shoes, he looked like an injured blind man. I climbed into the ambulance with a doctor and an orderly and a young man about my age who seemed haughty and aloof. He turned out to be the driver's helper on the long-distance truck that had hit D. The congestion was getting worse all the time as the ambulance cut across the Ginza (according to some statistics I saw recently, there were record crowds that Christmas Eve). Those who heard the siren and stopped to watch us pass, nearly all of them, shared a look of circumspectly solemn concern. In one corner of my dazed head I reflected that the so-called inscrutable Japanese smile, while it seemed likely to exist, did not. Meanwhile D lay unconscious on that wobbly stretcher, bleeding his life away.

When we arrived at the hospital, two orderlies who didn't even pause to change out of shoes into slippers rushed D away to some recess of the building. The same policeman as before appeared out of nowhere again and calmly asked me a lot of questions. Then I was permitted to go to D. The young worker from the truck had already found the room and was sitting on a bench in the corridor next to the door. I sat down next to him and we waited for a long time. At first he would only mutter about all the deliveries he still had to make, but when two hours had passed he began to complain that he was hungry in a surprisingly young voice, and my hostility toward him dwindled. We waited some more, then the banker arrived with his wife and three daughters, who were all dressed up to go to a party. Ignoring us, they went inside. All four of the women had fat, squat bodies and red faces; they reminded me of D's former wife. I continued to wait. It had been hours by then, and the whole time I had been tormented by suspicion—hadn't my employer intended to kill himself from the beginning? Before taking his life he had settled things with his ex-wife and former mistress, burned his manuscripts, toured the city saying goodbye to places he would miss—hadn't he hired me because he needed some good-natured help with those chores? Kept me from seeing his plan by inventing a monster baby floating in the sky? In other words, wasn't it the case that

259

my only real function had been to help D commit suicide? The young laborer had fallen asleep with his head on my shoulder and every minute or two he would convulse as though in pain. He must have been dreaming about running over a man with a truck.

It was pitch black outside when the banker appeared in the door and called me. I eased my shoulder from under the worker's head and stood up. The banker paid me my salary for the day and then let me into the room. D lay on his back with rubber tubes in his nostrils as in a joke. His face gave me pause: it was black as smoked meat. But I couldn't help voicing the doubt that had me so afraid. I called out to my dying employer: "Did you hire me just so you could commit sucide? Was all that about Aghwee just a cover-up?" Then my throat was clogged with tears and I was surprised to hear myself shouting, "I was about to believe in Aghwee!"

At that moment, as my eyes filled with tears and things began to dim, I saw a smile appear on D's darkened, shriveled face. It might have been a mocking smile and it might have been a smile of friendly mischief. The banker led me out of the room. The young man from the truck was stretched out on the bench asleep. On my way out, I slipped the thousand yen I had earned into his jacket pocket. I read in the evening paper the next day that the composer was dead.

And then it was this spring and I was walking down the street when a group of frightened children suddenly started throwing stones. It was so sudden and un-provoked, I don't know what I had done to threaten them. Whatever it was, fear had turned those children into killers, and one of them hit me in the right eye with a rock as big as a fist. I went down on one knee, pressed my hand to my eye and felt a lump of broken flesh. With my good eye I watched my dripping blood draw in the dirt in the street as though magnetically. It was then that I sensed a being I knew and missed leave the ground behind me like a kangaroo and soar into the teary blue of a sky that retained its winter brittleness. Good-bye, Aghwee, I heard myself whispering in my heart. And then I knew that my hatred of those frightened children had melted away and that time had filled my sky during those ten years with figures that glowed with an ivory-white light, I suppose not all of them purely innocent. When I was wounded by those children and sacrificed my sight in one eye, so clearly a gratuitous sacrifice, I had been endowed, if for only an instant, with the power to perceive a creature that had descended from the heights of my sky.